"Come, then!" cried Defarge, in a loudly echoing voice. "Patriots and friends, we are ready! The Bastille!"

With a roar, the living sea of people rose, wave on wave, and overflowed the city. Soon the prison of the Bastille was before it. Alarm bells ringing, drums beating, the sea raging and thundering on its new beach, the attack began.

Deep ditches, double drawbridge, massive stone walls, eight great towers, cannon, muskets, fire and smoke. In the fire and in the smoke, Defarge of the wine shop worked like a soldier. . . .

"To me, women!" cried his wife. "We can kill as well as the men when the place is taken!" Around Madame Defarge the women gathered, with a shrill, thirsty cry, all holding weapons, all armed alike with hunger and revenge.

A Background Note about *A Tale of Two Cities*

The events of *A Tale of Two Cities* take place from 1775 to 1793 in London, England, and Paris, France—the "two cities" of the title. When the novel opens, England and France are each about to be involved in major wars. In 1776, England would be at war with its American colonies, a conflict now known as the American Revolution. And in 1789, the French Revolution would begin, as the people of France rose up to overcome their oppressive government in one of the bloodiest times any country has ever known.

Travel in the late 1700s was very different from what we know today. There were no automobiles, trains, or airplanes. People traveled on horseback or in stagecoaches that also carried the mail from city to city—one of these was the "Dover mail." Trips between England and France involved crossing the English Channel, a 21-mile-wide body of water between Dover (England) and Calais (France), by a small boat somewhat like our ferryboats.

Names were also treated differently in the late 18th century. At this time, people usually called each other by their last names. In addition, because many of the characters are French, French names and titles occur often in *A Tale of Two Cities*. Lucie Manette, a major character, spells her name with an IE instead of a Y. You will also meet characters called *Monsieur* (meaning "Mr."), *Madame* ("Mrs."), *Mademoiselle* or *Mam'selle* ("Miss"), and titles of nobility such as *Marquis* and *Monseigneur* (My Lord).

Charles Dickens
A TALE OF TWO CITIES

Edited by Martin E. Goldstein,
with an Afterword by
Martin E. Goldstein and Janet M. Goldstein

 THE TOWNSEND LIBRARY

A TALE OF TWO CITIES

TP THE TOWNSEND LIBRARY

For more titles in the Townsend Library,
visit our website: **www.townsendpress.com**

Townsend Press, Inc.
1038 Industrial Drive
West Berlin, New Jersey 08091

ISBN 1-59194-034-6

Library of Congress Control Number:
2004105875

CONTENTS

BOOK THE FIRST: *Recalled to Life*

BOOK THE SECOND: *The Golden Thread*

BOOK THE THIRD: *The Track of a Storm*

AFTERWORD

A TALE OF TWO CITIES

BOOK THE FIRST:

Recalled to Life

CHAPTER
1

The Period

It was the best of times; it was the worst of times. It was the age of wisdom; it was the age of foolishness. It was the season of Light; it was the season of Darkness. It was the spring of hope; it was the winter of despair. Some people had everything to look forward to, while others had nothing to look forward to—much like today.

In France, in 1775, things were beginning to go swiftly downhill. The government was spending money without limits, gradually bankrupting the country. Church leaders entertained themselves with such "humane" actions as sentencing a youth to have his hands cut off, his tongue torn out with pincers, and his body burned alive—because he had not kneeled down, in the rain, to honor a procession of monks some fifty or sixty yards away.

There were already trees growing in France in 1775 that would soon be sawed into boards, to make a terrible instrument of death. This was the guillotine, which would slice off the heads of thousands of French nobility. And in the small farmlands outside of Paris sat many creaky carts in need of new paint. These time-worn vehicles were spattered with mud, snuffed about by pigs, and roosted in by poultry. But one day, they would carry lords and ladies to the guillotine, whose razor-sharp knife so swiftly separated an aristocrat's head from his body.

But in 1775, no one suspected that these trees and carts would one day be transformed into agents of death. No one dared suggest that France reshape itself, so that the small farmer, the tradesman, the ordinary citizen could have a decent life. This would have been considered unpatriotic by the aristocracy that ruled the land and the cardinals that ruled the church.

While France enjoyed a period of calm, England was the scene of wide disorder. Every night armed robbers plundered residents of the cities and the countryside. Families were publicly cautioned not to go out of town without putting their furniture in warehouses for security. Even the mayor of London was robbed of his possessions while strolling about the city. Jailed prisoners regularly fought battles with their guards. In a fruitless effort to preserve law and order, the hangman strung up countless villains. Some of these were ruthless murderers, while others had stolen only a few pennies— but they all received the same punishment.

CHAPTER 2

The Mail

On a Friday night in late November, 1775, the road to Dover lay shrouded in mist. As the Dover mail carriage lumbered up Shooter's Hill, the weary passengers walked uphill in the mud by the side of the coach. They trudged along not for exercise, but because the weight of the carriage had three times already brought the horses to a stop.

However, the coachman managed to persuade the beasts to continue on. So, with drooping heads and swishing tails, they mashed their way through the thick mud, floundering and stumbling along. As often as the driver rested them and brought them to a stand, the near horse violently shook his head, as if insisting that the coach could never get up the hill.

A steaming mist had crawled up the hill like an evil spirit. A clammy, intensely cold dampness filled the air, like the waves of an unwholesome sea. The mist was so dense that the coach driver could see only a few yards ahead.

The three passengers in the carriage were wrapped up to the cheekbones and over the ears, and wore heavy boots. Each traveler was so protected against the penetrating cold, that none could tell what the others looked like. No one spoke. In those days, travelers hesitated to break into conversation with strangers. They could never tell who might be ready to draw a pistol and rob them right on the spot.

The guard of the Dover mail stood on his own particular perch, beating his feet to keep warm, as the coach lumbered up Shooter's Hill. He kept an eye and a hand on the arms-chest before him, where several loaded guns lay on top of a layer of sharp swords.

"Wo-ho!" said the coachman, addressing the horses. "One more pull and you're at the top and be damned to you, for I have had trouble enough to get you to it—Joe!"

"Hallo," the guard replied.

"What time do you make it, Joe?"

"Ten minutes past eleven."

"And not atop of Shooter's yet! Tst! Yah! Get on with you!"

The lead horse, spurred by the whip, made a decided scramble for it, and the three other horses followed suit. This last burst carried the mail to the summit of the hill. The horses stopped to breathe again, and the guard got down to prepare the wheel for the descent.

"Tst, Joe!" cried the coachman in a warning

voice, looking down from his box.

"What is it, Tom?"

They both listened.

"I hear a horse cantering, Joe."

"I think the horse is galloping, Tom," replied the guard. "Gentlemen! In the king's name, all of you!" With this warning, he cocked his blunderbuss and made ready to defend the coach.

The stillness that accompanied the halting of the coach, added to the stillness of the night, made it very quiet indeed. The hearts of the passengers beat loud enough perhaps to be heard, for they too heard the distant hoofbeats.

The sound of a galloping horse came fast and furiously up the hill.

"So-ho!" the guard sang out, as loud as he could roar. "Yo there! Stop! I shall fire!"

The pace was suddenly halted and, with much splashing and slipping, a man's voice called from the mist, "Is that the Dover mail?"

"Never you mind what it is!" the guard retorted. "Who are you?"

"Is that the Dover mail?"

"Why do you want to know?"

"I want a passenger, if it is."

"What passenger?"

"Mr. Jarvis Lorry."

One of the passengers indicated that it was his name. The guard, the coachman, and the two other passengers eyed him distrustfully.

"Stay where you are," the guard called to the voice in the mist. "Passenger by the name of Lorry answer straight."

"What is the matter?" asked the passenger with a worried tone. "Who wants me? Is it Jerry?"

"Yes, Mr. Lorry."

"What is the matter?"

"A message sent after you from over yonder. T. and Co."

"I know this messenger, guard," said Mr. Lorry. "He may come close; there's nothing wrong."

"I hope there ain't, but I can't be so sure of that," said the guard gruffly. "Listen well, you! Come forward slowly, d'yuh hear? And if you've got holsters on your saddle, don't let me see your hand go near 'em. For I might make a mistake, and when I make one, it takes the form of lead. So now let's look at you."

The figures of a horse and rider came slowly through the swirling mist to the side of the mail, where the passenger stood. The rider stooped and handed the passenger a small folded paper. The rider's horse was tired, and both horse and rider were covered with mud, from the hoofs of the horse to the hat of the man.

"Guard!" said the passenger, in a tone of quiet confidence.

The watchful guard, with his right hand at the stock of his raised blunderbuss, his left around the barrel, and his eye on the horseman, answered curtly, "Sir."

"There is nothing to worry about. I belong to Tellson's Bank. You must know Tellson's Bank in London. I am going to Paris on business. May I read this?"

"If you be quick, sir."

In the light of the coach-lamp he read, first to himself and then aloud, "'Wait at Dover for Mam'selle.' It's not long, you see, guard. Jerry, say that my answer was RECALLED TO LIFE."

"That's a very strange answer," said Jerry.

"Take that answer back, and they will know that I received their message. Have a safe journey. Good night."

The coach lumbered on again, with heavier wreaths of mist closing round it as it began the descent. The guard soon replaced his gun in his arms-chest, but only after checking on the condition of the pistols that he wore in his belt.

"Tom!" the guard called softly over the coach-roof.

"Hallo, Joe."

"Did you hear the message?"

"I did, Joe."

"What did you make of it, Tom?"

"Nothing at all, Joe."

"That's a coincidence," the guard replied, "for I made the same of it myself."

Jerry, left alone in the mist and darkness, dismounted. As the exhausted mare rested, he wiped the mud from his face and shook the water out of his hat brim. He waited until the wheels of the mail coach were no longer within hearing and the night was quite still again. Then he turned to walk down the hill.

"After that there gallop from Temple Bar in London, old lady, I won't trust your fore-legs till I get you on the level," said this hoarse messenger, glancing at his mare. 'Recalled to life.' That's a Blazing strange message. If everyone were recalled to life, Jerry, you'd be in a Blazing bad way, Jerry!"

CHAPTER

3

The Night Shadows

The messenger rode back at an easy trot, stopping often at ale-houses on the way to drink. He talked to no one and kept his hat cocked over his eyes. His black eyes gave him a sinister look. He kept his chin and throat wrapped in a great muffler, which descended nearly to his knees.

The message that he carried puzzled him greatly. "Recalled to life." What could that mean? It was as dark and murky as the night shadows that surrounded him. So the rider continued on the road to London, where he was to deliver the message to the night watchman at Tellson's Bank. Soon after, the message would be conveyed to important officials at the bank. But as to what the message might mean to them—he could not say.

The coach passenger, Mr. Jarvis Lorry, who had given the message, was also thinking about Tellson's Bank. But his mind also turned to another subject. This was a man of forty-five, with sunken cheeks and hair prematurely white. The passenger, half asleep, imagined that he asked the ghostly individual, "Buried how long?"

The answer: "Almost eighteen years."

"You had abandoned all hope of being dug out?"

"Long ago."

"You know that you are recalled to life?"

"They tell me so."

"I hope you care to live?"

"I can't say."

"Shall I show her to you? Will you come and see her?"

At this point in the imaginary conversation, the man gave different answers. Sometimes he would say, "Wait! It would kill me if I saw her too soon." Sometimes he said, through tears, "Take me to her." Sometimes he said, "I don't know her. I don't understand."

Many times the passenger repeated this conversation in his mind, as the coach rattled on through the rain and mist. Sometimes nodding off to sleep, sometimes half awake, the passenger was suddenly aware of the faint gray light of morning.

He lowered the window, and looked out at the rising sun. There was a ridge of plowed land, with a plow upon it where it had been left last night when the horses were unyoked; beyond it lay a wood with red and golden leaves still on the trees. Though the earth was cold and wet, the sky was clear, and the sun rose bright.

"Eighteen years!" said the passenger, looking at the sun. "Imagine! To be buried alive for eighteen years!"

CHAPTER
4

The Preparation

When the mail coach arrived in Dover that afternoon, the doorman at the Royal George Hotel opened the coach door, as if to congratulate the passengers on completing such a journey.

By that time, there was only one adventurous traveler left to be congratulated. The two others had been set down at their respective roadside destinations.

"Will there be a ship to Calais, France, tomorrow?" asked the weary passenger.

"Yes, sir, if the weather holds, at about two in the afternoon, sir. Bed, sir?"

"I shall not go to bed till night; but I want a bedroom, and a barber."

The coach passenger removed his wrappings, revealing a gentleman of sixty. He was formally dressed in a brown suit of clothes, pretty well worn, but very well kept, with large square cuffs and large flaps to the pockets. He proceeded to the coffee shop, where the breakfast table was drawn before the fire. As was the style of the day, the gentleman wore on his head a wig that had the look of spun glass. Despite the uncomfortable journey of the previous day, he had a healthy color in his cheeks. His face, though lined, bore few traces of anxiety.

When his breakfast arrived, the gentleman said to the waiter, "I would like to reserve a room for a young lady who may come here at any time today. She may ask for Mr. Jarvis Lorry, or she may ask for a gentleman from Tellson's Bank. Please let me know."

"Yes, sir. Tellson's Bank in London, sir?"

"Yes."

When Mr. Lorry had finished his breakfast, he went out for a stroll on the beach. The rest of the day passed uneventfully. When it was dark, Mr. Lorry took his dinner before the coffee-room fire. Following the meal, he ordered a bottle of red wine, which he drank very slowly. Just as he was finishing the wine, he heard a rattling of coach wheels in the narrow street. The sound grew louder as the coach turned into the inn-yard.

In a very few minutes, the waiter came in to announce that Miss Manette had arrived from London, and was anxious to see the gentleman from Tellson's as soon as possible.

"So soon?"

Mr. Lorry took care to straighten his wig just right and followed the waiter to Miss Manette's chamber. It was a large, dark room, furnished with heavy dark tables.

The room was so dark that Mr. Lorry, picking his way over the well-worn carpet, supposed Miss Manette to be, for the moment, somewhere else. Then he noticed, standing by one of the tables, a young lady of not more than seventeen, in a riding-cloak, holding her straw traveling-hat by its ribbon in her hand. She had a short, slight, pretty figure; a quantity of golden hair; and a pair of blue eyes that met his own with an inquiring look. Suddenly he recalled the face of a child whom he had held in his arms on the passage across the English Channel to France, one cold time, when the hail drifted heavily and the sea ran high. Just as suddenly, the vision passed, and he made a formal bow to Miss Manette.

"Please take a seat, sir," she said, in a very clear and pleasant young voice, tinged with a slight foreign accent.

Mr. Lorry took her hand and kissed it, and then he sat down.

"I received a letter from the Bank, sir, yesterday. It informed me that there was new information concerning the property of my long-dead father, whom I never saw, and that I had to go to Paris. There I was to speak to a representative from the Bank, who was to go to Paris for that purpose."

"That representative is myself."

"As I was prepared to hear, sir."

She curtseyed to him (young ladies made

curtseys in those days) out of respect. He bowed to her once more.

"Sir, the Bank told me that you would explain to me the details of this matter, and that I would find these details quite surprising." She took a seat and prepared herself to hear what Mr. Lorry had to say.

"Miss Manette, I am a man of business and nothing more. It is my duty to tell you the story of one of our customers. He was a French gentleman, a man of science with many accomplishments. He was a doctor."

"Was he from the city of Beauvais, where my father lived?"

"Why, yes, from Beauvais. Like Monsieur Manette, your father, the gentleman was from Beauvais. Like Monsieur Manette, your father, the gentleman had an outstanding reputation in Paris. I had the honor of knowing him there. Our relations were business relations. I was at that time in our bank's French branch, and had been there for—oh! twenty years."

"At that time—may I ask, at what time, sir?"

"I speak, miss, of twenty years ago. He married an English lady, and I helped look after his business affairs. To go on—"

"But this sounds like my father's story, sir," Miss Manette said. "And I begin to think that when I was left an orphan, that it was you who brought me to England. I am almost sure it was you."

Mr. Lorry took the hesitating little hand that advanced to take his, and he gently drew it to his lips. He then conducted the young lady to her chair again. He stood looking down into her face while she sat looking up into his.

"Miss Manette, it *was* I. You have been in the care of Tellson's Bank ever since those days, and I have never seen you since.

"So far, miss, as you have remarked, this is the story of your dear dead father. Now comes the difference. If your father had not died when he did— Don't be frightened! How you jump up!"

She did, indeed, rise to her feet. And she caught his wrist with both her hands.

"Please," said Mr. Lorry, in a soothing tone, "please try to control your agitation. As I was saying, suppose Monsieur Manette had not died. Suppose he had suddenly and silently disappeared, because he had been secretly taken to prison. Well, then, the history of your father would have been the history of this unfortunate gentleman, the doctor from Beauvais."

"I beg you to tell me more, sir."

"I will. I am going to. You can bear it?"

"I can bear anything but the uncertainty you leave me in at this moment."

"Now this doctor's wife, a lady of great courage and spirit, suffered greatly on account of her husband's departure before her little child was born—"

"The little child was a—a daughter, sir?"

"A daughter, indeed. Now, suppose this lady wanted to spare her daughter the agony of knowing what horrors her father really experienced. Might not this great lady have told the child that her father was dead? No, don't kneel! In Heaven's name, why should you kneel to me!"

"For the truth. O dear, good, kind sir, for the truth!"

"Miss Manette, your mother took this course with you. And when she died—brokenhearted— she left you, at two years old, to grow to be beautiful and happy. You never needed to agonize over whether your father wore his heart out in prison, or wasted away there until he died.

"Your parents were not rich. There has been no new discovery of money, but—"

He felt his wrist held more tightly, and he stopped. The expression on the girl's face had deepened into one of pain and horror.

"But—your father has been found. He is alive! He has suffered much. No doubt he is greatly changed. He has been taken to the house of an old servant in Paris, and we are going there. My duty is to identify him—if I can. Your task is to restore him to life, love, duty, rest, comfort."

A shiver ran through her body, and from it through his. She said, in a low, distinct, awe-stricken voice, as if she were saying it in a dream, "I am going to see his Ghost! It will be his Ghost—not him!"

Mr. Lorry tried to comfort her. "You know

your father's story now, the best and the worst. You are on your way to the poor wronged gentleman. With a fair sea voyage, and a fair land journey, you will be soon at his dear side.

"Only one thing more," said Mr. Lorry. "He has been found under another name. It would be worse than useless now to make any inquiries, because it would be dangerous. Better not to mention the subject, anywhere or in any way. You must quickly take him out of France. But what is the matter? Miss Manette!"

The girl sat perfectly still and silent, as if in a daze. When Mr. Lorry called for assistance, a wild-looking woman who seemed all in red, with red hair and a red complexion, charged into the room. At once she detached Miss Manette from Mr. Lorry, by laying a brawny hand upon Mr. Lorry's chest and flinging him across the room.

"Why, look at you!" the woman in red cried to the inn servants who had come to help. "Why don't you go and fetch things, instead of staring at me?" As they fled from the room, in search of smelling salts, cold water and vinegar, the woman gently placed the young girl on the sofa and tended her with great care, whispering "my precious" and "my bird." She spread the girl's golden hair over her shoulders with great pride and care.

"And you," she said, indignantly turning to Mr. Lorry, "couldn't you tell her what you had to tell her without frightening her to death?"

"I hope she will do well now," said Mr. Lorry.

"No thanks to you if she does. My darling pretty."

The woman dismissed the servants and returned to caring for Miss Manette. Mr. Lorry made his exit with a certain sense of relief.

CHAPTER
5

The Wine Shop

A large cask of wine had been dropped and broken, in the street. The cask had fallen out of a cart, and its hoops had burst. It lay on the stones just outside the door of the wine shop, shattered like a walnut shell.

All the people close by stopped what they were doing and rushed to drink the wine. The rough, irregular cobblestones had dammed it into little pools. Crowds formed around each puddle, pushing against each other to get close. Some men kneeled down, made scoops of their two hands joined, and sipped. Others tried to help women to sip before the wine could run out between their fingers. Still others dipped in the puddles with little mugs, or even with handkerchiefs from women's heads. Some made small mud embankments, to stop the wine as it ran, or cut off little streams of wine that started away in new directions.

Others licked the wine-stained pieces of the cask, and even chewed the moister wine-rotted fragments.

A shrill sound of laughter echoed in the street while this wine game lasted. There were playful embraces, drinking of healths, shaking of hands, and even joining of hands and dancing.

When the wine was gone, these demonstrations ended, as suddenly as they had broken out. A man who had left his saw sticking in the firewood he was cutting, set it in motion again. A woman returned to a little pot of hot ashes, at which she had been trying to warm her starved fingers and toes. Men with bare arms, matted hair, and pale faces, who had emerged into the winter light, returned to their cellars. And a gloom gathered on the scene that appeared more natural to it than sunshine.

The wine was red wine. It had stained the ground of the narrow street in Saint Antoine, on the outskirts of Paris, where it was spilled. It had stained many hands, too, and many faces, and many naked feet, and many wooden shoes. Those who had drunk the most had a tigerish smear about the mouth. And one tall fellow, his face stained, scrawled upon a wall with his finger dipped in muddy wine—"BLOOD."

The time was to come, when *that* wine too would be spilled on the street stones, and when the stain of it would be red upon many there.

Saint Antoine was heavy with cold, dirt, sickness, ignorance, and want, especially the last.

People shivered at every corner. Children had old-looking faces and grave voices. And hunger was everywhere. There was barely enough oil for people to fry bits of potato. The baker's shelves held only small loaves of stale bread. The butcher sold only scraps of meat.

Yet many of the depressed citizens of Saint Antoine had eyes of fire. Their lips were tight with anger; their foreheads were as knotted as gallow ropes. Nothing in Saint Antoine was in a healthy condition, except tools and weapons. The cutler's knives and axes were sharp and bright, the blacksmith's hammers were heavy, and the gunmaker's stock was murderous.

The wine shop was a corner shop, in better condition than most others. Ernest Defarge, the owner of the wine shop, was standing outside it, looking on at the struggle for the lost wine. "It's not my business," he said, with a final shrug of the shoulders. "The people from the market did it. Let them bring another cask."

Then he noticed the tall fellow writing on the wall, and he called to him. "Say, my Gaspard, what are you doing? Are you mad?"

Defarge crossed the road and covered the word with a handful of mud. "Why do you write in the public streets? Is there no other place to write such words?" As he said this, he pointed to Gaspard's heart.

This wine-shop keeper was a thick-necked, tough-looking man of thirty. Although it was a bitterly cold day, he wore no coat. His shirtsleeves were rolled up, and his arms were bare to the elbows. He looked good-humored, but determined, too; a man of strong resolution and fixed purpose.

Madame Defarge, his wife, sat in the shop behind the counter. Madame Defarge was a stout woman, also aged about thirty, with a watchful eye. Her large hands were decorated with rings, and she wore large earrings. Sensitive to cold, she was wrapped in a coat, and a bright shawl was draped over her head. Her knitting was before her, but she had laid it down to pick her teeth with a toothpick. Madame Defarge said nothing when her husband came in. She only gave a slight cough and lifted her dark eyebrows in a way that communicated, "Some strangers are here."

The wine-shop keeper looked around and finally noticed an elderly gentleman and a young lady, who were seated in a corner. Other customers were there: two playing cards, two playing dominoes, three standing by the counter drinking wine. As he passed behind the counter, he saw that the elderly gentleman signaled to the young lady, "This is our man."

Monsieur Defarge pretended not to notice the two strangers, and fell into conversation with the three customers who were drinking at the counter.

"How goes it, Jacques?" said one of these three to Monsieur Defarge. "Is all the spilt wine swallowed?"

"Every drop, Jacques," answered Monsieur Defarge.

Madame Defarge, picking her teeth with her toothpick, coughed once again, and raised her eyebrows a little higher than before.

"It is not often," said the second of the three drinkers, "that many of these miserable beasts know the taste of wine—or of anything but black bread and death. Is it not so, Jacques?"

"It is so, Jacques," Monsieur Defarge responded.

Yet again Madame Defarge, still using her toothpick, made a slight cough and raised her eyebrows even higher.

"Ah! So much the worse!" the last of the three drinkers said. "A bitter taste it is that such poor creatures always have in their mouths, and hard lives they live, Jacques. Am I right, Jacques?"

"You are right, Jacques," was the response of Monsieur Defarge.

At this point Madame Defarge put her toothpick aside, kept her eyebrows up, and slightly rustled in her seat.

"Gentlemen," said her husband, who had kept his eyes upon her, "good day. The chamber that you wished to see is on the fifth floor. The doorway of the staircase is here," pointing with his hand, "near the window of my establishment. But, now that I remember, one of you has already been there, and can show the way. Gentlemen, adieu!"

They paid for their wine and left. Soon after,

the elderly gentleman advanced from his corner, and requested a word.

"Willingly, sir," said Monsieur Defarge, and quietly stepped with him to the door.

Their conference was very short. Almost at the first word, Monsieur Defarge looked surprised and paid close attention. After only a minute, he nodded and went out. The gentleman then beckoned to the young lady, and they followed him. Madame Defarge knitted with nimble fingers and steady eyebrows, and saw nothing.

Mr. Jarvis Lorry and Miss Manette, emerging from the wine shop, joined Monsieur Defarge in the doorway to which he had directed his three customers just before. In the entryway, Monsieur Defarge bent down on one knee to the child of his old master, and put her hand to his lips. It was a gentle action, but not at all gently done. A very remarkable transformation had come over him in a few seconds. He now looked like an angry, dangerous man.

"It is very high; it is a little difficult. Better to begin slowly," said Monsieur Defarge to Mr. Lorry, as they began climbing the stairs.

"Is he alone?" Mr. Lorry whispered.

"Alone! God help him, who would be with him?" said Defarge.

"Is he always alone, then?"

"Yes."

"By his own choice?"

"By his own necessity. As he was when he was released to me, so he is now."

"He is greatly changed?"

"Changed!"

The keeper of the wine shop struck the wall with his hand, and muttered a tremendous curse. No direct answer could have been half so forceful. Mr. Lorry's spirits grew heavier and heavier, as he and his two companions climbed higher and higher.

As the three of them inched higher, they passed by the doors of other rooms where poor people lived. Outside each door lay a pile of refuse that gave off a sickening odor.

At last, they reached the top of the staircase and stopped to rest. There was one more staircase, even steeper and narrower, to be climbed, before the attic was reached. The keeper of the wine shop stopped here and took a key from his pocket.

"The door is locked then, my friend?" said Mr. Lorry, surprised.

"Yes," was the grim reply of Monsieur Defarge.

"Why is the door locked?"

"Why! Because he has lived so long, locked up, that he would be frightened—rave—tear himself to pieces—die—come to I know not what harm—if his door was left open."

"Is it possible!" exclaimed Mr. Lorry.

"Is it possible!" repeated Defarge, bitterly. "Yes. And a beautiful world we live in, when it *is* possible, and when many other such things are possible, and not only possible, but done—every day. Long live the Devil. Let us go on."

They went up slowly and softly. The staircase was short. It ended, after an abrupt turn, at a single door. There they discovered three men intently looking into the room through some holes in the wall. Hearing footsteps close by, these three turned around. They were the three Jacques who had been drinking in the wine shop.

"I forgot them," explained Monsieur Defarge. "Leave us, good boys; we have business here."

The three glided by, and went silently down.

There was no other door on that floor. When the keeper of the wine shop went straight to this one, Mr. Lorry asked him in an angry whisper, "Do you make a show of Monsieur Manette?"

"I show him, in the way you have seen, to a chosen few."

"Is that well?"

"*I* think it is well."

"Who are the few? How do you choose them?"

"I choose them as real men, of my name—Jacques is my name—to whom the sight is likely to do good."

With a warning gesture to keep them back, Defarge knocked two or three times upon the door. Then he put the key clumsily into the lock, and turned it as heavily as he could.

The door slowly opened inward, and he looked into the room and said something. A faint voice answered.

Defarge looked back over his shoulder and

beckoned them to enter. Mr. Lorry put his arm securely round Miss Manette's waist and held her. He felt that she was about to faint.

"Come in, come in!" Mr. Lorry said.

"I am afraid of it," she answered, shuddering.

"Of it? What?"

"I mean of *him*. Of my father."

He lifted her a little and hurried her into the room. He sat her down just within the door, and held her as she clung to him.

The attic was dim and dark. A small window in the roof was opened slightly. So little light was in the room, that it was difficult, on first coming in, to see anything. Only someone used to such a small portion of light could perform any work in such darkness. But delicate work was being done in the attic. For, with his back toward the door, and his face toward the window, a white-haired man sat on a low bench, leaning forward, very busy, making shoes.

CHAPTER
6

The Shoemaker

"Good day!" said Monsieur Defarge, looking down at the white head that bent low over the shoemaking.

It was raised for a moment, and a very faint voice responded, as if at a distance: "Good day!"

"You are still hard at work, I see?"

After a long silence, the head was lifted for another moment, and the voice replied, "Yes—I am working." This time, a pair of haggard eyes had looked at the questioner, before the face had dropped again.

The faintness of the voice was pitiable and dreadful. It was not the faintness of physical weakness. Rather, it was the faintness of solitude and disuse. It was like the last feeble echo of a sound made long ago, like a once beautiful color faded to a poor weak stain. So sunken and suppressed it was, that it was like a voice underground.

"I want," said Defarge, "to let in a little more light here. You can bear a little more?"

The shoemaker stopped his work, looked around without speaking, and finally looked at the speaker.

"What did you say?"

"You can bear a little more light?"

"I must bear it, if you let it in."

The window was opened a little more. A broad ray of light fell into the attic. It showed the workman with an unfinished shoe upon his lap. His few common tools and various scraps of leather were at his feet and on his bench. He had a white beard, raggedly cut, but not very long; a hollow face; and exceedingly bright eyes. His yellow rags of shirt lay open at the throat and showed his body to be withered and worn. He, and his old canvas coat, and his loose stockings, and all his torn clothing had faded to such a dull shade of parchment-yellow, that it would have been hard to say which was which.

He had put up a hand between his eyes and the light, and his very bones seemed transparent. So he sat, with a steadfastly vacant gaze, pausing in his work.

"Are you going to finish that pair of shoes today?" asked Defarge, motioning to Mr. Lorry to come forward.

"What did you say?"

"Do you mean to finish that pair of shoes today?"

"I can't say that I mean to. I suppose so. I don't know."

The question reminded him of his work, and he bent over it again.

Mr. Lorry came silently forward, leaving Miss Manette by the door. When he had stood, for a minute or two, by the side of Defarge, the shoemaker looked up. He showed no surprise at seeing another figure, and he once more bent over the shoe.

"You have a visitor," said Defarge.

The shoemaker looked up as before, but without removing a hand from his work.

"Come!" said Defarge. "Here is monsieur, who knows a well-made shoe when he sees one. Show him that shoe you are working on. Take it, monsieur."

Mr. Lorry took it in his hand.

"Tell monsieur what kind of shoe it is and the maker's name."

There was a longer pause than usual before the shoemaker replied:

"I forget what it was you asked me. What did you say?"

"I said, could you describe the kind of shoe for monsieur?"

"It is a lady's shoe. It is a young lady's walking shoe. It is in the present style. I never saw such a shoe. I have been working from a drawing." He glanced at the shoe with some pride.

"And the maker's name?" said Defarge.

The shoemaker laid the knuckles of the right hand in the hollow of the left, and then the knuckles of the left hand in the hollow of the right. After he spoke, he sank into a vacancy. Recalling him from this was like recalling some very weak person from a faint.

"Did you ask me for my name?"

"I did."

"One Hundred and Five, North Tower."

"Is that all?"

"One Hundred and Five, North Tower."

With a weary sound that was not a sigh, nor a groan, he bent to work again, until the silence was again broken.

"You are not a shoemaker by trade?" said Mr. Lorry, looking steadfastly at him.

His haggard eyes turned to Defarge as if he would have transferred the question to him. But as no help came from that quarter, they turned back on the questioner.

"I am not a shoemaker by trade? No, I was not a shoemaker by trade. I—I learned it here. I taught myself. I asked permission to—"

For a minute or two his mind drifted away, and he fell silent. His eyes came slowly back, at last, to the face from which they had wandered. When they rested on it, he looked startled. Then he resumed, in the manner of a sleeper just awakened, "I asked permission to teach myself. I obtained it, with much difficulty, after a long while, and I have made shoes ever since."

As he held out his hand for the shoe that had been taken from him, Mr. Lorry said, still looking steadily in his face, "Monsieur Manette, do you remember nothing of me?"

The shoe dropped to the ground, and the shoemaker sat looking intently at the questioner.

Mr. Lorry laid his hand upon Defarge's arm. "Look at me. Is there no old banker, no old business, no old servant, no old time, rising in your mind, Monsieur Manette?"

The captive of many years sat looking from Mr. Lorry to Defarge and back again. For a flickering moment, his face signaled that he recalled something from his distant past. But darkness had fallen on him once again. His eyes sought the ground and looked about him in the old way. Finally, with a long, deep sigh, he took the shoe up, and resumed his work.

"Have you recognized him, monsieur?" asked Defarge in a whisper.

"Yes; for a moment. At first I thought it quite hopeless, but I have unquestionably seen, for a single moment, the face that I once knew so well. Hush! Let us draw further back. Hush!"

The girl had moved closer to the bench on which the white-haired man sat. Not a word was spoken; not a sound was made. She stood, like a spirit, beside him, as he bent over his work.

It happened, after a while, that he had to exchange the instrument in his hand for his shoemaker's knife. He had taken it up, and was stooping to work again, when his eyes caught the skirt of her dress. He looked up and saw her face. Mr. Lorry and Defarge started forward, but she stopped them with a motion of her hand. She had no fear of his striking at her with the knife, though they had.

He stared at her with a fearful look. After a while his lips began to form some words, though no sound proceeded from them. Soon, in between his quick and labored breathing, he was heard to say, "What is this?"

With the tears streaming down her face, Miss Manette put her two hands to her lips, and kissed them to him.

"You are not the jailer's daughter?"

She sighed. "No."

"Who are you?"

Not yet trusting the tones of her voice, she sat down on the bench beside him. He shrank back, but she laid her hand upon his arm. A strange thrill struck him when she did so. He put the knife down softly as he sat staring at her.

Her golden hair, which she wore in long curls, had been hurriedly pushed aside, and fell down over her neck. Advancing his hand by little and little, he took it up and looked at it. In the midst of the action he went astray, and, with another deep sigh, fell to work at his shoemaking.

But not for long. Releasing his arm, Miss Manette placed her hand upon his shoulder. He looked at it, two or three times, as if to be sure that it was really there. Then he laid down his work, put his hand to his neck, and took off a blackened string with a scrap of folded rag attached to it. He opened this carefully on his knee. It contained a very little quantity of hair, not more than one or two long golden hairs.

He took her hair into his hand again, and looked closely at it. "It is the same. How can it be! When was it! How was it!" He turned her to the light and looked at her.

"She had laid her head upon my shoulder, that night when I was summoned out—she had a fear of my going, though I had none—and when I was brought to the North Tower, they found these hairs upon my sleeve. 'You will leave me them? They can never help me to escape in the body, though they may in the spirit.' Those were the words I said. I remember them very well."

He formed this speech with his lips many times before he could utter it. But when he did find spoken words for it, they came to him coherently, though slowly.

"How was this?—WAS IT YOU?"

Once more, the two spectators jumped in their seats, as he turned upon her with a frightful suddenness. But she sat perfectly still in his grasp, and only said, in a low voice, "I beg you, good gentlemen, do not come near us. Do not speak; do not move!"

"Hark!" he exclaimed. "Whose voice was that?"

His hands released her as he uttered this cry, and went up to his white hair, which they tore in a frenzy. He refolded his little packet of hair and tried to secure it in his pocket; but he still looked at her, and gloomily shook his head.

"No, no, no; you are too young, too blooming. It can't be. See what I am. These are not the hands she knew, this is not the face she knew, this is not a voice she ever heard. No, no. She was— and *he* was—before the slow years of the North Tower—ages ago. What is your name, my gentle angel?"

Encouraged by his softened tone and manner, his daughter fell upon her knees before him, with her appealing hands upon his chest.

"O, sir, at another time you shall know my name, and who my mother was, and who my father, and how I never knew their hard, hard history. But I cannot tell you at this time, and I cannot tell you here. All that I may tell you, here and now, is, that I pray to you to touch me and to bless me. Kiss me, kiss me! O my dear, my dear!"

His cold white head mingled with her radiant hair, which warmed and lighted it as though it were the light of Freedom shining on him.

"If you hear in my voice any resemblance to a voice that once was sweet music in your ears, weep for it, weep for it! If you touch, in touching my hair, anything that recalls a beloved head that lay on your chest when you were young and free, weep for it, weep for it! If, when I hint to you of a home that is before us, where I will be true to you with all my duty and with all my faithful service, I bring back the remembrance of a home long desolate, while your poor heart pined away, weep for it, weep for it!"

She held him closer round the neck, and rocked him like a child.

"If, when I tell you, dearest dear, that your agony is over, and that I have come here to take you from it, and that we go to England to be at peace and at rest, I cause you to think of your useful life laid waste, weep for it, weep for it! And if, when I shall tell you my name, and about my father who is living, and about my mother who is dead, you learn that I kneel to my honored father, and I never knew of his suffering, weep for it, weep for it! Good gentlemen, thank God! I feel his sacred tears upon my face, and his sobs strike against my heart. O, see! Thank God for us, thank God!"

He had sunk into her arms. It was a sight so touching, yet so terrible in the tremendous wrong and suffering which had gone before it, that the two onlookers covered their faces.

When the quiet of the attic had returned, they came forward to raise the father and daughter from the ground. He had gradually dropped to the floor exhausted. She had nestled down with him, that his head might lie upon her arm. Her hair, drooping over him, shielded him from the light.

"If, without disturbing him," she said, raising

her hand to Mr. Lorry as he stooped over them, after repeated blowings of his nose, "all could be arranged for our leaving Paris at once—"

"But, consider. Is he fit for the journey?" asked Mr. Lorry.

"More fit for that, I think, than to remain in this city, so dreadful to him."

"It is true," said Defarge. "More than that; Monsieur Manette is, for many reasons, best out of France. Shall I hire a carriage and post-horses?"

"That's business," said Mr. Lorry. "I had better do it."

"Then be so kind," urged Miss Manette, "as to leave us here. You see how calm he has become, and you cannot be afraid to leave him with me now. I will take care of him until you return."

Both Mr. Lorry and Defarge then departed to secure a carriage and traveling papers.

Then, as the darkness closed in, the daughter laid her head down on the hard ground close at her father's side and watched him. The darkness deepened and deepened, and they both lay quiet, until a light gleamed through the chinks in the wall.

Mr. Lorry and Monsieur Defarge had made preparations for the journey. They had brought with them traveling cloaks, bread and meat, wine, and hot coffee. Monsieur Defarge put these supplies, and the lamp he carried, on the shoemaker's bench. Then he and Mr. Lorry roused the captive and assisted him to his feet.

Whether he knew what had happened,

whether he knew that he was free, were questions that could not be answered. They tried speaking to him. However, he was so confused, and so very slow to answer, that they agreed, for the present, to question him no more. He had a wild, lost manner of occasionally clasping his head in his hands, which had not been seen in him before. Yet he had some pleasure in the mere sound of his daughter's voice, and he always turned toward it when she spoke.

In the submissive way of one long accustomed to obey orders, he ate and drank what they gave him to eat and drink. He put on the cloak and other traveling clothes that they gave him to wear. He readily responded to his daughter's drawing her arm through his, and took—and kept—her hand in both his own.

They began to descend; Monsieur Defarge going first with the lamp, Mr. Lorry closing the little procession. They had not walked down many steps of the long main staircase when Dr. Manette stopped and stared at the roof and the walls.

"You remember the place, my father? You remember coming up here?"

"What did you say?"

But, before she could repeat the question, he murmured an answer as if she had repeated it.

"Remember? No, I don't remember. It was so very long ago."

He had no recollection whatever of his having been brought from his prison to that house. They heard him mutter, "One Hundred and Five, North Tower." When he looked about him, it evidently was for the strong fortress walls which had long entombed him. On their reaching the courtyard, he instinctively altered his tread, as if he expected a drawbridge. When there was no drawbridge, and he saw the carriage waiting in the open street, he dropped his daughter's hand and clasped his head again.

No crowd was about the door. Only one soul was to be seen, and that was Madame Defarge—who leaned against the doorpost, knitting.

The prisoner had gotten into a coach, and his daughter had followed him, when he asked for his shoemaking tools and the unfinished shoes. Madame Defarge immediately called to her husband that she would get them, and went, knitting, out of the lamplight, through the courtyard. She quickly brought them down and handed them in.

Defarge directed the coach driver, "To the Barrier!" The driver cracked his whip, and they clattered away.

They passed by lighted shops, happy crowds, illuminated coffeehouses, and theater doors, to one of the city gates. Soldiers with lanterns were waiting at the guardhouse. "Your papers, travelers!"

"See here then, Monsieur the Officer," said Defarge, getting down, and taking him gravely aside, "these are the papers of monsieur inside, with the white head. They were entrusted to me, with him, at the—"

He dropped his voice. There was a flutter among the military lanterns, and one of them peered into the coach. "It is well. Forward!" exclaimed the soldier. "Adieu!" from Defarge. And so they departed the city.

Beneath a ceiling of stars, the shadows of the night were broad and black. All through the cold and restless journey, the three of them attended the buried man who had been dug out. They could not help but wonder what powers were forever lost to him, and what were capable of restoration—the old inquiry:

"I hope you care to be recalled to life?"

And the old answer:

"I can't say."

A TALE OF TWO CITIES

Book the Second:

The Golden Thread

CHAPTER
1

Five Years Later

Tellson's Bank in London was an old-fashioned place, even in the year 1780. It was very small, very dark, and very ugly. But the owners of the bank were proud of its smallness, proud of its darkness, and proud of its ugliness. Any one of these owners would have disinherited his son for suggesting that the bank be made larger and brighter. In this respect the House was much like England itself, which often disinherited its sons for suggesting improvements in laws and customs that had long been highly objectionable.

Outside Tellson's was an odd-job-man, named Jerry Cruncher, with a grim, red face and spiky hair. He was never absent during business hours, unless upon an errand as a porter or messenger. Then he was represented by his son, also named Jerry, a boy of twelve who was his exact image.

On one particular March morning, Mr. Cruncher prepared to leave his apartment in

Hangingsword Alley, London. He reached down to put on his shoes, which were spattered with mud. It was strange that, while he often came home after banking hours with clean shoes, the same shoes were covered with mud the next morning.

Red-eyed and grim, as if he had had an unpleasant night, Jerry Cruncher worried down his breakfast rather than ate it. Toward nine o'clock, he smoothed his ruffled appearance. Looking as respectable and business-like as he could, he set out in pursuit of his daily occupation.

It could scarcely be called a trade, in spite of his description of himself as "an honest tradesman." His entire stock consisted of a wooden stool, made out of a broken-backed chair cut down, and a handful of straw, grabbed from a passing vehicle, to keep the cold and wet from Cruncher's feet.

At a quarter before nine on this windy March morning, Jerry Cruncher and his son were at their assigned place. Before long an important-looking individual from Tellson's Bank cried out a window, "Porter wanted!"

"Hooray, father! Here's an early job to begin with!" young Jerry cried.

As his father left, young Jerry muttered to himself, "Al-ways rusty! His fingers is al-ways rusty! Where does my father get all that iron rust from? He don't get no iron rust here!"

CHAPTER
2

A Sight

"You know the Old Bailey well, no doubt?" said one of the oldest of clerks to Jerry the father.

"Yes, sir," answered Jerry. "I *do* know the Bailey."

"Just so. And you know Mr. Lorry."

"I do know Mr. Lorry, sir."

"Very well. Find the door where the witnesses go in, and show the doorkeeper this note for Mr. Lorry. He will then let you in."

"Into the court, sir?"

"Into the court."

"Am I to wait in the court, sir?" he asked.

"I am going to tell you. The doorkeeper will pass the note to Mr. Lorry. Then you make some gesture that will attract Mr. Lorry's attention, and show him where you stand. Then remain there until he wants you."

"Is that all, sir?"

"That's all. He wishes to have a messenger at

hand. This is to tell him you are there."

As the ancient clerk deliberately folded the note and handed it to Mr. Cruncher, the latter remarked, "I suppose they'll be trying forgeries this morning?"

"Treason!"

"That's quartering," said Jerry. "Barbarous!"

"It is the law," remarked the ancient clerk. "It is the law. Take care of your chest and voice, my good friend, and leave the law to take care of itself. I give you that advice."

"It's the damp, sir, what settles on my chest and voice," said Jerry. "I leave you to judge what a damp way of earning a living mine is."

"Well, well," said the old clerk, "we all have our various ways of gaining a livelihood. Some of us have damp ways, and some of us have dry ways. Here is the letter. Go along."

Jerry took the letter. Informing his son of his destination, he went his way.

The jail by Old Bailey was a vile place, in which most kinds of atrocities and evils were common. Dreadful diseases were bred there, which came into court with the prisoners and infected those within their reach. Sometimes, the judge in the black cap pronounced his own doom as certainly as the prisoner's, and even died before him. For the rest, the Old Bailey was famous as a kind of deadly inn-yard, from which pale travelers set out continually, in carts and coaches, on a violent passage to another world. The Old Bailey was also known for the pillory and the whipping-post, two wise old institutions—or so the authorities believed.

Making his way through the bustling crowd, with the skill of a man accustomed to make his way quietly, the messenger Cruncher found the door he was looking for. He handed his letter through a small window designed for that purpose. Then, after some delay, he managed to squeeze his way into court.

"What's on?" he asked the man next to him, in a whisper.

"The treason case."

"The quartering one, eh?"

"Ah!" responded the man, with obvious pleasure. "He'll be drawn on a hurdle to be half hanged. Then he'll be taken down and sliced before his own face, and then his insides will be taken out and burnt while he looks on, and then his head will be chopped off, and he'll be cut into quarters. That's the sentence."

"If he's found guilty, you mean to say?" Jerry added.

"Oh, they'll find him guilty," said the other. "Don't you be afraid of that."

The doorkeeper soon made his way to Mr. Lorry, with the note in his hand. Mr. Lorry sat at a table, among some gentlemen in wigs. Not far away sat the prisoner's lawyer, who had a great bundle of papers before him. Nearly opposite sat another wigged gentleman with his hands in his pockets, who stared continually at the ceiling of the court. After some gruff coughing and rubbing his chin and waving his hand, Jerry attracted the notice of Mr. Lorry, who had stood up to look for him, and who quietly nodded and sat down again.

Presently, the judge entered the chamber. Two jailers brought in the prisoner, who took his place at the bar.

Everybody present, except the one wigged gentleman who looked at the ceiling, stared at him. Eager faces strained around pillars and corners to get a sight of him. Spectators in back rows stood up, not to miss a hair of him. People on the floor of the court laid their hands on the shoulders of the people before them to get a clearer view. If he had been threatened by a less horrible sentence, he would have been much less fascinating to the bloodthirsty spectators.

The object of all this attention was a good-looking young man of about twenty-five, gentlemanly in appearance, with a sun-bronzed cheek and a dark eye. He was plainly dressed in black, or very dark gray, and his hair, which was long and dark, was gathered in a ribbon at the back of his neck. The prisoner bowed to the judge and stood quietly.

The prisoner, Charles Darnay, had yesterday pleaded "Not Guilty" to an indictment accusing him of being a traitor to the Crown. Specifically, he was accused of revealing to the French what forces Britain were about to send to Canada and

North America for the purpose of protecting its American colonies.

The accused, who was (and who knew he was) being mentally hanged, beheaded, and quartered, by everybody there, did not flinch. Nor did he assume any theatrical air in it. He was quiet and attentive. He watched the opening proceedings with a grave interest, and stood with his hands resting calmly on the slab of wood before him.

There was a mirror over the prisoner's head, to throw the light down upon him. Crowds of the wicked and the wretched had been reflected in it, and had passed from its surface and this earth's together. A change in his position made him conscious of a bar of light across his face. To avoid the glare, he turned his face to his left. There he spied two figures, a young lady of little more than twenty, and a gentleman who was evidently her father. The man's appearance was remarkable for the absolute whiteness of his hair, and a certain indescribable intensity of face.

His daughter had one of her hands drawn through his arm, as she sat by him, and the other pressed upon it. She had drawn close to him, frightened by the surroundings, and pitying the prisoner. Her face clearly showed her terror and compassion for the danger in which he stood.

The prisoner fixed such a stare upon these two, that the spectators could not help but notice. A whisper went through the crowd: "Who are they?"

Jerry, the messenger, who had been sucking the rust off his fingers in his absorption, stretched his neck to hear who they were. The crowd about him had asked the nearest official. The answer made its way back to him: "Witnesses."

"For which side?"

"Against."

"Against what side?"

"The prisoner's."

The judge leaned back in his seat and looked steadily at the man whose life was in his hands. The Attorney General, who was to argue the case against the prisoner, rose to spin the rope, grind the axe, and hammer the nails into the scaffold.

CHAPTER
3

A Disappointment

Mr. Attorney General stated before the jury that the prisoner before them, though young in years, was old in treasonable practices. That the prisoner had passed back and forth between France and England on secret business that he could not honestly explain. That a person, who was beyond fear and beyond reproach, discovered the nature of the prisoner's schemes, and, struck with horror, resolved to expose the traitor. That this patriot persuaded the prisoner's servant to remove secret military papers from the prisoner's pockets and desk. That this patriot would be brought before them. That he (Mr. Attorney General) expected the defense attorney to attempt to damage this admirable witness's credibility. That the evidence would show the prisoner obtained lists of his Majesty's forces, and of their disposition and preparation, both by sea and land.

That he had repeatedly provided such information to a hostile power. That the proof would go back five years, and would show the prisoner already engaged in these traitorous missions even before the very first battle between the British troops and the Americans. That, for these reasons, the jury, being a loyal jury (as he knew they were), and being a responsible jury (as THEY knew they were), must positively find the prisoner guilty.

When the attorney general ceased, a buzz arose in the court as if a cloud of great blue-flies were swarming about the prisoner, in anticipation of what he was soon to become. When silence returned to the courtroom, the attorney general called the unimpeachable patriot to the witness box.

This key witness, named John Barsad, was examined by the attorney general's assistant, known as the solicitor general. Unsurprisingly, the solicitor general demonstrated him to be above reproach. The witness was prepared to withdraw, when the defense attorney begged to ask him a few questions. The wigged gentleman, sitting opposite, continued to gaze at the ceiling of the court.

The defense attorney began his questioning of the witness. Had he ever been a spy himself? No; he scorned the suggestion. What did he live upon? His property. Where was his property? He didn't precisely remember where it was. What was it? None of your business. Had he inherited it? Yes, he had. From whom? Distant relation. Very distant? Rather. Ever been in prison? Certainly not.

Never in a debtors' prison? Didn't see what that had to do with it. Never in a debtors' prison?— Come, once again. Never? Yes. How many times? Two or three times. Not five or six? Perhaps. Of what profession? Gentleman. Ever been kicked? Might have been. Frequently? No. Ever kicked downstairs? Well, once. Kicked on that occasion for cheating at dice? The drunken liar who made the accusation said so, but it was not true. Ever live by gambling? Not more than other gentlemen do. Ever borrow money of the prisoner? Yes. Ever pay him? No. Sure he saw the prisoner with these lists of military forces? Certain. Knew no more about the lists? No. Had not obtained them himself, for instance? No. Expect to get anything by this evidence? No. Not in regular government pay and employment, to lay traps? Oh dear no. No motives but motives of sheer patriotism? None whatsoever.

The virtuous servant, Roger Cly, was next sworn in. He stated that he took employment as the prisoner's serving man four years ago. He began to have suspicions of the prisoner, and to keep an eye upon him, soon afterward. In arranging his clothes, while traveling, he had seen similar lists to these in the prisoner's pockets, over and over again. He had taken these lists from the drawer of the prisoner's desk. He had not put them there first. He had seen the prisoner show these identical lists to French gentlemen at Calais, and similar lists to French gentlemen both at Calais and Boulogne. He loved his country and had therefore given information against the prisoner. He himself had never been suspected of stealing so much as a silver teapot. He had known the last witness seven or eight years, merely a coincidence. He was a true Briton, and hoped there were many like him.

The blue-flies buzzed again, and Mr. Attorney General called Mr. Jarvis Lorry.

"Mr. Jarvis Lorry, are you a clerk in Tellson's Bank?"

"I am."

"On a certain Friday night in November, 1775, were you traveling between London and Dover by the mail coach?"

"I was."

"Were there any other passengers in the mail?"

"Two."

"Did they get out on the road in the course of the night?"

"They did."

"Mr. Lorry, look upon the prisoner. Was he one of those two passengers?"

"He was not."

"Does he resemble either of these two passengers?"

"Both were so wrapped up, and the night was so dark, and we were all so quiet, that I cannot say even that."

"Mr. Lorry, look again upon the prisoner. Supposing him wrapped up as those two passengers were, can you say for sure he was not one of them?"

"I cannot."

"Mr. Lorry, look once more upon the prisoner. Have you seen him, to your certain knowledge, before?"

"I have."

"When?"

"I was returning from France a few days afterward. At Calais, the prisoner came on board the packet-ship in which I returned, and made the voyage with me."

"At what hour did he come on board?"

"At a little after midnight."

"Were you traveling alone, Mr. Lorry, or with any companion?"

"With two companions. A gentleman and lady. They are here."

"They are here. Had you any conversation with the prisoner?"

"Hardly any. The weather was stormy, and the passage long and rough. I lay on a sofa, almost from shore to shore."

"Miss Manette!"

The young lady, to whom all eyes had been turned before, and were now turned again, stood up where she had sat. Her father rose with her, and kept her hand drawn through his arm.

"Miss Manette, look upon the prisoner. Have you seen the prisoner before?"

"Yes, sir."

"Where?"

"On board of the packet-ship just now referred to, sir, and on the same occasion."

"You are the young lady just now referred to?"

"Oh! Most unhappily, I am!"

"Miss Manette, had you any conversation with the prisoner on that passage across the Channel?"

"Yes, sir."

"Repeat it."

There was silence. She faintly began: "When the gentleman came on board—"

"Do you mean the prisoner?" inquired the judge, frowning.

"Yes, my Lord."

"Then say 'the prisoner.'"

"When the prisoner came on board, he noticed that my father"—she turned her eyes lovingly to him as he stood beside her—"was much fatigued and very weak. My father was so weak that I was afraid to take him out in the air. I had made a bed for him on the deck near the cabin steps, and I sat on the deck at his side to take care of him. There were no other passengers that night but we four. The prisoner was so kind. He asked permission to advise me how I could shelter my father from the wind and weather. I had not known how to do it well. He did it for me. He expressed great gentleness and kindness for my father's state, and I am sure he felt it."

"Let me interrupt you for a moment. Had he come on board alone?"

"No."

"How many were with him?"

"Two French gentlemen."

"Had the three of them spoken together?"

"They had conferred together until the last moment, when it was necessary for the French gentlemen to return to their boat."

"Had any papers been exchanged among them, similar to these lists?"

"Some papers had been exchanged, but I don't know what papers."

"Like these in shape and size?"

"Possibly, but indeed I don't know. They stood whispering very near to me, but I did not hear what they said."

"Now, tell us more about your conversation with the prisoner, Miss Manette."

"He told me that he was traveling on business of a delicate and difficult nature, which might get people into trouble, and that he was therefore traveling under an assumed name. He said that this business might, at intervals, take him back and forth between France and England for a long time to come."

"Did he say anything about America, Miss Manette? Be particular."

"He tried to explain to me how America's war for independence had arisen. He said that, so far as he could judge, England's position was wrong and foolish. He added, in a joking way, that perhaps George Washington might gain almost as great a name in history as our own monarch, George the Third."

Mr. Attorney General now told the judge that he deemed it necessary to call the young lady's father, Dr. Manette, to testify. The judge called the doctor to the stand.

"Dr. Manette, look upon the prisoner. Have you ever seen him before?"

"Once. When he stayed at my lodgings in London. Some three years, or three and a half years ago."

"Can you identify him as your fellow passenger on board the packet-ship, or tell us about his conversation with your daughter?"

"Sir, I can do neither."

"Is there any special reason for your being unable to do either?"

He answered, in a low voice, "There is."

"Has it been your misfortune to undergo a long imprisonment, without trial, or even accusation, in your native country, Dr. Manette?"

He answered, in a tone that touched every heart, "A long imprisonment."

"Were you newly released on the occasion in question?"

"They tell me so."

"Have you no remembrance of the occasion?"

"None. My mind is a blank, from some time— I cannot even say what time—when I employed myself, in my captivity, in making shoes, to the time when I found myself living in London with my dear daughter here. She had become familiar to me, when a gracious God restored my faculties. I am quite unable even to say how she had become familiar. I have no remembrance of the process."

Mr. Attorney General sat down, and the father and daughter sat down together.

The case then took an unusual turn. The prosecuting attorney general was trying to prove that the prisoner went down, with some fellow plotter, in the Dover mail coach on that Friday night in November five years ago. Then, he said, the prisoner left the coach in the night, as a trick, at a place where he did not remain. From that spot the prisoner secretly traveled to a garrison and dockyard, where he collected military information to provide to the enemies of England. To prove this point beyond any doubt, the attorney general called a witness who said he saw the prisoner, at the precise time required, in the coffee room of a hotel in that garrison-and-dockyard town, waiting for another person. The prisoner's lawyer then began to cross-examine this witness. Just then, the wigged gentleman who had all this time been looking at the ceiling of the court, wrote a word or two on a little piece of paper, twisted it up, and tossed it to the prisoner's attorney. After reading what was scrawled upon the scrap of paper, the defense attorney resumed his questioning of the witness.

"You say again you are quite sure that it *was* the prisoner?"

The witness was quite sure.

"Look well upon that gentleman," pointing to him who had tossed the paper over, "and then look well upon the prisoner. How say you? Do they not look very much like each other?"

To the astonishment of the witness, as well as everybody else in the courtroom, the resemblance was undeniable. Then might it not be the case that the witness, on that stormy night in 1775, had actually seen someone other than the defendant? Soon, the witness and his testimony were destroyed.

Mr. Cruncher had by this time taken quite a lunch of rust off his fingers in his following of the evidence. He had now to listen to the defense counsel's final statement of his case to the jury. Here the lawyer maintained that the so-called patriot, Barsad, was a villain who agreed to make up a story in return for money. How the virtuous servant, Cly, was his friend and fellow scoundrel. That the prisoner did indeed make trips between England and France, but only because he was visiting relatives in France. In sum, the lawyer told the jury, the case against the prisoner was a total lie, and the prisoner should be judged not guilty.

The attorney general, in his remarks to the jury, insisted on the very opposite, and begged the jury to declare the prisoner guilty as charged.

And now the jury retired to reach its verdict, and the great flies swarmed again.

Those who remained in the court room were

caught up in a great excitement as the jury delib-
erated. There was much talking and moving
about. But one individual, Mr. Carton, who had
so long sat looking at the ceiling of the court,
remained still and continued to gaze upward.

Yet this Mr. Carton took in more of the details
of the scene than he appeared to take in. When
Miss Manette's head dropped upon her father's
chest, he was the first to see it, and cried out,
"Officer! Look to that young lady. Help the gentleman to take her out. Don't you see she is about
to fall!"

There was much sympathy for her as she was
removed, and much sympathy for her father. It
had evidently been a great distress to him, to have
the days of his imprisonment recalled. He had
shown strong internal agitation when he was questioned. As the two exited the chamber, the jury's
foreman announced that the jury were not agreed
and needed more time.

The trial had lasted all day, and the lamps in
the court were now being lighted. A rumor circu-
lated that the jury would be out a long while.
Many spectators left for dinner, and the well-
guarded prisoner withdrew to the back of the dock
to await the verdict.

Mr. Lorry, who had gone out when the young
lady and her father went out, now reappeared, and
addressed Jerry.

"Jerry, if you wish to take something to eat,
you can. But stay close by. You will be sure to hear

when the jury come in. Don't be a moment behind them, for I want you to take the verdict back to the bank. You are the quickest messenger I know, and will get to the bank long before I can."

Mr. Carton then approached and touched Mr. Lorry on the arm.

"How is the young lady?"

"She is greatly distressed, but her father is comforting her. She feels the better for being out of court."

"I'll tell the prisoner so. It won't do for a respectable bank gentleman like you to be seen speaking to him publicly, you know."

Carton hailed the prisoner. "Mr. Darnay. You will naturally be anxious to hear of the witness, Miss Manette. She will do very well. You have seen the worst of her distress."

"I am deeply sorry to have been the cause of it. Could you tell her so for me?"

"Yes, I will, if you ask it."

"I do ask it. Accept my cordial thanks."

"What," said Carton, "do you expect the jury to decide, Mr. Darnay?"

"The worst."

"It's the wisest thing to expect, and the likeliest. But I think their request for additional time is in your favor."

An hour and a half passed. After digesting a small meal, Jerry had dropped into a doze. Suddenly, a loud murmur and a rapid tide of people pressed up the stairs that led to the court, carrying Jerry along.

"Jerry! Jerry!" Mr. Lorry was already calling at the door when he got there.

"Here I am, sir!"

Mr. Lorry handed him a paper through the crowd. "Quick! Have you got it?"

"Yes, sir."

Hastily written on the paper was the word "ACQUITTED."

"If you had sent the message 'Recalled to Life,' again," muttered Jerry, as he turned, "I should have known what you meant, this time."

He had no opportunity to say, or so much as think, anything else, until he was clear of the Old Bailey. The crowd came pouring out with a vehemence that nearly took him off his legs. A loud buzz swept into the street, as if the baffled blue-flies were dispersing in search of other carrion.

CHAPTER
4

Congratulatory

In front of the Old Bailey, Dr. Manette, his daughter Lucie, Mr. Lorry, and the defense attorney, Mr. Stryver, gathered round Mr. Charles Darnay—just released—congratulating him on his escape from death.

Dr. Manette, who now stood tall, no longer resembled the stooped-over shoemaker of the attic in Paris. Yet from time to time a gloom came over him, the product of his imprisonment in the Bastille. Only his daughter had the power of charming this mood from his mind. She was the golden thread that united him to his past and his present. The sound of her voice, the look of her face, the touch of her hand, had a strong beneficial influence with him—almost always. She could recall some occasions when her power had failed; but they were few, and she believed them over.

Mr. Darnay kissed the hand of Lucie Manette

fervently and gratefully for the words she had spoken at the trial. He also warmly thanked Mr. Stryver, his defense counsel.

As they spoke, Dr. Manette was staring at Darnay. On the doctor's face was an intent look that slowly deepened into a frown of dislike and distrust. With this strange, almost fearful expression, his thoughts had wandered away.

"Shall we go home, my father?" Lucie asked.

With a long breath, he answered, "Yes."

Mr. Lorry stood alone with the acquitted prisoner, when Sydney Carton, who had been leaning against the wall where its shadow was darkest, stepped up to where Mr. Lorry and Mr. Darnay stood upon the pavement.

The former said goodbye to the others and made his way to Tellson's. The new arrival, Carton, who smelled strongly of port wine, remarked to Darnay, "This is a strange chance that throws you and me together. This must be a strange night to you, standing alone here with your twin on these street stones?"

"I hardly seem," returned Charles Darnay, "to belong to this world again."

"I don't wonder at it. It's not so long since you were pretty far advanced on your way to another. You speak faintly."

"I begin to think I *am* faint."

"Then why the devil don't you dine? I dined, myself, while those idiots were deliberating which world you should belong to—this, or some other.

Let me show you the nearest tavern to dine well at."

Drawing Darnay's arm through his own, Carton took him down Ludgate Hill to Fleet Street and into a tavern. Here, they were shown into a little room, where Charles Darnay was soon regaining his strength with a good plain dinner and good wine. Carton sat opposite him with his separate bottle of port wine, and his half-joking manner.

"Do you feel, yet, that you belong to this world again, Mr. Darnay?"

"Yes, I do feel that."

"It must be an immense satisfaction!"

He said it bitterly, and filled up his large glass again. "As to me," Carton continued, "the greatest desire I have, is to forget that I belong to the world. It has no good in it for me—except wine like this—nor I for it. So we are not much alike in that particular. Indeed, I begin to think we are not much alike in any particular, you and I."

Confused by the emotion of the day, and sitting across from someone who looked so much like himself, Darnay was at a loss how to answer.

"Now your dinner is done," Carton presently said, "why don't you offer a toast?"

"What toast? To whom?"

"Why, the name is on the tip of your tongue. It must be. I'll swear it's there."

"Miss Manette, then!"

"Miss Manette, then!"

Looking his companion full in the face while he drank the toast, Carton flung his glass over his shoulder against the wall, where it shivered to pieces. He then ordered another.

"That's a fair young lady to be pitied by and wept for by! How does it feel? Is it worth being tried for one's life, to be the object of such sympathy and compassion, Mr. Darnay?"

Darnay did not answer.

"She was mightily pleased to have your message, when I gave it to her. Not that she showed she was pleased, but I suppose she was."

This remark reminded Darnay that this disagreeable companion had, of his own free will, been of great help to him. Darnay thanked him for it.

"I neither want any thanks, nor merit any," Carton replied. "I don't even know why I did it. Mr. Darnay, let me ask you a question."

"Certainly. It is a small payment for what you have done."

"Do you think I particularly like you?"

"Really, Mr. Carton," returned the other, "I have not asked myself the question."

"But ask yourself the question now."

"You have acted as if you do; but I don't think you do."

"*I* don't think I do," said Carton.

"Nevertheless," said Darnay, "I hope that is no reason to prevent my calling for the bill and for us to part with good feeling."

"Are you paying for both of us?" asked Carton. When Darnay nodded his head, Carton instructed the waiter to bring him more wine and to wake him at ten o'clock.

After paying, Charles Darnay rose and wished Carton good night. Without returning the wish, Carton rose too, and said, "A last word, Mr. Darnay: you think I am drunk?"

"I think you have been drinking, Mr. Carton."

"Think? You know I have been drinking."

"Since I must say so, I know it."

"Then you shall likewise know why. I am a disappointed drudge, sir. I care for no man on earth, and no man on earth cares for me."

"That is much to be regretted. You might have used your talents better."

"Maybe so, Mr. Darnay; maybe not. You don't know what the future may bring. Good night!"

When he was left alone, this strange being took up a candle, went to a mirror that hung against the wall, and looked closely at his reflection.

"Do you like Darnay?" he muttered at his own image. "Why should you like a man who happens to resemble you? There is nothing in *you* to like; you know that. How can you like someone who shows you what you have fallen away from, and what you might have been! Change places with him, and would you have been looked at by those blue eyes as he was? Would you have sparked such sympathy from her as he did? Admit it—you hate the fellow."

He turned to his wine for consolation, drinking it all in a few minutes. Soon he fell asleep with his head on his arms, with his hair straggling over the table, and the candle dripping down upon him.

CHAPTER
5

The Jackal

Those were drinking days, and most men drank hard. The defense counsel Stryver was no exception. In addition, he was known to lack the skill of summarizing cases and evidence—a skill every lawyer needs. Yet no matter what abilities Stryver lacked or how late he stayed up drinking, he always was surprisingly well prepared for court the next morning.

Sydney Carton, idlest and most unpromising of men, was Stryver's great friend. What the two drank together might have floated a ship. Whenever Stryver argued a case, Carton was there, with his hands in his pockets, staring at the ceiling of the court. After court, the two frequently sat drinking late into the night. Next morning, Carton would head stealthily and unsteadily to his lodgings. Many observed that although Sydney Carton would never be a lion, he was an amazingly good jackal. In that capacity, as a follower, he was of great service to Stryver.

But let us return to the tavern, where Darnay's departure left Carton drifting off into a wine-soaked sleep.

"Ten o'clock, sir," said the man at the tavern, whom Carton had asked to wake him—"ten o'clock, sir."

"What do you mean? Ten o'clock at night?"

"Yes, sir. Your honor told me to call you."

"Oh! I remember. Very well, very well."

With considerable effort, Carton got up, tossed his hat on, and walked rather unsteadily to the place where Stryver lived.

Wearing slippers and a dressing gown, Stryver greeted him at the door. "You are a little late," said Stryver.

"About the usual time, maybe a quarter of an hour later."

They went into a dingy room lined with books and littered with papers, where there was a blazing fire. A kettle steamed upon the stove. Among the papers stood a table, with plenty of wine upon it, and brandy and rum and sugar and lemons.

"You have had your bottle, I perceive, Sydney."

"Two tonight, I think. I have been dining with the day's client; or seeing him dine—it's all one!"

"That was a clever point, Sydney, that you brought to bear upon the identification. How did you think of it?"

"I thought he was rather a handsome fellow, and I thought I should have been much the same sort of fellow, if I had had any luck."

Mr. Stryver laughed until his stomach shook.

"You and your luck, Sydney! Get to work; get to work."

The jackal loosened his shirt, went into an adjoining room, and came back with a large jug of cold water, a basin, and a towel or two. Soaking the towels in the water, and partially wringing them out, he wrapped them around his head, sat down at the table, and said, "Now I am ready!"

"Not much legal work to be done tonight," said Mr. Stryver, happily, as he looked among his papers.

"How much?"

"Only two sets of them."

"Give me the hardest first."

"There they are, Sydney. Fire away!"

The lion then arranged himself on his back on a sofa on one side of the drinking-table, while the jackal sat at his own paper-littered table on the other side of it, with the bottles and glasses ready at hand. Both visited the drinking-table regularly, but each in a different way. The lion kept staring at the fire, occasionally glancing at a lighter document. The jackal, with knitted brows and intent face, read and summarized the difficult papers— first one set, then the other—and offered his summaries to the grateful lion.

It was not until three in the morning that the

work was finished. "And now we have done, Sydney, let us fill our glasses again," said Mr. Stryver.

The jackal removed the towels from his head, shook himself, yawned, shivered, and did what he was told.

"You did very well today, Sydney, with those crown witnesses. Every question worked."

"I always do well, do I not?" Sydney replied.

"I won't deny it. What has roughened your temper? Have another drink to smooth it."

Again the jackal did what he was told.

'The old seesaw Sydney of old Shrewsbury School," Stryver teased. "Up one minute and down the next; now cheerful, and now depressed!"

"Ah," sighed Carton, "yes! The same Sydney, with the same luck. Even in school, I did homework for other boys, and seldom did my own."

"Carton," said his friend in an earnest tone, "your way is, and always was, a lame way. You lack energy and purpose. Look at me."

"Oh, bother!" returned Sydney, with a lighter and more good-humored laugh, "don't *you* lecture me!"

"How have I done what I have done?" said Stryver. "How do I do what I do?"

"Partly through paying me to help you, I suppose. But you were always in the front rank, and I was always behind."

"I had to get into the front rank. I was not born there, was I?"

"I was not present at the ceremony; but my opinion is you were," said Carton. At this, they both laughed.

"Let us talk of other matters," Carton continued.

"Let us toast the pretty witness," said Stryver, holding up his glass.

"Pretty witness," Carton muttered, looking down into his glass. "I have had enough of witnesses today and tonight. Who's your pretty witness?"

"The lovely doctor's daughter, Miss Manette."

"*She* pretty?"

"Is she not?"

"No."

"Why, man alive, she was the admiration of the whole Court!"

"Damn the admiration of the whole Court! Who made the Old Bailey a judge of beauty? She is a golden-haired puppet!"

Mr. Stryver looked at him with sharp eyes and slowly drew a hand across his reddish face. "Do you know, Sydney," he said, "I rather thought, at the time, that you sympathized with the golden-haired puppet, and were quick to see what happened to the golden-haired puppet?"

"Quick to see what happened! If a girl, puppet or no puppet, begins to faint within a yard or two of a man's nose, he can see it quick enough. I'll join you in your toast, but I deny the beauty. And now I'll have no more drink. I'll get to bed."

Carton stepped out into the morning's faint light and made his way to his rooms. As he walked, he had a vision, for a moment, of what could have been his life's story: honorable ambition, self-denial, fame—even love. But a moment later, the vision was gone. He climbed the stairs to his room and threw himself down in his clothes on a neglected bed, its pillow wet with wasted tears.

Sadly, sadly, the sun rose. It rose upon no sadder sight than this man of good abilities and strong emotions, who could not put either to good use. He was aware of the blight upon him, but he had resigned himself to let it eat him away.

CHAPTER
6

Hundreds of People

Dr. Manette was now living, and seeing patients, in a large corner house on a quiet street in London, not far from Soho Square. One fine Sunday afternoon, four months after Darnay's trial, Mr. Jarvis Lorry walked from his residence to dine with the doctor. Over time, Mr. Lorry had become the doctor's friend, and they often spent Sundays together.

Lucie lived with her father. She had chosen the furniture and decorations for the house, and her little touches everywhere created an extremely pleasant feeling for any visitor.

There were three rooms on each floor. The first was the best room, and in it were Lucie's birds, flowers, books, desk, worktable, and box of watercolors. The second was the doctor's consulting-room, used also as the dining room. The third was the doctor's bedroom. In a corner of that room stood the disused shoemaker's bench and tray of tools—much as it had stood on the fifth floor of the dismal house by the wine shop, in the district of Saint Antoine in Paris.

"I wonder," said Mr. Lorry, looking about, "why he keeps that reminder of his sufferings about him!"

"And why wonder at that?" came an abrupt inquiry.

These words were uttered by Miss Pross, that wild-looking red woman whom Mr. Lorry had first met at the Royal George Hotel at Dover. She was Lucie's companion and servant. The profession was a respectable one. The promise of free room and board, plus some spending money, appealed to persons who had little other opportunity to earn a living.

"How do you do?" inquired that lady then— sharply, yet without ill will.

"I am pretty well, I thank you," answered Mr. Lorry meekly; "how are you?"

"I am very much put out about my Ladybird."

"May I ask the cause?"

"I don't want dozens of people who are not at all worthy of Ladybird, to come here looking after her," said Miss Pross.

"*Do* dozens come for that purpose?"

"Hundreds," said Miss Pross. "I have lived with the darling since she was ten years old. It's really very annoying that all sorts of people, who are not in the least degree worthy of her, are always turning up." She continued, "The only man worthy of my Ladybird was my brother Solomon, if he hadn't made a mistake in life."

Mr. Lorry knew the truth: Solomon was a heartless scoundrel who had stolen everything Miss Pross possessed, using her money to gamble. He had then abandoned her in her poverty, without any feelings of guilt. Miss Pross, on the other hand, was a totally unselfish and devoted creature. Her continued belief in Solomon (deducting a mere trifle for this "slight mistake") was quite a serious matter with Mr. Lorry.

"As we are alone for the moment," Mr. Lorry said, when they had got back to the drawing room, "let me ask you a question. Does the doctor, in talking with Lucie, ever refer to the time when he made shoes at his bench?"

"Never."

"And yet he keeps that bench and those tools beside him?"

"Ah!" returned Miss Pross, shaking her head. "But I can't say that he thinks about it."

"Do you believe he does?"

"I do," said Miss Pross.

"Do you suppose," Mr. Lorry went on, "that Dr. Manette has any theory of his own about why he was imprisoned? Or the name of the person responsible?"

"I don't suppose anything about it but what Ladybird tells me."

"And that is—?"

"That she thinks he has."

"Do you not think it remarkable that Dr. Manette, unquestionably innocent of any crime, should never speak about his imprisonment? Not even with his daughter?"

"Well! To the best of my understanding," said Miss Pross, "he is afraid of the whole subject."

"Afraid?"

"It's plain enough, I should think, why he may be. It's a dreadful memory."

"True," said he, "and fearful to reflect upon. Yet I wonder whether it is good for Dr. Manette to keep it all shut up within him."

"Can't be helped," said Miss Pross, shaking her head. "Touch that string, and he instantly changes for the worse. Better leave it alone. Sometimes, he gets up in the dead of the night, and we hear him walking up and down, walking up and down, in his room. Ladybird has learned to know then that his mind is walking up and down, walking up and down, in his old prison. She hurries to him, and they go on together, walking up and down, walking up and down, until he is quiet. But he never says a word of the true reason of his restlessness, to her, and she finds it best not to hint at it to him. In silence they go walking up and down together, until her love and company have made him calm."

The corner where Dr. Manette lived was so designed that the footsteps of anyone outside echoed off the walls and could be heard in the house. At that very moment, familiar footsteps could be heard.

"Here they are!" said Miss Pross, rising to end the conversation. "And now we shall have hundreds of people pretty soon!"

Dr. Manette and Lucie did indeed appear at the front door, and Miss Pross stood ready to receive them.

Miss Pross was a pleasant sight, despite being wild, and red, and grim. She took off Lucie's hat and blew the dust off it, and folded her scarf neatly. Then she smoothed Lucie's rich hair with as much pride as she might have taken in her own hair, if she had been vain. Lucie was a pleasant sight, too, hugging her and thanking her, and protesting against her taking so much trouble for her. The doctor was a pleasant sight too, looking on, telling Miss Pross how she spoiled Lucie. Mr. Lorry was a pleasant sight too, beaming at all this in his little wig. But no hundreds of people came to visit, as Miss Pross had predicted.

Dinnertime came, and still no hundreds of people. In the modest household, Miss Pross did the cooking. Her dinners, half English and half French, never failed to please.

It was an extremely warm day. After dinner, Lucie proposed that they have their wine outside in the shade.

Still, the hundreds of people did not present themselves. Mr. Darnay did present himself, while they were sitting outside; however, he was only *one*.

Dr. Manette received him kindly, and so did Lucie. The doctor was feeling very well, and he looked especially young. He had been talking all day, on many subjects, and with unusual energy. The likeness between him and Lucie was very strong at such times, as they sat side by side, she leaning on his shoulder, and he resting his arm on the back of her chair.

"Dr. Manette," said Mr. Darnay, as they sat under the shade tree, "have you seen much of the Tower of London?"

"Lucie and I have been to the great prison, but only as tourists. We have seen enough of it to know that it holds great interest."

"*I* have been there, as you remember," said Darnay, with a smile, "for another purpose, which did not allow me to see much of it. They told me a curious thing when I was imprisoned there."

"What was that?" Lucie asked.

"Some workmen, making repairs, came upon an old dungeon, which had been forgotten for many years. Every stone of its inner wall was covered by writing which had been carved by prisoners—dates, names, complaints, and prayers. Upon a corner stone, one prisoner, who was later executed, had cut, as his last work, three letters. They were done with some very poor instrument, and hurriedly, with an unsteady hand. At first, they were read as D. I. C.; but, after a careful examination, the last letter was found to be G. There was no record of any prisoner with those initials.

Finally, it was suggested that the letters were not initials, but a complete word: DIG. The floor under the inscription was examined very carefully. In the earth, beneath a stone, were the ashes of a paper, along with the ashes of a small leather case or bag. What the unknown prisoner had written no one will ever know. But he had written something, and hidden it away to keep it from the jailer."

"My father," exclaimed Lucie, "you are ill!"

Dr. Manette had suddenly stood up, with his hand to his head. His manner and his look quite terrified them all.

"No, my dear, not ill. There are large drops of rain falling, and they startled me. We had better go in."

He recovered himself almost instantly and said nothing more. But as they entered the house, Mr. Lorry thought he noticed on the doctor's face, as it turned toward Charles Darnay, the same troubled look that had been upon it when the doctor had seen Darnay in court four months ago.

Miss Pross prepared tea, and yet no hundreds of people arrived. Mr. Sydney Carton had appeared, but he made only *two*.

The night was so hot, that although they sat with doors and windows open, they were overpowered by heat. When they finished tea, they all moved to one of the windows and looked out into the heavy twilight. Lucie sat by her father; Darnay sat beside her; Carton leaned against a window.

The curtains were long and white, and some of the thunder and wind that whirled into the room blew them up to the ceiling and waved them like ghostly wings.

"The raindrops are still falling, large, heavy, and few," said Dr. Manette. "It comes slowly."

"It comes surely," said Carton.

They spoke softly, as people in a dark room, watching and waiting for lightning, always do.

There was a great hurry in the streets of people speeding away to get shelter before the storm broke. The wonderful corner for echoes, where the doctor and Lucie lived, resounded with the echoes of footsteps coming and going.

"What a crowd of people, and yet we cannot see anyone!" said Darnay, when they had listened for a while.

"Is it not impressive, Mr. Darnay?" asked Lucie. "Sometimes, I have sat here in the evening, until I have imagined—but even talk of an imaginary feeling makes me shudder tonight, when all is so black and solemn—"

"Let us shudder too. Tell us what it is."

"It will seem nothing to you. I have sometimes sat alone here in the evening, listening, until I have imagined the echoes to be all the footsteps that are coming, one day, into our lives."

"There is a great crowd coming one day into our lives, if that be so," Sydney Carton added, in his moody way.

The footsteps did not cease, and their pace

became more and more rapid. The corner echoed and re-echoed with the tread of feet. Some, as it seemed, were under the windows; some, as it seemed, were in the room; some coming, some going, some breaking off, some stopping altogether—all in the distant streets, and not one within sight.

"Are all these footsteps destined to come to all of us, Miss Manette, or are we to divide them among us?"

"I don't know, Mr. Darnay; I told you it was a foolish idea. When I have allowed myself to have such thoughts, I have been alone. Then I have imagined them the footsteps of the people who are to come into my life, and my father's."

"There is a great crowd bearing down upon us, Miss Manette, and I see them—by the lightning." Carton added the last words, after a vivid flash.

"And I hear them!" he added again, after a peal of thunder. "Here they come, fast, fierce, and furious!"

It was the rush and roar of rain. Carton became quiet, for no voice could be heard over it. A memorable storm of thunder and lightning broke. There was constant crash, and fire, and rain, until after the moon rose at midnight.

"What a night it has been! Almost a night, Jerry," said Mr. Lorry, "to bring the dead out of their graves."

"I never see the night myself, master, what

would do that," answered Jerry.

"Good night, Mr. Carton," said Mr. Lorry, as he left, accompanied by Jerry. "Good night, Mr. Darnay. Shall we ever see such a night again, together!"

Perhaps. Perhaps, see the great crowd of people with its rush and roar, bearing down upon them, too.

CHAPTER
7

Monseigneur
in Town

Monseigneur, one of the great lords in power at the Court of the King of France, was holding his reception, as he did every two weeks, in his grand mansion in Paris. Monseigneur was in his inner room, his sanctuary of sanctuaries, the Holiest of Holiests to the crowd of worshippers outside. He was about to drink his chocolate. Monseigneur could swallow a great many things easily, and some discontented citizens thought he was rather rapidly swallowing France. Be that as it may, his morning's chocolate could not so much as get into the throat of Monseigneur, without the aid of four strong men besides the cook.

Yes. It took four men, all ablaze with gorgeous decorations upon their shirts and jackets. One servant carried the chocolate-pot into Monseigneur's sacred presence. A second stirred the chocolate with the little instrument he bore for that function.

A third presented a napkin. A fourth poured the chocolate out.

Monseigneur had dined out last night and had attended the theater. Monseigneur went out for entertainment most nights. In fact, Monseigneur devoted much more time to amusing himself than to attending to his official duties as a high government official. Such affairs of state he found tiresome in the extreme. His idea of looking after the welfare of France was simply to let things run their course.

This life of lazy self-indulgence had steadily chipped away at Monseigneur's grand fortune, inherited from his ancestors. To reverse this tide, Monseigneur decided to ally himself with an extremely rich landowner. Accordingly, Monseigneur had taken his own sister from a convent, just before she had taken her vows, and had bestowed her as a prize upon the very rich landowner. Although fabulously wealthy, this man was not of noble blood like Monseigneur. Therefore, Monseigneur looked down upon him with the greatest contempt.

This landowner lived extremely well. Thirty horses stood in his stables. Twenty-four male servants attended him, while six women waited on his wife. This landowner was one of the guests at Monseigneur's lavish gathering. The crowd included military officers who knew nothing of military tactics, naval officers with no idea of a ship, and civil servants without a notion of how to run a government. High church officials were also present, many of whom led loose lives. There were doctors there as well, who made great fortunes by selling fake remedies for imaginary illnesses.

Such were the kinds of people with whom Monseigneur regularly associated. Such were the kinds of people that governed France and set the rules for society. Among this crowd of liars and fakers, there was a single redeeming factor—all the company at Monseigneur's residence were beautifully dressed. Great attention was paid to the shaping and powdering of hair. Cosmetics were artfully applied. The men wore gleaming swords. The well-turned-out gentlemen wore little ornaments that clinked as they slowly moved about, like precious little bells. That ringing, combined with the rustle of silk and brocade and fine linen, was enough to drive Saint Antoine, and the hunger of its poor people, far away.

Monseigneur, having eased his four men of their burdens and taken his chocolate, came forth to greet his guests. Then, what submission, what cringing and fawning, what base humiliation! Offering a word of promise here and a smile there, Monseigneur passed through his rooms and mingled with the company.

Eventually, the gathering broke up, and the guests departed. The last guest to leave was a man of about sixty, handsomely dressed and haughty in manner, with a face like a fine mask. This person went downstairs into the courtyard, got into his carriage, and ordered his coachman to drive quickly away. He took particular pleasure in seeing the common people scatter before his horses, often barely escaping from being run down. So his man drove as if he were charging an enemy.

With a wild rattle and clatter, the carriage dashed through streets and swept around corners, with women screaming before it, and men clutching each other and pulling children out of its way. At last, racing around a street corner by a fountain, one of its wheels came to a sickening little jolt. There was a loud cry from a number of voices, and the horses reared and plunged.

Except for the horses' behavior, the carriage probably would not have stopped. Carriages were often known to drive on, leaving their wounded behind. But the frightened valet had got down in a hurry, and there were twenty hands holding the horses' bridles.

"What has gone wrong?" said Monsieur, calmly looking out.

A tall man had caught up a bundle from among the feet of the horses. He laid it on the base of the fountain and howled over it like a wild animal.

"Pardon, Monsieur the Marquis!" said a ragged and submissive man, "it is a child."

"Why does he make that disagreeable noise? Is it his child?"

"Excuse me, Monsieur the Marquis—it is a pity—yes."

As the tall man suddenly got up from the

ground, and ran toward the carriage, Monsieur the Marquis clapped his hand for an instant on his sword-hilt.

"Killed!" shrieked the man, in wild desperation, extending both arms above his head, and staring at him. "Dead!"

The people surrounded the carriage and looked at Monsieur the Marquis. Nobody said a word. After the first cry, they had been silent, and they remained so. Monsieur the Marquis looked at the crowd as if they had been rats that had come out of their holes.

He took out his purse. "It is extraordinary to me," said the Marquis, "that you people cannot take care of yourselves and your children. One or the other of you is forever in the way. How do I know what injury you have done to my horses? See! Give him that."

He threw out a gold coin for the valet to pick up, and all the heads craned forward that all the eyes might look down at it as it fell. The tall man called out again, with a most unearthly cry, "Dead!"

He was distracted by the quick arrival of another man, for whom the rest made way. On seeing him, the miserable creature fell upon his shoulder, sobbing and crying, and pointing to the fountain. There, some women were stooping over the motionless bundle and moving gently about it. They were as silent, however, as the men.

"I know all," said the new arrival in a comforting tone of voice. "Be a brave man, my Gaspard! It is better for the poor child to die, this way, than to live. It has died in a moment, without pain. Could it have lived an hour as happily?"

"You are a wise man, you there," said the Marquis, smiling. "What is your name?"

"Defarge."

"Of what trade?"

"Monsieur the Marquis, vendor of wine."

"Pick up that, wise man and vendor of wine," said the Marquis, throwing him another gold coin, "and spend it as you will. The horses there; are they all right?"

Without troubling himself to look at the crowd a second time, Monsieur the Marquis leaned back in his seat. He was just being driven away, like a gentleman who had accidentally broken something and had paid for it, when he was suddenly disturbed by a coin flying into his carriage.

"Stop!" said Monsieur the Marquis. "Hold the horses! Who threw that?"

He looked at the spot where Defarge, the vendor of wine, had just stood. But the wretched father was crawling on the pavement in that spot. The figure that stood beside him was the figure of a dark, stout woman, knitting.

"You dogs!" said the Marquis. "I would ride over any of you very willingly, and exterminate you from the earth. If I knew which brute threw the coin at my carriage, I would have him crushed under the wheels."

The people were frightened by long and hard experience of what such a man could do to them, within the law and beyond it. Not a voice, or a hand, or even an eye was raised. Among the men, not one. But the woman who stood knitting looked up steadily, and looked the Marquis in the face. It would be beneath his dignity to take notice of her. His scornful eyes passed over her, and over all the other rats. He leaned back in his seat again, and said to his coachman, "Go on!"

CHAPTER
8

Monseigneur in the Country

Monsieur the Marquis in his traveling carriage, conducted by four post-horses and two coachmen, made his way toward his castle. Nearby was a little village at the bottom of a hill.

The village had its one poor street, with its poor brewery, poor tannery, poor tavern, poor stable yard for relays of post-horses, poor fountain. It had its poor people too. All its people were poor, and many of them were sitting at their doors, shredding spare onions and the like for supper. Others were at the fountain, washing leaves, and grasses, and any such small products of the earth that could be eaten. Their poverty was increased by the taxes they had to pay: to the state, to the church, to the Marquis, among many others.

The hill was so steep that the carriage gradually slowed to a walking pace. At the steepest point of the hill, there was a little burial ground, with a cross and a new large figure of Our Saviour on it. It was a poor figure in wood, done by some unskilled country carver. Like the people who lived there—like the carver, perhaps—it was dreadfully thin.

Before this figure, a woman was kneeling. She turned her head as the carriage came up to her, rose quickly, and presented herself at the carriage door.

"It is you, Monseigneur! Monseigneur, a petition."

With an exclamation of impatience, Monseigneur looked out. "How, then! What is it? Always petitions!"

"Monseigneur. For the love of the great God! My husband, the forester."

"What of your husband, the forester? Always the same with you people. He cannot pay something?"

"He has paid all, Monseigneur. He is dead."

"Well! He is quiet. I cannot restore him to you."

"Alas, no, Monseigneur! But he is buried over there, under a little heap of poor grass."

"Well?"

"Monseigneur, there are so many little heaps of poor grass."

"Again, well?"

She looked like an old woman, but she was young, and filled with passionate grief. She clasped her knotted hands together with wild energy, and laid one of them on the carriage door—tenderly, caressingly, as if it could be expected to feel the appealing touch.

"Monseigneur, hear me! My husband died of poverty. So many die of poverty; so many more will die of poverty."

"Again, well? Do you expect *me* to feed them?"

"Monseigneur, the good God knows; but I don't ask it. My petition is, that a piece of stone or wood, with my husband's name, may be placed over his grave. Otherwise, the place will be quickly forgotten. It will never be found when I die of the same poverty. I shall be laid under some other heap of poor grass. Monseigneur, they are so many, they increase so fast, there is so much want. Monseigneur! Monseigneur!"

At a signal from the Marquis, the valet shoved the woman away from the door, and the horses broke into a brisk trot. Shortly thereafter, the carriage stopped, and an attendant opened the great door of the castle to the Marquis.

"Monsieur Charles, whom I expect; is he arrived from England?"

"Monseigneur, not yet."

CHAPTER
9

The Gorgon's Head

The castle of Monsieur the Marquis was a massive structure. Before the entrance lay a large stone courtyard. Two staircases made of stone swept down to a stone terrace before the main entrance. It was a stony business altogether, with heavy stone banisters, and stone urns, and stone flowers, and stone faces of men, and stone heads of lions, facing in all directions.

Up the broad flight of stone steps, Monsieur the Marquis ascended. The great door to the castle clanged behind him. He crossed a hall grim with old spears, swords, and long hunting knives. Heavy riding-rods and riding-whips were also displayed, which had laced the backs of many a peasant when the lord was angry.

Monsieur the Marquis, with his torch-bearer going on before, walked to his personal suite of rooms: his bed chamber and two others. All these rooms had high vaulted ceilings as well as all the luxuries befitting a marquis in a luxurious age and country. A supper table was set for two in the third room.

"My nephew," said the Marquis, glancing at the elaborate table laden with dishes, "has not arrived. Nevertheless, leave the table as it is. I shall be ready in a quarter of an hour."

In a quarter of an hour Monseigneur sat down alone to his lavish and choice supper. His chair was opposite to the window, and he had taken his soup, and was raising his glass of Bordeaux wine to his lips, when a faint sound made him put it down.

"What is that?" he asked one of the servants.

"Monseigneur? That?"

"Outside the blinds. Open the blinds."

It was done.

"Well?"

"Monseigneur, it is nothing. The trees and the night are all that are here."

"Good," said the master. "Close the blinds again."

That was done too, and the Marquis went on with his supper. He was halfway through it, when he again stopped with his glass in his hand, hearing the sound of wheels.

"Ask who has arrived."

It was the nephew of Monseigneur. He was to be told (said Monseigneur) that supper awaited him and that he should come to dine. In a little while, he entered the room. He had been known in England as Charles Darnay.

Monseigneur received him in a courtly manner, but they did not shake hands.

"You left Paris yesterday, sir?" he said to Monseigneur, as he took his seat at table.

"Yesterday. And you?"

"I come direct."

"From London?"

"Yes."

"You have been a long time coming," said the Marquis, with a smile.

"On the contrary; I come direct."

"Pardon me! I mean, not a long time on the journey; but a long time intending the journey."

"I have been detained by"—the nephew stopped a moment in his answer—"various business."

"Without doubt," said his elegant uncle.

So long as a servant was present, no other words passed between them. When coffee had been served and they were alone, the nephew looked at the uncle, saw a face that revealed no feeling, and began to speak.

"I have come back, sir, as you probably know, pursuing the object that took me away. It carried me into great and unexpected peril. However, it is a sacred object, and if it had carried me to death, I hope it would have sustained me."

"Not to death," said the uncle; "it is not necessary to say, to death."

"I doubt, sir," returned the nephew, "whether,

if it had carried me to the brink of death, you would have cared to stop me."

The uncle's face turned grim and menacing at that remark. Nevertheless, he made a graceful if unconvincing gesture of protest.

"Indeed, sir," pursued the nephew, "for all I know, you may have plotted to make my activities look more suspicious than they actually were."

"No, no, no," said the uncle, pleasantly.

"In effect, sir," pursued the nephew, "I believe it to be at once your bad fortune, and my good fortune, that has kept me out of a prison in France. Furthermore, I believe that if you had as much influence at the royal court as you once did, you would have arranged for me to be imprisoned for life."

"That is possible," said the uncle, "for the honor of the family. These favors from the Court are sought by so many, and they are granted to so few! It used not to be so, but France in all such things is changed for the worse. Not long ago our fathers held the right of life and death over the common masses. From this room, many such dogs were taken out to be hanged. We have lost many privileges. All very bad, very bad!"

The Marquis comforted himself with a gentle little pinch of snuff. He shook his head sadly.

"Our family has behaved so badly toward our fellow citizens, both in the old time and today," said the nephew, gloomily, "that I believe our name to be more hated than any name in France."

"Let us hope so," said the uncle. "If they hate

us, that is a sign of respect."

"Every face I see," insisted the nephew, "is a face expressing fear and slavery."

"A compliment," said the Marquis, "to the glory of our family. Hah!" He took another gentle little pinch of snuff and lightly crossed his legs. "Fear and slavery, my friend," added the Marquis, "will keep the dogs obedient to the whip, as long as this roof"—he looked upward at it—"shuts out the sky."

That might not be so long as the Marquis supposed. If the Marquis could see a picture of his castle, and fifty others like it, only a few years into the future, he would not have been able to identify it from the ghastly, fire-charred ruins. Little could he have known that the lead in its roof would be turned into bullets that would shut out the sky from the eyes of a hundred thousand victims.

"Meanwhile," said the Marquis, "I will preserve the honor of the family, if you will not. But you must be tired. Shall we end our conversation for the night?"

"A moment more."

"An hour, if you please."

"Sir," said the nephew, "we have done wrong, and are reaping the fruits of wrong."

"*We* have done wrong?" repeated the Marquis, with an inquiring smile. He delicately pointed, first to his nephew, then to himself.

"Yes," his nephew answered. "Even in my father's time, we did a world of wrong, injuring every human creature who came between us and our pleasure. Why need I speak of my father's time, when it is also your time, since you were brothers? I find myself bound to a system that is repulsive to me. What I wish to do is to execute the last request of my dear mother's lips, and obey the last look of my dear mother's eyes. She begged me to have mercy on less fortunate souls."

The Marquis stood looking quietly at his nephew, with his snuff box in his hand. Every fine straight line in the clear whiteness of his face was cruelly, craftily, and closely compressed. His finger stabbed his nephew several times on his chest, as though his finger were the fine point of a small sword. Finally he said, "My friend, I will die, preserving the system by which I have lived. You should be sensible and accept your natural destiny. But you are lost, Monsieur Charles, I see."

"This castle and France are lost to me," said the nephew, sadly. "I reject them. What are they but a wilderness of misery and ruin!"

"Hah!" said the Marquis, glancing round the luxurious room.

"To the eye, it is fair enough. However, in reality it is a crumbling tower of waste, mismanagement, extortion, debt, mortgage, oppression, hunger, nakedness, and suffering."

"Hah!" said the Marquis again, in a well-satisfied manner. "Tell me, under your new philosophy, what do you intend to do with yourself?"

"I must do what others of my countrymen, even those with noble blood, may have to do some day—work."

"In England, for example?"

"Yes. The family honor, sir, is safe from me in France. The family name can suffer from me in no other, for I do not use it abroad."

"England is very attractive to you, seeing how poorly you have prospered there," he observed then, turning his calm face to his nephew with a smile. "You know another French citizen who has found a refuge there? A doctor?"

"Yes."

"With a daughter?"

"Yes."

"Yes," said the Marquis. "You are tired. Good night! I look forward to the pleasure of seeing you again in the morning. Sleep well! Light Monsieur my nephew to his chamber there!" he ordered a servant. "And burn Monsieur my nephew in his bed, if you will," he added to himself. He rang his little bell again, and summoned his valet to his own bedroom.

After the valet had come and gone, Monsieur the Marquis walked back and forth in his loose chamber robe, preparing himself for sleep. Rustling about the room, his softly-slippered feet making no noise on the floor, he moved like a well-groomed tiger. At last he crept into his lair and went to bed.

The stone faces on the castle walls stared blindly at the black night. Out on the road, the graves marked by little heaps of poor grass were undistinguishable from one another. In the village, the hungry peasants dreamed of banquets, as the starved usually do, and of ease and rest, as the driven slave and the yoked ox may.

At last the sun touched the tops of the still trees and poured its radiance over the hill. In the glow, the water of the castle fountain seemed to turn to blood, and the stone faces turned red.

When the sun was fully risen, movement began in the village. Windows opened, and people came forth shivering—chilled, as yet, by the morning air. Some villagers came to the fountain; some, to the fields. Some led the bony cows out to such pasture as could be found by the roadside. In the church could be found a kneeling figure or two.

The castle also awoke, but a bit later. Doors and windows were thrown open. Horses in their stables looked round over their shoulders at the light and freshness pouring in. Leaves sparkled and rustled at iron-grated windows. Dogs pulled hard at their chains and reared, impatient to be let loose.

All these trivial incidents belonged to the routine of life at the castle. But there was nothing routine about the ringing of the castle's great bell, or the sudden scurrying up and down stairs by the castle attendants so early in the morning, or the quick saddling of horses and riding away.

The ringing of the castle bell meant that something important had happened there. All the people of the village were at the fountain, standing about in their depressed manner and whispering.

What could all this mean?

It meant that there was one stone face too many, up at the castle. That stone face lay on the pillow of Monsieur the Marquis. It was like a fine mask, suddenly startled, made angry, and then terrified. Driven into the heart of the Marquis, now as cold as stone, was a knife. Round its handle was a scrap of paper on which was scrawled:

"Drive him fast to his tomb. This, from Jacques."

CHAPTER
10

Two Promises

Twelve months later, Charles Darnay was living in England. He had established himself there as a teacher of French to young men who wanted to learn the language and literature. Darnay was willing to work hard, so he did well, and he earned respect.

He had loved Lucie Manette from the hour of his danger. He had never heard a sound so sweet and dear as the sound of her compassionate voice. He had never seen a face so tenderly beautiful as hers. But he had not yet spoken to her of his love. One summer day, Darnay turned into the quiet corner in Soho where Dr. Manette and his daughter lived. He had resolved to tell Dr. Manette of his love for Lucie. It was late in the day, and he knew Lucie to be out with Miss Pross.

He found the doctor reading in his armchair at a window. The doctor's health had improved markedly. He was now both strong and energetic. He studied much, slept little, and was cheerful even when tired. At the sight of Darnay, the doctor laid aside his book and held out his hand.

"Charles Darnay! We have been hoping to see you. Mr. Stryver and Sydney Carton were both here yesterday, and they said you would visit soon."

"I am obliged to them," he answered. "Miss Manette—"

"Is well," said the doctor, as he stopped short, "and your return will delight us all. She has gone out on some household matters, but will soon be home."

"Dr. Manette, I knew she would not be at home. I took the opportunity of her being away from home to speak to you."

"Yes?" said the doctor. "Bring your chair here and speak."

Darnay brought the chair, but appeared to find the speaking less easy. "I have had the happiness, Dr. Manette, of being among friends here," he began, "for some year and a half. So I hope the topic on which I am about to touch may not—"

The doctor put out his hand to stop him. When he had kept it so a little while, he said, drawing it back, "Is Lucie the topic?"

"She is."

"It is hard for me to speak of her at any time. It is very hard for me to hear her spoken of in that tone of yours, Charles Darnay."

"It is a tone of ardent admiration, true respect, and deep love, Dr. Manette!" Darnay said.

There was a brief silence before her father replied, "I believe it. I do you justice; I believe it."

His uneasiness was so evident that Charles Darnay hesitated. "Shall I go on, sir?"

Another silence. "Yes, go on."

"You anticipate what I would say. But you cannot know how earnestly I say it, how earnestly I feel it, without knowing my secret heart, and the hopes and fears and anxieties I keep there. Dear Dr. Manette, I love your daughter fondly, dearly, devotedly, without any gainful purpose. If ever there were love in the world, I love her. You have loved yourself. Let your old love speak for me!"

The doctor sat with his face turned away and his eyes bent on the ground. At the last words, he stretched out his hand again, hurriedly, and cried: "Not that, sir! Let that be! I beg of you, do not recall that!"

His cry was so like a cry of actual pain, that it rang in Charles Darnay's ears long after he had ceased. He motioned with the hand he had extended, and it seemed to be an appeal to Darnay to pause. The latter so received it, and remained silent.

"I ask your pardon," said the doctor, in a subdued tone, after some moments. "I do not doubt your loving Lucie. You may be sure of that."

He turned toward Darnay in his chair, but did not look at him, or raise his eyes. His chin dropped upon his hand, and his white hair overshadowed his face. "Have you spoken to Lucie?"

"No."

"Nor written?"

"Never."

"It is thoughtful of you to bring the matter to me. I thank you." He offered his hand, but his eyes did not go with it.

"I know," said Darnay, respectfully, "that between you and Miss Manette, there is an unusual and touching affection. Since in her childhood she had no parent, she is now devoted to you. I know that when she is clinging to you, the hands of baby, girl, and woman, all in one, are round your neck. I know that in loving you, she loves her brokenhearted mother, loves you through your dreadful trial and in your blessed restoration. I have known this, night and day, since I have known you in your home."

Her father sat silent, with his face bent down. His breathing was a little quickened, but he repressed all other signs of agitation.

"Dear Dr. Manette, always knowing this, always seeing her and you with this hallowed light about you, I have withheld my feelings as long as I could. But I love her. Heaven is my witness that I love her!"

"I believe it," answered her father, mournfully. "I have thought so before now. I believe it."

"But do not believe," said Darnay, "that if fortune were to make her my wife, I would put any separation between her and you. Besides, I know that would be hopeless and base."

The doctor looked up for the first time since the beginning of the conversation. A struggle was evidently in his face. It was a struggle that occasionally colored his face with dark doubt and dread.

"You speak so feelingly and so manfully, Charles Darnay, that I thank you with all my heart, and will open all my heart—or nearly so. Have you any reason to believe that Lucie loves you?"

"None. As yet, none."

"Do you seek any guidance from me?"

"I ask none, sir. But I have thought it possible that you might have it in your power, if you should deem it right, to give me some. May I ask, sir, if you think she is—" As he hesitated, her father supplied the rest.

"Is sought by any other suitor?"

"It is what I meant to say."

Her father considered a little before he answered:

"You have seen Mr. Carton here, yourself. Mr. Stryver is here too, occasionally. If any seek her favor, it can only be one of these."

"Or both," said Darnay.

"I had not thought of both. I do not think it likely that either seeks her hand. Now, is there anything you want from me?"

"Yes, please. If Miss Manette should ever speak her heart to you, and tell you that she loves me, that you will tell her my feelings."

"I promise," said the doctor, "without any condition. I believe your object to be, purely and truthfully, as you have stated it. I believe your intention is to strengthen, not to weaken, the ties between me and my daughter. If she should ever tell me that you are essential to her perfect happiness, I will give her to you. If there were—Charles Darnay, if there were—"

The young man had taken his hand gratefully. Their hands were joined as the doctor's voice faded into silence. So strange was the look upon his face when he had stopped speaking, that Darnay felt his own hand turn cold in the hand that slowly released and dropped it.

"You said something to me," said Dr. Manette, breaking into a smile. "What was it you said to me?"

For the moment Darnay was at a loss how to answer, but then he replied: "I wish to confide something else to you. My present name, though slightly changed from my mother's, is not my own. I wish to tell you my real name, and why I am in England."

"Stop!" said the doctor.

"I wish it, that I may the better deserve your trust, and have no secret from you."

"Stop!"

For an instant, the doctor had his two hands at his ears. For another instant, he placed his two hands on Darnay's lips.

"Tell me when I ask you, not now. If your suit

should prosper, if Lucie should love you, you shall tell me on your marriage morning. Do you promise?"

"Willingly."

"Give me your hand. She will be home directly, and it is better she should not see us together tonight. Go! God bless you!"

It was dark when Charles Darnay left him. It was an hour later and darker when Lucie came home. She hurried into the room alone—for Miss Pross had gone straight upstairs—and was surprised to find his reading chair empty.

"My father!" she called to him. "Father dear!"

No answer came, but she heard a low hammering sound in his bedroom. She looked in at his door and came running back frightened, crying to herself in terror, "What shall I do? What shall I do?"

Her uncertainty lasted only a moment. She hurried back, tapped at his door, and softly called to him. The noise ceased at the sound of her voice. He presently came out to her, and they walked up and down together for a long time.

She came down from her bed to look at him that night. He was sleeping heavily, and his tray of shoemaking tools, and his old unfinished work, were all as usual.

CHAPTER
11

A Companion Picture

"Sydney," said Mr. Stryver, on that same night, "mix another bowl of wine punch. I am going to tell you something that will surprise you. I intend to marry."

"*Do* you?" Sydney Carton replied. He had been working very hard for many evenings to finish Mr. Stryver's legal matters before the courts closed for their annual vacation.

"Yes. And not for money. What do you say to that?"

"I don't have much to say at all. Who is she?"

"Guess."

"Do I know her?"

"Guess."

"I am not going to guess, at five o'clock in the morning, with my brains all caught up in your legal matters."

"Well then, I'll tell you," said Stryver, rising

slowly to a sitting position on the sofa. "The young lady is Miss Manette. She will have in me a man already pretty well-off, and a man of some distinction. It is a piece of good fortune for her, but she is worthy of good fortune. Are you amazed?"

Carton, helping himself to a large quantity of wine punch, replied, "Why should I be amazed?"

"Well!" said his friend Stryver, "you take it more calmly than I thought you would. Yes, Sydney, I have had enough of this style of life. It must be pleasant for a man to have a home to go to. Furthermore, I feel that Miss Manette will do me credit. So I have made up my mind."

CHAPTER
12

The Fellow of Delicacy

Having decided to bring such good fortune into Lucie Manette's life, Mr. Stryver resolved to make this known to her before he left London for his vacation. Accordingly, one evening he set out in the direction of Soho to inform Miss Manette of her glorious future.

The path he walked took him by Tellson's Bank, where Mr. Lorry worked. Mr. Stryver knew that Mr. Lorry was a close friend of the Manettes. So he decided to acquaint the banker with his intentions and ask his opinion. Mr. Stryver entered the dark and gloomy establishment and immediately found Mr. Lorry.

"Hallo!" said Mr. Stryver. "How do you do? I hope you are well!"

Using his banker's tone of voice, Mr. Lorry said, "How do you do, Mr. Stryver?" and shook hands. "Can I do anything for you?"

"I have come for a personal, not a business, purpose."

"Oh indeed!" said Mr. Lorry.

"I am going to make an offer of myself in marriage to your agreeable little friend, Miss Manette."

"Oh dear me!" cried Mr. Lorry, rubbing his chin, and looking at his visitor in a doubtful way.

"Oh dear me, sir?" repeated Stryver, drawing back. "What do you mean by that, Mr. Lorry?"

"My meaning," answered the man of business, "is, of course, friendly. But—really, you know, Mr. Stryver—" Mr. Lorry paused and shook his head at him.

"Well!" said Stryver, slapping the desk with an angry hand. "If I understand you, Mr. Lorry, I'll be hanged!"

Mr. Lorry adjusted his little wig at both ears and inquired, "Were you going there now?"

"Immediately!" said Stryver, with a thump of his fist on the desk.

"Then I think I wouldn't, if I were you."

"Why?" said Stryver.

"Because," said Mr. Lorry, "I wouldn't go without having some cause to believe that I should succeed. Instead," he continued, "allow me to visit the Manettes and make some inquiries on your behalf. I'll go tonight and let you know what I discover."

"All right," said Stryver. "I won't go up there now. I shall look forward to your report to me later."

Mr. Lorry called on Mr. Stryver that night at ten o'clock.

"Well," said the good-natured banker, "I have been to Soho. And I was correct. My previous opinion was confirmed."

"I am sorry to hear it," returned Mr. Stryver. "Young women have been equally foolish before, and have regretted their foolishness later, in poverty and obscurity. Mr. Lorry, you cannot control the absurd ideas and silliness of empty-headed girls. Now, let us say no more about it. And I am really very much obliged to you for giving me your advice."

CHAPTER
13

The Fellow of No Delicacy

Sydney Carton often visited the Manette household. While there, he was usually solemn, even sad. When he spoke, he spoke well. But the familiar cloud, of caring for nothing, always seemed to be upon him.

Yet he did care something for the streets and stones that surrounded the Manettes' house. Many a night he unhappily wandered there, when wine had brought him no satisfaction. Many a dreary daybreak revealed his solitary figure lingering there.

As it was August, Mr. Stryver had left London for his vacation. One morning, Sydney's Soho wanderings took him to Dr. Manette's door.

He was shown upstairs and found Lucie at her work, alone. She had never been completely at ease with him. As they exchanged greetings, she observed a change in Carton's face.

"I fear you are not well, Mr. Carton!"

"I am not. But the life I lead, Miss Manette, does not promote health. What can be expected of one who has no regular habits and drinks to excess?"

"Is it not—forgive me—a pity to live no better life?"

"God knows it is a shame!"

"Then why not change it?"

Looking gently at him again, she was surprised and saddened to see that there were tears in his eyes. There were tears in his voice too, as he answered: "It is too late for that. I shall never be better than I am. I shall sink lower, and be worse."

He leaned an elbow on her table and covered his eyes with his hand. The table trembled in the silence that followed.

She had never seen him softened, and was much distressed. He realized this and said, "Please forgive me, Miss Manette. I break down because of what I want to say to you. Will you hear me?"

"If it will do you any good, Mr. Carton. If it would make you happier, it would make me very glad!"

"God bless you for your sweet compassion!"

He removed his hand from his face after a little while, and spoke steadily. "Don't be afraid to hear what I have to say. I am like one who died young. All my life might have been."

"No, Mr. Carton. I am sure that the best part of your life might still be. I am sure that you might be much, much worthier of yourself."

"Although I know better, I shall never forget that you said this."

He quickly went on: "If it had been possible, Miss Manette, that you could have returned my love, I would have been a happy man. But I would also have known that, despite my happiness, I would bring you to misery, disgrace you, pull you down with me. I know very well that you can have no tenderness for me. I ask for none. I am even thankful that it cannot be."

"Without it, can I not save you, Mr. Carton? Can I not recall you—forgive me again!—to a better course? Can I in no way repay your confidence?"

He shook his head. "If you will hear me just a little more, all you can ever do for me is done. I wish you to know that you have been the last dream of my soul. The sight of you with your father, and of this home, has stirred old memories that I thought had died out of me. Since knowing you, I have had vague ideas of beginning again and abandoning my wasteful ways. I know this is all a dream. I will never change. But I wish you to know that you inspired such thoughts."

"Oh Mr. Carton, think again! Try again!"

"Miss Manette, I distress you. I shall not detain you much longer. Will you let me believe, when I recall this day, that you allowed me to share this confidence with you? Will you tell no one of this conversation, not even the dearest one you shall ever know?"

"If that is what you wish, yes."

"My last request is this. I wish you to know that for you, and for those dear to you, I would do anything. I would welcome any sacrifice. Soon you will form new ties, the strongest ties any person can have. When you gaze into your loved ones' eyes, remember that there is a man who would give his life, to keep a life you love beside you!"

He said, "Farewell!" and a last "God bless you!" and left her.

CHAPTER
14

The Honest Tradesman

Jerry Cruncher, accompanied by his son, spent much of his time upon a stool perched outside Tellson's Bank on Fleet Street. There he awaited assignments from the bankers within.

One morning, when Mr. Cruncher was so engaged, a rowdy crowd of people came pouring down Fleet Street in his direction. "Young Jerry," said Mr. Cruncher, turning to his son, "it's a buryin'."

"Hooray, father!" cried Young Jerry.

"What d'ye mean? What are you hooraying at?" said Mr. Cruncher. To show his displeasure, he smacked Young Jerry on the ear.

"I warn't doing no harm," Young Jerry protested, rubbing his cheek.

"Drop it then," said Mr. Cruncher. Get on top of that there seat, and look at the crowd."

His son obeyed, and the crowd approached.

They were yelling and hissing around a dingy hearse and dingy mourning coach. Only one mourner sat in the coach, and that gentleman was dressed in dingy clothes that blended well with his vehicle. Around that mourner the crowd made ugly faces and kept calling out: "Yah! Spies! Tst! Yaha! Spies!"

Funerals had always a remarkable attraction for Mr. Cruncher. He always became excited when a funeral passed Tellson's. Such an unusual funeral naturally excited him greatly, and he asked of the first man who passed near him:

"What is it, sir? What's it about?"

"I don't know," said the man. "Spies! Yaha! Tst! Spies!"

He asked another man. "Who is it?"

"I don't know," returned the man, clapping his hands to his mouth and screaming out at the top of his lungs, "Spies! Yaha! Tst, tst! Spies!"

At length, a person better informed explained that the funeral was the funeral of one Roger Cly.

"Was *he* a spy?" asked Mr. Cruncher.

"Old Bailey spy," returned his informant. "Yaha! Tst! Yah! Old Bailey spies!"

"Why, to be sure!" exclaimed Jerry, recalling the trial of Charles Darnay. "I've seen him. Dead, is he?"

"Dead as mutton," returned the other, "and can't be too dead. Drag 'em out, there! Spies! Pull 'em out, there! Spies!"

This idea greatly appealed to the onlookers. They mobbed the two vehicles, forcing the procession to come to a halt. When the crowd opened the coach doors, the one mourner barely managed to flee with his life. In his place, eight members of the crowd piled in, including a chimney sweep, a seller of meat pies, and Jerry Cruncher himself.

Thus, with beer drinking, pipe smoking, and song roaring, the disorderly procession went its way to the burying ground at the old church of Saint Pancras. There the deceased Roger Cly was laid to rest.

The crowd then broke up, but not without breaking various shop windows and pulling down whatever railings it could reach. Many then retired to pubs and ale-houses, where they celebrated the events of the day.

Mr. Cruncher did not assist at these closing sports. Instead, he remained behind in the church-yard to confer with the gravediggers. On his way home that night, Mr. Cruncher made a brief stop at the office of a surgeon he dealt with from time to time.

The evening meal completed, Mrs. Cruncher asked her husband, "Are you going out tonight?"

"Yes, I am."

"May I go with you, Father?" asked his son, briskly.

"No, you mayn't. I'm a-going—as your mother knows—a-fishing. That's where I'm going to. Going a-fishing."

"Your fishing rod gets rather rusty; don't it, Father?"

"Never you mind."

"Shall you bring any fish home, Father?"

"If I don't, you'll have short rations, tomorrow," replied Mr. Cruncher, shaking his head. "That's enough questions for you. I ain't a-going out till you've been long in bed."

In time Young Jerry was ordered to bed. Not long after, Mrs. Cruncher also retired for the night. Mr. Cruncher sat in his chair and smoked his pipe, as the sky turned from gray to pitch black. Toward one o'clock, he rose up from his chair, took a key from his pocket, opened a locked closet, and brought forth a sack, a crowbar, a rope and chain, and other fishing tackle of that nature. Carrying these articles with him, he extinguished the light and went out.

Young Jerry, who had only pretended to go to sleep, heard his father go out and followed him. For cover, he kept as close as he could to house fronts, walls, and doorways. After a short while, another man joined his, and then a third.

The three went on, and Young Jerry went on, until they stopped before an iron gate by a churchyard. All three men nimbly climbed over the gate. They lay on the ground a little—listening, perhaps. Then, they moved away on their hands and knees.

When the three men had moved a short distance into the graveyard, Young Jerry approached the gate, holding his breath. Crouching down in a corner, and looking in, he made out the three "fishermen" creeping through the grass. The gravestones in the churchyard looked on like ghosts in white, while the church tower itself peered down like the ghost of a monstrous giant. They did not creep far before they stopped and stood upright. And then they began to fish.

They fished with a spade, at first. Then Mr. Cruncher began to work some instrument like a great corkscrew. The men bent over their quarry. With great effort, they managed to haul it up to the surface. Young Jerry very well knew what it would be. But, when he saw it, and saw his parent about to wrench it open, he was so frightened that he ran away like the wind.

In his terror, he imagined that the coffin he had seen was chasing him. He pictured it as hopping on behind him, upright, upon its narrow end, always about to overtake him. It hid in doorways too. It got into shadows on the road, and lay on its back to trip him up. All this time it was gaining on him, so that when the boy got to his own door, he felt half dead. And even then it would not leave him, but followed him upstairs with a bump on every stair, scrambled into bed with him, and bumped down, dead and heavy, on his chest when he fell asleep.

There was no fish for breakfast the next morning, and not much of anything else. Mr. Cruncher was in a bad temper. But by then, the terrors of the night had fled from Young Jerry's mind. He got himself brushed and washed at the usual hour, and he set off with his father to pursue their normal occupation.

"Father," said Young Jerry, as they walked along, "what's a Resurrection-Man?"

Mr. Cruncher came to a stop on the pavement before he answered, "How should I know?"

"I thought you knowed everything, Father," said the boy, innocently.

"Hem! Well," replied Mr. Cruncher, "he's a tradesman."

"What's his goods, father?" asked Young Jerry.

"His goods," said Mr. Cruncher, after turning it over in his mind, "is a branch of scientific goods."

"Persons' bodies, ain't it, Father?" asked the lively boy.

"I believe it is something of that sort," said Mr. Cruncher.

"Oh, Father, I should so like to be a Resurrection-Man when I'm quite growed up!"

Mr. Cruncher was soothed. "It depends upon how you dewelop your talents. Be careful to dewelop your talents, and never to say no more than you can help to nobody, and there's no telling what you may not come to be fit for." As Young Jerry, thus encouraged, went on ahead, to place the stool in the shadow of the Bar, Mr. Cruncher added to himself, "Jerry, you honest tradesman, there's hopes wot that boy will be a blessing to you yet!"

CHAPTER
15

Knitting

One early afternoon, two dusty men passed through the streets of Saint Antoine. One of them was Monsieur Defarge. The other, in a blue cap, was a repairer of roads. Full of thirst, the two entered Monsieur Defarge's wine shop, where a small group of men were sitting at tables.

"Good day, gentlemen!" said Monsieur Defarge.

"Good day!" was the joint reply.

"It is bad weather, gentlemen," said Defarge, shaking his head.

The customers sat silent. One man got up and went out.

"My wife," said Defarge aloud, addressing Madame Defarge, "I have traveled a good distance with this good mender of roads, called Jacques. I met him—by accident—a day and half's journey out of Paris. He is a good man. Give him something to drink!"

A second man got up and went out. Madame Defarge set wine before the mender of roads called Jacques. He saluted the company with his blue cap and drank. He unwrapped some dark bread he had carried with him and bit off chunks, which he ate with his thin wine. A third man got up and went out.

Defarge refreshed himself with some wine. When the man in the blue cap had finished eating and drinking, Defarge said to him, "Come see the apartment that I have chosen for you. It will suit you just fine."

The two men walked out of the wine shop into the street, across a courtyard, up a steep staircase, and into a room. This was the very same room where Dr. Manette had stayed, making shoes.

The chamber was vacant, of course. However, the three men who had gone out of the wine shop singly were there. They were the very same individuals who had once looked in at Dr. Manette through the holes in the wall.

Defarge closed the door carefully and spoke in a subdued voice. "Jacques One, Jacques Two, Jacques Three! This is the witness I left Saint Antoine to meet. We shall call him Jacques Five. He will tell you all. Speak, Jacques Five!"

"I saw him," began the mender of roads, blue cap in hand, "a year ago this summer. He clung to the bottom of the coach in which the Marquis was traveling. He was very tall. Next day the Marquis is stabbed. The tall man disappears."

"He was well hidden," said Defarge, "but at

last he is unluckily found. Go on!"

"I am again at work upon the hillside, and the sun is about to go to bed. I am collecting my tools to head to my cottage in the village below, when I raise my eyes, and see six soldiers coming over the hill. In the midst of them is a tall man with his arms tied to his sides—like this!"

He then represented a man with his elbows bound fast at his hips, with cords that were knotted behind him.

"When they advance quite near to me, I recognize the tall man, and he recognizes me. But I do not show the soldiers that I recognize the tall man. He does not show the soldiers that he recognizes me. 'Come on!' says the officer, pointing to the village, 'bring him to his tomb!' and they bring him faster. I follow. His arms are swollen because of being bound so tight. Also, he is lame. Because he is lame, and consequently slow, they drive him with their guns—like this!"

He imitated the action of a man's being pushed forward by the butt-ends of muskets.

"As they descend the hill, he falls. They laugh and pick him up again. His face is bleeding and covered with dust, but he cannot touch it. This makes the soldiers laugh again. They bring him into the village, past the mill, and up to the prison at the top of the hill. All the village sees the prison gate open in the darkness of the night, and swallow him—like this!"

He opened his mouth as wide as he could, and

shut it with a loud snap of his teeth.

"Next morning," went on the mender of roads, "I go to fix the roads with my tools upon my shoulder, eating my black bread as I go. When I pass the prison, I see him, high up, behind the bars of an iron cage, bloody and dusty. He has no hand free to wave to me. I dare not call to him."

Defarge and the three Jacques glanced at one another. The looks of all of them were dark and revengeful, as they listened to the worker's story.

"Go on, Jacques," said Defarge.

"He remains up there in his iron cage some days. The villagers steal glances at him, for they are fearful. There is whispered talk that he will be executed for murdering Monseigneur the Marquis. One old man says at the fountain, that his right hand, armed with the knife, will be burnt off before his face. Into wounds which will be made in his arms, his chest, and his legs, there will be poured boiling oil, melted lead, hot resin, wax, and sulfur. Finally, he will be torn limb from limb by four strong horses. That old man says that all this was actually done to a prisoner who tried to kill a former king. But how do I know if he lies? I am not a scholar."

"Listen," said one of the Jacques. "The name of that prisoner was Damiens, and it was all done in public here in Paris. There was a large crowd, which included many ladies of quality and fashion. They stayed all day until nightfall, when he had lost two legs and an arm, and still breathed!"

"Enough!" said Defarge. "Go on."

"Well! At length, on Sunday night, workmen raise a gallows forty feet high. All work is stopped. All the villagers assemble there. At midday, the roll of drums. Soldiers bring the prisoner to the hanging ground. He is bound as before, and in his mouth there is a gag. He is hanged there forty feet high—and is left hanging."

They looked at one another, as he used his blue cap to wipe some sweat off his face.

After a gloomy silence, the first Jacques said, "Good! You have acted and spoken faithfully. Will you wait for us a little, outside the door?"

"Very willingly," said the mender of roads, who left the room.

"How say you, Jacques?" demanded Number One. "To be recorded?"

"To be recorded, as doomed to destruction," returned Defarge.

"The castle and all the race?" inquired the first.

"The castle and all the race," returned Defarge. "Extermination."

"Are you sure," asked Jacques Two, of Defarge, "that no danger can arise from our method of keeping the record? Without doubt it is safe, for no one except ourselves can read it. But shall we always be able to read it—or, I ought to say, will she?"

"Jacques," returned Defarge, "if madame my wife undertook to keep the record in her memory alone, she would not lose a word of it. Knitted, in her own stitches and her own symbols, it will always be as plain to her as the sun. Trust Madame Defarge. It would be easier for the weakest fool that lives, to erase himself from existence, than to erase one letter of his name or crimes from the knitted register of Madame Defarge."

There was a murmur of confidence and approval. Then one of the Jacques asked, "Is this simple fellow to be sent back soon? I hope so. He is not too bright. Is he not a little dangerous?"

"He knows nothing," said Defarge. "Let him remain with me. I will take care of him and set him on his way. He wishes to see the fine world—the King, the Queen, and Court. Let him see them on Sunday."

"What?" exclaimed Jacques, staring. "Is it a good sign, that he wishes to see royalty and nobility?"

"Jacques," said Defarge; "show a cat milk, if you wish her to thirst for it. Show a dog his natural prey, if you wish him to bring it down one day."

When Sunday came, the Defarges accompanied the mender of roads to Versailles. Here a gigantic palace housed the king and queen and thousands of lords and ladies of royal blood. All the way there, Madame Defarge continued to knit. As the crowd that afternoon waited to see the carriage of the King and Queen, Madame Defarge kept on with her knitting.

"You work hard, madame," said a man near her.

"Yes," answered Madame Defarge. "I have a good deal to do."

"What do you make, madame?"

"Many things."

"For instance—"

"For instance," returned Madame Defarge, calmly, "shrouds."

After a while, the king and queen of France arrived in their golden coach. They were accompanied by a glittering assembly of laughing ladies and fine lords, all in jewels and elegant silks. Along with the crowd, the mender of roads cried "Long live the King" and "Long live the Queen."

"Bravo!" said Defarge, clapping him on the back when it was over. "You are a good boy!"

The mender of roads was beginning to wonder whether he should have cheered.

"You are the fellow we want," said Defarge. "You make these fools believe that the nobility will reign for ever. Then, they will treat the people worse, and their reign is sooner ended."

CHAPTER
16

Still Knitting

At the end of the day, the Defarges picked their way through the mud and garbage that lined the streets of Saint Antoine and returned home. On the way, Monsieur Defarge held a brief and private conversation with a policeman he knew well.

Madame Defarge inquired of her husband, "Say then, what did Jacques of the police tell you?"

"The authorities are sending a spy to our neighborhood, to report on our activities. Additional spies might follow."

"Eh well!" said Madame Defarge, raising her eyebrows with a cool business air. "It is necessary to register him. What is his name?"

"He is English."

"So much the better. His name?"

"Barsad," said Defarge.

"Barsad," repeated madame. "Good. First name?"

"John."

"John Barsad," repeated madame, after murmuring it once to herself. "Good. His appearance—is it known?"

"Age, about forty years; height, about five feet nine; black hair; dark complexion; rather handsome features; eyes dark, face thin, long, and pale; nose long, but not straight, inclining toward the left cheek; expression, therefore, sinister."

"It is a portrait!" said madame, laughing. "He shall be registered tomorrow."

The next afternoon saw Madame Defarge in her usual place in the wine shop, busily knitting away. Today, however, a rose lay beside her. There were a few customers sprinkled about. The day was very hot, and flies buzzed about the wine shop.

A new customer entered the wine shop. At that instant, Madame Defarge laid down her knitting and pinned the rose in her headdress. The moment Madame Defarge took up the rose, the other customers stopped talking and gradually began to leave.

"Good day, madame," said the newcomer.

"Good day, monsieur."

She said it aloud, but added to herself, as she resumed her knitting: "Hah! Good day, age about forty, height about five feet nine, black hair, generally rather handsome features, dark complexion, eyes dark, thin, long and pale face, long nose but not straight, having a peculiar inclination toward the left cheek which imparts a sinister expression! Good day, one and all!"

"May I have a little glass of cognac and some

cool fresh water, madame."

Madame set the two glasses before the customer and resumed her knitting.

The visitor watched her fingers for a few moments and declared, "You knit with great skill, madame. May one ask what it is for?"

"It helps pass the time," said madame, still looking at him with a smile while her fingers moved nimbly.

"Not for any particular purpose?"

"I may find a use for it one day. If I do—well, I'll use it!"

The effect of the rose on the wine shop's regular customers was remarkable. Two men had entered separately, and had been about to order a drink, when, catching sight of the flower, they went away. Furthermore, all the customers who had been there when the visitor entered were now gone. The spy had kept his eyes open, but he could not figure out why everyone had left.

"JOHN," thought madame, checking off her work as her fingers knitted, and her eyes looked at the stranger. "Stay long enough, and I shall knit 'BARSAD' before you go."

"You have a husband, madame?"

"I have."

"Children?"

"No children."

"Business seems bad?"

"Business is very bad; the people are so poor."

"Ah, the unfortunate, miserable people! So oppressed, too—as you say."

"As *you* say," madame retorted, correcting him, and deftly knitting an extra something into his name that promised him no good.

"Pardon me. Certainly it was I who said so, but you naturally think so. Of course."

"*I* think?" returned madame, in a high voice. "I and my husband have enough to do to keep this wine shop open, without thinking. All we think, here, is how to live. That is the subject *we* think of."

The spy continued to sip his cognac. Trying to gather any information he could, he then said, "A bad business this, madame, of Gaspard's execution. Ah! poor Gaspard!" With a sigh of great compassion.

"My faith!" returned madame, coolly and lightly, "if people use knives for such purposes, they have to pay for it. He knew beforehand what the penalty was. He has paid the price."

Lowering his voice, the spy continued, "I believe there is much compassion and anger in this neighborhood, concerning the poor fellow. Just between us, is that not so?"

"Oh, here is my husband!" said Madame Defarge.

As the keeper of the wine shop entered, the spy greeted him with "Good day, Jacques!" Defarge stopped short and stared at him.

"Good day, Jacques!" the spy repeated.

"You deceive yourself, monsieur," replied the keeper of the wine shop. "You mistake me for another. That is not my name. I am Ernest Defarge."

"I was saying to madame that they tell me there is—and no wonder!—much sympathy and anger in Saint Antoine, regarding the unhappy fate of poor Gaspard."

"No one has told me so," said Defarge, shaking his head. "I know nothing of it."

The spy, well practiced in his craft, asked for another glass of cognac. Madame Defarge poured it out for him, took to her knitting again, and hummed a little song over it.

"The pleasure of conversing with you, Monsieur Defarge, reminds me," pursued the spy, "that I have some familiarity with your name."

"Indeed!" said Defarge, with much indifference.

"Yes, indeed. When Dr. Manette was released, you, his old servant, took care of him, I know. He was delivered to you."

"That is so," said Defarge.

"It was to you," said the spy, "that his daughter came. And it was from your care that his daughter took him, accompanied by an Englishman named Lorry, of the bank of Tellson and Company, to England."

"Such is the fact," repeated Defarge.

"Very interesting recollections!" said the spy. "I know Dr. Manette and his daughter in England."

"Yes?" said Defarge.

"You don't hear much about them now?" said the spy.

"No," said Defarge.

"In effect," madame struck in, looking up from her work and her little song, "we never hear about them. We received the news of their safe arrival, and another letter or two. Since then, they have gradually taken their road in life—we, ours—and we have not corresponded."

"Then let me inform you," replied the spy, that Miss Manette is going to be married—to one who, like herself, is French by birth. And speaking of Gaspard (ah, poor Gaspard! It was cruel, cruel!), it is a curious thing that she is going to marry the nephew of Monsieur the Marquis. He is now the present Marquis, but the English do not know this. He is Mr. Charles Darnay. D'Aulnais is the name of his mother's family."

Madame Defarge knitted steadily, but this news had a visible effect upon her husband. The spy saw his hand shaking, and he made a note of it in his mind.

Having made, at least, this one observation, and doubting he would learn anything else of value, Mr. Barsad paid for his drinks and took his leave.

"Can it be true," said Defarge, in a low voice, looking down at his wife as he stood smoking with his hand on the back of her chair: "what he has said of Ma'amselle Manette?"

"As he has said it," returned madame, lifting her eyebrows a little, "it is probably false. But it may be true."

"If it is," Defarge began, "then I hope her husband will stay out of France when the great upheaval comes."

"Her husband's destiny," said Madame Defarge, with her usual composure, "will take him where he is to go."

With those words she rolled up her knitting and removed the rose from her hair. Shortly afterwards, the usual crowd filtered in to the wine shop.

In the evening, as darkness closed around, church bells rang. From the palace courtyard came the distant beating of military drums, as the women sat knitting, knitting. Darkness surrounded them. Another darkness was closing in, as surely, all over France. In this darkness, the church bells, now ringing so pleasantly, would be melted into thundering cannon. The drums would drown out the voices of the powerful. And the women would gather around a structure yet unbuilt, where they would sit knitting, knitting, counting dropping heads.

CHAPTER
17

One Night

It was the night before Lucie was to be married. She had reserved this last evening for her father, and they sat alone in the garden in the moonlight.

"You are happy, my dear father?"

"Quite, my child."

"And I am very happy tonight, dear father. I am deeply happy in the love that Heaven has so blessed—my love for Charles, and Charles's love for me. But if my marriage would cause a separation between us, I should be more unhappy than I can tell you." She clasped him by the neck, and laid her face upon his chest.

The doctor tenderly kissed her and declared, "My future is far brighter, Lucie, with your marriage, than it could have been—nay, than it ever was—without it. How could my happiness be perfect, while yours was incomplete? In my wildest thoughts, I never imagined the happiness that I have known with you, and that we have before us."

He embraced her and humbly thanked Heaven for having given her to him. After a time, they went into the house.

No one was invited to the wedding next day except Mr. Lorry. The only bridesmaid was Miss Pross. Once married, Lucie and Charles would live at Dr. Manette's house, occupying the upper rooms.

Dr. Manette was very cheerful at supper that evening. Eventually, the time came for him to bid Lucie good night, and they separated. But, a few hours after midnight, Lucie came downstairs and crept into his room to see if he were all right.

She found the doctor quietly asleep, his white hair spread on the untroubled pillow. She set her candle aside and kissed him gently. She prayed that she might always be true to him, took up her candle, and glided out of the room.

CHAPTER
18

Nine Days

The marriage day shone brightly, and the wedding party was making preparations to go to church. Mr. Darnay was conferring with Dr. Manette in the latter's room. This gave Mr. Lorry an opportunity to draw Lucie aside and say, "Rest assured that you leave your good father in hands as earnest and as loving as your own. We shall take extremely good care of him during your honeymoon in Warwickshire." That said, he planted a delicate kiss upon her forehead and made ready to go off to church.

The door of the doctor's room opened, and he came out with Charles Darnay. The doctor was deadly pale—which had not been the case when they went in together. However, he seemed otherwise undisturbed. Nevertheless, Mr. Lorry feared that the old air of dread had lately passed over him, like a cold wind.

Dr. Manette gave his arm to his daughter and escorted her downstairs to the coach which Mr. Lorry had hired. The rest followed in another carriage, and soon, in a nearby church, Charles Darnay and Lucie Manette were happily married.

They returned home to breakfast, and all went well. In due course it was time for the newly married couple to leave. Lucie and her father embraced, her golden hair mingling with his white hair. Her father comforted her, and said at last, gently removing himself from her arms, "Take her, Charles! She is yours!"

Her agitated hand waved to them from the carriage window, and she was gone.

Dr. Manette, Mr. Lorry, and Miss Pross were left quite alone. When they turned into the welcome shade of the cool old hall, Mr. Lorry observed a great change in the doctor. It was as though Lucie's waving arm had struck him a poisoned blow.

"I think," Mr. Lorry whispered to Miss Pross, after anxious consideration, "I think we had best not speak to him just now. I must look in at Tellson's. I will go there at once and come back soon. Then, we will take him for a ride into the country and dine there, and all will be well."

Two hours later, Mr. Lorry returned from the bank. He ascended the old staircase and approached the doctor's room. There he was stopped by a low sound of knocking.

"Good God!" he said, startled. "What's that?"

Miss Pross, with a terrified face, was at his ear.

"O me, O me! All is lost!" she cried, wringing her hands. "What is to be told to Lucie? He doesn't recognize me, and he is making shoes!"

Mr. Lorry said what he could to calm her and entered the doctor's room. The bench was turned toward the light, and his head was bent down. He was very busy.

"Dr. Manette. My dear friend, Dr. Manette!"

The doctor looked at him for a moment—half inquiringly, half as if he were angry at being spoken to—and bent over his work again.

He had laid aside his coat. His shirt was open at the throat, as it used to be when he did that work. Even the old haggard expression had returned to his face. He worked steadily, impatiently, as if he had been interrupted.

Mr. Lorry glanced at the work in the shoemaker's hand, and observed that it was a shoe of the old size and shape. He took up another that was lying by him, and asked what it was.

"A young lady's walking shoe," the doctor muttered, without looking up. "It ought to have been finished long ago. Let it be."

"But—Dr. Manette. Look at me!"

He obeyed, in the old submissive manner, without pausing in his work.

"You know me, my dear friend? Think again. This is not your proper occupation. Think, dear friend!"

The doctor did not answer. He looked up, for an instant at a time, when he was requested to do so. But then he would return immediately to his work. Mr. Lorry resolved to watch him attentively, in the hope that the doctor would recover. He notified Tellson's that he would be absent for a time, and began to keep watch over Dr. Manette.

Mr. Lorry was not long in discovering that it was worse than useless to speak to the doctor. Therefore, he contented himself with sitting silently, reading, writing, and observing him.

Dr. Manette took what was given him to eat and drink and worked, that first day, until it was too dark to see. When he put his tools aside until morning, Mr. Lorry rose and said to him, "Will you go out?"

He looked down at the floor on either side of him in the old manner, looked up in the old manner, and repeated in the old low voice, "Out?"

"Yes, for a walk with me. Why not?"

The doctor did not reply. Miss Pross and Mr. Lorry divided the night into two watches. They observed him from the adjoining room. He paced up and down for a long time before he lay down. When he did finally lie down, he fell asleep. The next morning he awoke and went straight to his bench.

On the second day, Mr. Lorry greeted him cheerfully and brought up topics they had recently talked about. Again, the doctor made no reply. When it became dark, Mr. Lorry asked him as before, "Dear Doctor, will you go out?"

As before, he repeated, "Out?"

"Yes; for a walk with me. Why not?"

The doctor made no reply, but he made it clear that he did not care to leave the house. The third day came and went, as did the next six. The doctor's condition did not change. Mr. Lorry's heart grew heavier and heavier. He observed that the shoemaker was growing more skillful, and that he had never been so intent on his work, as on that ninth evening.

CHAPTER
19

An Opinion

On the morning of the tenth day, Mr. Lorry was surprised to see that the shoemaker's bench and tools had been put aside. Dr. Manette sat reading at the window.

Mr. Lorry decided to greet the doctor as if nothing unusual had occurred. Miss Pross agreed. If Dr. Manette continued to behave normally, Mr. Lorry would then try to learn what had caused his relapse, and if it might happen again.

When the breakfast was cleared away, Mr. Lorry spoke. "My dear Manette, I am anxious to have your opinion on a matter of concern to me. The case involves a particularly dear friend of mine. Please advise me well for his sake—and above all, for his daughter's—his daughter's, my dear Manette."

"If I understand," said the doctor, in a subdued tone, "some mental shock—?"

"Yes!"

"Be explicit," said the doctor. "Spare no detail."

"My dear Manette, it is the case of an old and a severe shock to the mind. In time the sufferer recovered, although he is not sure how. Unfortunately, there has been"—he paused and took a deep breath—"a slight relapse."

The doctor, in a low voice, asked, "For how long?"

"Nine days and nights."

"How did it show itself? I assume," glancing at his hands, "that he resumed an old behavior connected with the shock?"

"Exactly."

"Now, did you ever see him," asked the doctor in the same low voice, "engaged in that behavior originally?"

"Once."

"And when the relapse fell on him, was he in most respects—or in all respects—as he was then?"

"I think in all respects."

"You spoke of his daughter. Does his daughter know of the relapse?"

"No. It has been kept from her, and I hope will always be kept from her. It is known only to myself, and to one other who may be trusted."

The doctor grasped his hand and murmured, "That was very kind."

Neither spoke for a while. Finally, Mr. Lorry said, "I am a mere man of business, and I know little about such matters. Tell me, how does this relapse come about? Is there danger of another? Could a repetition be prevented? How should a repetition be treated? Please tell me how to help my friend. I want to be useful."

Dr. Manette sat for a moment, deep in thought.

"I think," said the doctor, speaking with an effort, "that the relapse you have described, my dear friend, was expected by its subject."

"Was it dreaded by him?" Mr. Lorry ventured to ask.

"Very much," he said with a shudder. "You have no idea how such a fear weighs on the sufferer's mind."

"Would he," asked Mr. Lorry, "feel better if he could tell someone about it?"

"I think so. But it is next to impossible. Quite impossible."

"Now," said Mr. Lorry, gently laying his hand on the doctor's arm, after a short silence on both sides, "what is the cause of this attack?"

"I believe," returned Dr. Manette, "that something brought to mind a memory that caused the attack in the first place. This is what the sufferer must have feared."

"Would he remember what took place during the relapse?" asked Mr. Lorry, with natural hesitation.

The doctor shook his head and answered, in a low voice, "Not at all."

"Now, as to the future," hinted Mr. Lorry.

"As to the future," said the doctor, recovering firmness, "I should have great hope. Since a merciful Heaven restored him so soon, I should hope that the worst was over."

"Well, well! That's good comfort," said Mr. Lorry. "There are two other points on which I am anxious to be instructed. I may go on?"

"You cannot do your friend a better service."

"First of all, he is a studious person, unusually energetic. He reads a great deal. He conducts experiments. Now, does he do too much?"

"I think not. The more his mind is occupied with healthy things, the less it would be in danger of turning in an unhealthy direction."

"You are sure that he is not under too great a strain?"

"I am quite sure of it."

"Now for my second question. When suffering under the affliction we have been considering, let us say my friend turned to"—Mr. Lorry hesitated a bit—"blacksmith's work. Whenever he is deeply troubled, he turns to his forge. Now, might it be a good idea to remove that forge from his presence?"

The doctor shaded his forehead with his hand and tapped his foot nervously on the ground.

"He has always kept it by him," said Mr. Lorry, with an anxious look at his friend. "Now, would it not be better that he should let it go?"

Still, the doctor, with shaded forehead, tapped his foot nervously on the ground.

"You do not find it easy to advise me?" said Mr. Lorry.

"You see," said Dr. Manette, turning to him after an uneasy pause, "it is very hard to explain the workings of this poor man's mind. He once relied on the forge to relieve intense mental pain. Even now, when I believe he is more hopeful of himself than ever, he fears that one day he might need that old employment. Not having the forge close by would terrify him."

"But is it not possible that keeping the forge close by might encourage the return of his dreaded disorder?"

There was another silence.

"I would not keep it," said Mr. Lorry. "I would recommend him to get rid of it. I am sure it does no good. I only want your approval. For his daughter's sake, my dear Manette!"

The doctor did not answer. He seemed uncomfortable, even fearful. Finally he replied, "In *her* name, then, let it be done. But I would not take it away while he was present. Let it be removed when he is not there."

The conversation ended. For the next three days, Dr. Manette remained perfectly well. On the day after that, he went away to join Lucie and her husband.

That night, Mr. Lorry went into the doctor's room with a hatchet, saw, chisel, and hammer. Miss Pross held a candle. Mr. Lorry hacked the shoemaker's bench to pieces, which they burned in the kitchen fire. They then buried the tools, shoes, and leather in the garden. They looked, and felt, like accomplices in a horrible crime.

CHAPTER
20

A Plea

W hen the newly-married pair came home, the first person to offer his congratulations was Sydney Carton. He looked as careless as he had before, but there was a new air of faithfulness about him. After commending the couple, he said to Darnay privately, "I wonder if you would allow such a worthless fellow as myself to visit this house from time to time. I would not abuse the privilege. I wouldn't come more than, say, four times a year."

The new husband agreed. They shook hands upon it, and Sydney turned away to join the rest of the company.

When he was gone, Charles Darnay mentioned this conversation to Lucie, Mr. Lorry and Miss Pross. In relating the conversation, Darnay referred to Sydney Carton as a careless and reckless man—exactly as he seemed to the outside world.

Later that night, Lucie and Charles retired to their own chamber. There, Charles noticed that his wife seemed unusually thoughtful. "Is something troubling you, my love?" he asked.

"I think, Charles," Lucie answered, "that poor Mr. Carton deserves more consideration and respect than you expressed for him tonight. I would ask you, dearest, to be very generous with him always, and to be lenient with his faults. He has a heart he very, very seldom reveals, and there are deep wounds in it. My dear, I have seen it bleeding. I am sure that he is capable of good things, even noble things."

She looked so beautiful, as she expressed faith in this lost man, that her husband could have looked at her as she was for hours.

"And, my dearest Love!" she urged, as she clung to him and rested her head upon his chest, "remember how strong we are in our happiness, and how weak he is in his misery!"

"I will always remember it, dear Heart! I will remember it as long as I live."

CHAPTER
21

Echoing Footsteps

The corner where the doctor lived was a wonderful corner for echoes. All the sounds from the street could be heard. Ever busily winding the golden thread which bound her husband, and her father, and herself, and her old companion, in a life of quiet bliss, Lucie sat in the still house, listening to the echoing footsteps of years.

As the years passed, a new Lucie was born into the family. Then the echoes held the tread of her tiny feet and the sound of her prattling words. The shady house was sunny with a child's laugh.

Ever busily winding the golden thread that bound them all together, Lucie heard, in the echoes of years, only friendly and soothing sounds. Her husband's step was strong and prosperous among them; her father's, firm and equal.

Even when there were sad sounds in the echoes, they were not harsh or cruel. Lucie and Charles's second child, a son, was born with golden

hair, like her own. Sadly, he did not thrive. On the last day of his life, he said, with a radiant smile, "Dear papa and mamma, I am very sorry to leave you both, and to leave my pretty sister; but I am called, and I must go!" And so he departed this Earth, and the rustling of an angel's wings was blended with the other echoes.

The mother took comfort and delight in her little Lucie. As she performed a daily task or played with a doll, she chattered in the tongues of the Two Cities that were blended in her life.

The echoes rarely answered to the actual tread of Sydney Carton. Some half-dozen times a year, at most, he claimed his privilege of coming in uninvited, and would sit among them through the evening, as he had once done often.

No man ever really loved a woman, lost her, and remained her faithful friend, when she was a wife and a mother, whose children did not have feelings for him. Carton was the first stranger to whom little Lucie held out her chubby arms. The little boy had spoken of him, almost with his last breath: "Poor Carton! Kiss him for me!"

Mr. Stryver shouldered his way through the law, like some great engine forcing itself through stormy seas. He dragged his useful friend Carton, like a towed boat, in his wake. As the boat usually has a rough voyage, mostly under water, Sydney had a swamped life. Stryver grew rich. He married a wealthy widow with three boys, who had nothing particularly shining about them but the straight hair of their dumpling heads.

These were among the echoes to which Lucie Darnay listened in the echoing corner, until her little daughter was six years old. The echoes of her father, her husband, and her child, in their united home, filled with loving kindness, were music to her. Her father often told her that he found her more devoted to him married than single. Her husband often marveled that no cares and duties seemed to interfere with her love and help. He would ask, "What is the magic secret, my darling, of your being everything to all of us, yet never seeming to be hurried, or to have too much to do?"

But there were other echoes, from a distance, that rumbled menacingly in the corner all through this space of time. And now, about little Lucie's sixth birthday, they began to have an awful sound, as of a great storm in France with a dreadful sea rising.

On a night in mid-July, 1789, Mr. Lorry came in late from Tellson's and sat down by Lucie and her husband in the dark window. It was a hot, wild night. All three remembered a previous Sunday night when they had looked at the lightning from the same place.

"I began to think," said Mr. Lorry, "that I should have to pass the night at Tellson's. There is such an uneasiness in Paris, that we have more business than we can handle! Our customers in France cannot transfer their property to us fast enough. There is positively a mania among some of them for sending it to England."

"That has a bad look," said Darnay.

"Yes, but we don't know the reason."

Tea was served, and the group sat quietly and looked out on the still street.

But in Saint Antoine across the sea, there was neither quiet nor stillness. A tremendous roar arose from the throat of Saint Antoine. A forest of naked arms struggled in the air like shriveled branches of trees in a winter wind. Fingers reached for every weapon that became available.

No one could have said who gave them out and where they came from. But guns were being distributed—twenty at a time, over the heads of the crowd. So were cartridges, gunpowder, iron bars, knives, axes, pikes, and every other kind of weapon. People who could lay hold of nothing else used their bleeding hands to force stones and bricks from walls. Every pulse and heart in Saint

Antoine was at high-fever heat. Every living creature there saw life as worthless, and was passionately ready to sacrifice it.

A whirlpool of boiling waters has a center point. All this raging circled around Defarge's wine shop. Defarge himself was already begrimed with gunpowder and sweat. Every human drop in the swirling caldron was sucked toward the place where Defarge issued orders and issued weapons.

"Keep near to me, Jacques Three," cried Defarge. "You, Jacques One and Two, separate, and put yourselves in front of as many of these patriots as you can. Where is my wife?"

"Here you see me!" said madame, calm as ever, but not knitting today. Madame Defarge's right hand held an axe, and in her belt were a pistol and a knife.

"Where are you going, my wife?"

"I go," said madame, "with you, for now. You shall see me at the head of women, in a little while."

"Come, then!" cried Defarge, in a loudly echoing voice. "Patriots and friends, we are ready! The Bastille!"

With a roar, the living sea of people rose, wave on wave, and overflowed the city. Soon the prison of the Bastille was before it. Alarm bells ringing, drums beating, the sea raging and thundering on its new beach, the attack began.

Deep ditches, double drawbridge, massive stone walls, eight great towers, cannon, muskets, fire and smoke. In the fire and in the smoke,

Defarge of the wine shop worked like a soldier.

One drawbridge down! "Work, comrades all! Work, Jacques One, Jacques Two, Jacques One Thousand, Jacques Two Thousand, Jacques Five-and-Twenty Thousand!" Thus shouted Defarge of the wine shop, still at his gun, which had grown hot after two hours.

"To me, women!" cried his wife. "We can kill as well as the men when the place is taken!" Around Madame Defarge the women gathered, with a shrill thirsty cry, all holding weapons, all armed alike with hunger and revenge.

The battle for the Bastille raged. Cannon, muskets, fire and smoke. Boom, smash, and rattle, and the furious sounding of the living sea. But, still the deep ditch, and the single drawbridge, and the massive stone walls, and the eight great towers.

And still Defarge of the wine shop at his gun, grown doubly hot after four fierce hours.

A white flag from within the fortress. Surrender! Suddenly, the sea of attackers rose immeasurably wider and higher. It swept Defarge over the lowered drawbridge, past the massive stone outer walls, in among the eight great towers.

So powerful was the force of the ocean bearing him on, that Defarge could not turn his head until he landed in the outer courtyard of the Bastille. There, against an angle of a wall, he struggled to look about him. Jacques Three was nearly at his side. Madame Defarge, still leading her women, was a bit further on, her knife in her hand.

"The prisoners!"

"The records!"

"The secret cells!"

"The instruments of torture!"

"The prisoners!"

Of all these cries, "The prisoners!" was the cry most given by the sea that rushed in. When the prison officers were captured, Defarge laid his strong hand on the shoulder of one of these men, separated him from the rest, and pushed him against the prison wall.

"Show me the North Tower!" said Defarge. "Quick!"

"I will faithfully," replied the man, "if you will come with me. But there is no one there."

"What is the meaning of One Hundred and Five, North Tower?" asked Defarge. "Quick!"

"The meaning, sir?"

"Does it mean a captive, or a place of captivity? Or do you mean that I shall strike you dead?"

"Kill him!" croaked Jacques Three, who had joined Defarge.

"Monsieur, it is a cell."

"Show it to me!"

"Come this way, then."

Through gloomy vaults where the light of day had never shone, past hideous doors of dark dens and cages, down and then up steep rugged stairs of stone and brick, Defarge, the guard, and Jacques Three went as quickly as they could. Finally the guard stopped at a low door, turned a key in a lock, and swung the door slowly open. As they all bent their heads and passed in, he said: "One Hundred and Five, North Tower!"

There was a small, heavily-grated, unglazed window high in the wall. A stone screen blocked it, so that the sky could be seen only by stooping low and looking up. There was a small chimney, heavily barred across, a few feet within. There was a heap of old feathery wood ashes on the hearth. There were a stool, and table, and a straw bed. There were the four blackened walls and a rusted iron ring in one of them.

"Pass that torch slowly along these walls, that I may see them," said Defarge to the guard.

The man obeyed, and Defarge followed the light closely with his eyes.

"Stop!—Look here, Jacques!"

"A. M.!" croaked Jacques Three, as he read excitedly.

"Alexandre Manette," said Defarge. "And here he wrote 'a poor physician.' And it was he, without doubt, who scratched a calendar on this stone. What is that in your hand? A crowbar? Give it to me!"

Turning on the worm-eaten stool and table, he beat them to pieces in a few blows.

"Hold the light higher!" he said angrily to the guard. "Look among those fragments with care, Jacques. And see! Here is my knife," throwing it to him; "rip open that bed, and search the straw. Hold the light higher, you!"

Defarge looked up the chimney. He struck and pried at its sides with the crowbar and worked at the iron grating across it. In a few minutes, some mortar and dust came dropping down, which he averted his face to avoid. Defarge reached cautiously into the chimney, turning his hand this way and that.

"Nothing in the wood, and nothing in the straw, Jacques?"

"Nothing."

"Let us collect them together, in the middle of the cell. So! Light them, you!"

The guard put his torch to the little pile, which blazed high and hot. Stooping again to come out at the low-arched door, they left it burning, and returned to the courtyard. Soon they were in the raging flood once more.

They found it surging and tossing, in quest of Defarge himself. Saint Antoine wanted to have its wine shop keeper join those guarding the prison governor.

In the howling universe of passion and contention that surrounded this grim old officer, there was but one quite steady figure. It was a woman. "See, there is my husband!" she cried, pointing him out. "See Defarge!" She stood close to the grim old officer, and remained close to him as the crowd bore him through the streets. She remained close to him when he was brought near his destination. She remained close to him when the stabs and blows fell heavy on him. She was so close to him when he dropped dead under it, that she put her foot upon his neck, and with her cruel knife—long ready—cut off his head.

Saint Antoine's blood was up, and the blood of tyranny and domination by the iron hand was down. It was down on the steps of the Hotel de Ville where the governor's body lay. It was down on the sole of the shoe of Madame Defarge, where she had stepped on the body to steady it for mutilation. "Lower the lamp yonder!" cried Saint Antoine, after glaring round for a new means of death. "Here is one of his soldiers to be left on guard!" The swinging sentinel hung from a lamp-post, and the sea rushed on.

It was a sea of black and threatening waters. Its depths were still unmeasured; its forces were still unknown. It was a remorseless sea of swaying shapes, voices of vengeance, and faces hardened in the furnaces of suffering until there was no room for pity.

In the ocean of faces, there were two groups—each seven in number—different from the rest. Seven prisoners, suddenly released by the storm that had burst their tomb, were carried high overhead. They did not understand what was happening. They were frightened, lost, wondering, and amazed, as if the Day of Judgment had come, and those who rejoiced around them were lost spirits. There were seven other faces carried even higher—seven dead faces. These were the faces on the heads of the Bastille guards.

Seven prisoners released, seven gory heads on pikes; the keys of the accursed fortress of the eight strong towers; some discovered letters and other memorials of prisoners of old time, long dead of broken hearts—the loudly echoing footsteps of Saint Antoine escort these through the Paris streets in mid-July, 1789. Now, Heaven protect Lucie Darnay, and keep these feet far out of her life! For, they are headlong, mad, and dangerous. And in the years so long after the breaking of the cask at Defarge's wine shop door, they are not easily purified when once stained red.

CHAPTER
22

The Sea Still Rises

A week passed, during which life in Saint Antoine returned to normal. Madame Defarge, with her arms folded, sat looking at the wine shop and the street. In both, there were several groups of loungers, dirty and miserable, but now with a feeling of power along with their distress. This power was the power to destroy. Every thin bare arm, which had been without work before, now knew it could strike terror in the hearts of others. The fingers of the knitting women were vicious, knowing that they could tear.

Beside Madame Defarge sat another woman, busily knitting. She was the short, rather plump wife of a starved grocer and the mother of two children. She had already earned the complimentary name of The Vengeance.

"Listen!" said The Vengeance. "Someone is coming."

"It is Defarge," said madame. "Silence, patriots!"

Defarge came in breathless, pulled off a red cap he wore, and looked around him. "Listen, everywhere!" said madame again. "Listen to him!" All those within the wine shop had sprung to their feet.

"Say then, my husband. What is it?"

"Does everybody here recall old Foulon, the government official who told the famished people that they might eat grass? The one who died, and went to Hell?"

"Everybody!" from all throats.

"The news is of him. He is among us!"

"Among us! And dead?"

"Not dead! He feared us so much—and with reason—that he spread stories that he had died. He even staged a grand mock funeral. But they have found him alive, hiding in the country, and have brought him in. I have seen him just now. He is a prisoner. I have said that he had reason to fear us. Say all! *Had* he reason?"

A chorus of angry shouts answered, "Yea!"

A moment of profound silence followed. Defarge and his wife looked steadily at one another. The Vengeance stooped, brought out a drum from behind the counter and began to beat it.

"Patriots!" said Defarge, in a determined voice, "are we ready?"

Instantly Madame Defarge's knife was in her belt. The drum was beating in the streets. The

Vengeance, uttering terrific shrieks, and flinging her arms about her head furiously, was rushing from house to house, rousing the women.

The men were terrible to look upon, as they caught up what weapons they had, and came pouring down into the streets. But the women were a sight to chill the boldest. They ran from their homes, leaving families and household tasks behind, urging themselves on with the wildest cries and actions. "Foulon alive! Foulon, who told the starving people they might eat grass! Foulon, who told my old father that he might eat grass, when I had no bread to give him! Foulon, who told my baby it might suck grass, when these breasts were dry with want! Hear me, my dead baby and my withered father. I swear on my knees, on these stones, to avenge you on Foulon! Husbands, and brothers, and young men, give us the blood of Foulon! Tear Foulon to pieces, and dig him into the ground, that grass may grow from him!" With these cries, women, lashed into blind frenzy, whirled about, striking and tearing at their own friends until they dropped into a passionate swoon. Their men had to save them from being trampled under foot.

Within a quarter of an hour not a human creature remained in Saint Antoine except a few old women and wailing children.

The other inhabitants had all filled the Hall of Examination where old Foulon, ugly and wicked, was being held and questioned. The Defarges, husband and wife, The Vengeance, and Jacques Three pressed up close to where he was.

"See!" cried madame, pointing with her knife. "See the old villain bound with ropes. See the bunch of grass tied to his back. Ha, ha! That was well done. Let him eat grass now!" Madame put her knife under her arm, and clapped her hands, as if she were at a play.

A few men had managed to climb up the outside of the building and peer in through the windows. They told the crowd outside the building what was happening. Soon the neighboring streets echoed with the clapping of hands.

Finally, after hours had passed, the sun rose so high that a kindly ray, as of hope or protection, shone directly down upon the old prisoner's head. This angered the onlookers. Defarge suddenly leaped over a railing and held the miserable wretch in a deadly embrace. Madame Defarge immediately followed, grasping one of the ropes with which he was tied. The cry went up all over the city, "Bring him out! Bring him to the lamp!"

So they brought him. They dragged him down, and up, and headfirst on the steps of the building; on his knees, on his feet, on his back. He was struck at, stifled by the bunches of grass and straw that were thrust into his face by hundreds of hands. He was torn, bruised, panting, bleeding, as he begged for mercy. Soon he was hauled to the nearest street corner where one of the fatal lamps swung. There Madame Defarge let him go—as a cat might have done to a mouse—and looked at him silently while they got him ready, and while he pleaded with her. The women were passionately screeching at him, and the men were sternly calling out to have him killed with grass in his mouth. Once, he went aloft, and the rope broke, and they caught him shrieking. Twice, he went aloft, and the rope broke, and they caught him shrieking. Then, the rope was merciful, and held him. His head was soon upon a pike, with grass enough in the mouth for all Saint Antoine to dance at the sight of.

Nor was this the end of the day's bad work. Foulon's son-in-law, another of the people's enemies, was coming into Paris, guarded by five hundred men. Saint Antoine wrote his crimes on flaming sheets of paper, seized him, set his head and heart on pikes, and carried the three bloody prizes of the day, in wolf-procession, through the streets. When night fell, the men and women came back to the children, wailing and breadless. Then, long lines of customers appeared at the miserable bakers' shops, patiently waiting to buy bad bread. While they waited with stomachs faint and empty, they congratulated one another on the triumphs of the day. Gradually, these strings of ragged people frayed away. Dim lights began to shine in high windows, and slender fires were made in the streets, at which neighbors cooked their scanty meals.

It was almost morning, when the last group of customers left Defarge's wine shop. Monsieur

Defarge said to his wife, in husky tones, while locking the door, "At last it is come, my dear!"

"Eh well!" returned madame. "Almost."

Saint Antoine slept. The Defarges slept. Even The Vengeance slept with her starved grocer, and the drum was at last silent.

CHAPTER
23

Fire Rises

The mender of roads continued to work in the village. The prison on the hill above was not so dominant as before. There were soldiers to guard it, but not many. There were officers to guard the soldiers, but not one of them knew what the soldiers would do if orders were given.

The countryside was in ruins. Every green leaf, every blade of grass and blade of grain, was as shriveled and poor as the people. Everything was bowed down, dejected, oppressed, and broken. Homes, fences, farm animals, men, women, children, and the soil that bore them—all worn out.

As the mender of roads worked, alone, in the dust, he saw a rough figure approaching on foot. He was a shaggy-haired man, tall, grim, rough-looking, covered with mud and dampness and moss and leaves. The man came upon the mender of roads, like a ghost, at noon, as he sat on his heap of stones under a bank to take a rest.

The man looked at him, looked at the village in the hollow, at the mill, and at the prison on the hill. When he had identified these objects, he said, "How goes it, Jacques?"

"All well, Jacques."

They shook hands, and the man sat down on the heap of stones.

"No dinner?"

"Nothing but supper now," said the mender of roads, with a hungry face.

"It is the fashion," growled the man. "There is no dinner anywhere."

He took out a blackened pipe, filled it, lighted it with flint and steel, pulled at it until it was in a bright glow. Then, suddenly, he held it from him and dropped something into it from between his finger and thumb, that blazed and went out in a puff of smoke.

"Tonight?" said the mender of roads.

"Tonight," said the man, putting the pipe in his mouth.

"Where?"

"Here."

He and the mender of roads sat on the heap of stones looking silently at one another for a little while.

"Show me!" said the traveler then, moving to the brow of the hill.

"Well! About two leagues beyond the summit of that hill above the village."

"Good. When do you finish work?"

"At sunset."

"Will you wake me before you leave? I have walked two nights without resting. Let me finish my pipe, and I shall sleep like a child."

"Surely."

The traveler smoked his pipe out, put it in his pocket, slipped off his great wooden shoes, and lay down on his back on the heap of stones. He soon was fast asleep.

The road-mender (who wore a red cap now, in place of his blue one) continued to work. The figure on the heap of stones fascinated him. The bronze face, the shaggy black hair and beard, the coarse woolen red cap, the rough mismatched clothes, the powerful frame, and the desperate compression of the lips in sleep, inspired the mender of roads with awe. Stooping down beside him, the road-mender tried to get a peep at secret weapons hidden in his clothes. This effort failed, however, for he slept with his arms crossed. Fortified towns with their stockades, guard houses, gates, trenches, and drawbridges, would be powerless against such a person. And when the mender of roads raised his eyes to the horizon, he saw, in his mind's eye, similar figures that no obstacle could stop, marching all over France.

The man slept on, indifferent to showers of hail and intervals of brightness. At last, the sun was low in the west, and the sky was glowing. Then, the mender of roads, having packed up his tools, roused him.

"Good!" said the sleeper, rising on his elbow. "Two leagues beyond the summit of the hill?"

"About."

"About. Good!"

The mender of roads went to the village. He was soon at the fountain, squeezing himself in among the lean cattle brought there to drink, and whispering to all the villagers. When the village had taken its poor supper, it did not creep to bed, as it usually did, but came out of doors again, and remained there. Many people whispered; others looked expectantly at the sky in one direction only. Monsieur Gabelle, chief government official of the village, became uneasy. He went out on his house-top alone and looked in that direction too.

The night deepened. The trees surrounding the old castle moved in a rising wind, as though they threatened the massive building. Uneasy rushes of wind went through the hall, among the old spears and knives, passed up the stairs, and shook the curtains of the bed where the last Marquis had slept. East, west, north, and south, through the woods, four heavy-treading, unkempt figures moved cautiously and met in the court-yard. Four lights broke out there, and moved away in different directions, and all was black again.

But not for long. Soon, the castle began to be strangely visible by some light of its own. Then, a flickering streak appeared behind the front, show-ing where railings, arches, and windows were. Then it soared higher and grew broader and brighter. Soon, from the great windows, flames burst forth, and the stone faces awakened, staring out of fire.

There was spurring and splashing through the darkness, and a horse and rider stood at Monsieur Gabelle's door. "Help, Gabelle! Help, every one!" The church bell rang impatiently, but help did not appear. The mender of roads, and two hundred and fifty particular friends, stood with folded arms at the fountain, looking at the pillar of fire in the sky. "It must be forty feet high," said they, grimly, and did not move.

The rider from the castle clattered away through the village to the prison on the hill. At the gate, a group of officers and soldiers were looking at the fire. "Help, gentlemen—officers! The castle is on fire. Valuable objects may be saved from the flames! Help, help!" The officers looked at the soldiers, who looked at the fire. No orders were given. The officer in charge said, "It must burn."

As the rider rattled down the hill again and through the street, the village was glowing. The mender of roads, and the two hundred and fifty particular friends, had been inspired by the idea of lighting up. They had darted into their houses and were putting candles in every dull little pane of glass.

The castle was left to flame and burn. In the roaring and raging of the fire, a red-hot wind seemed to be blowing the structure away. As the flames rose, the stone faces seemed to be in torment.

When great masses of stone and timber fell, one face became hidden, then struggled out of the smoke again. It could have been the face of the cruel Marquis, burning at the stake.

The castle burned. The nearest trees burned and shriveled. Molten lead and iron boiled in the marble basin of the castle's fountain. The water ran dry. Great holes and splits branched out in the solid walls. Birds, dazed, wheeled about and dropped into the furnace. Four fierce men trudged away, east, west, north, and south, along the night-enshrouded roads, guided by the beacon they had lighted, toward their next destination. The illuminated village had seized hold of the church bell and rang it for joy.

Within a hundred miles, there were several other fires. In their light many a village official was strung up and left dangling until death put an end to his misery. Other villagers and townspeople were less fortunate than the mender of roads and his fellows. Soldiers attacked them with success and strung them up in their turn. But the fierce figures were steadily traveling east, west, north, and south. And wherever they went, fires burned.

CHAPTER
24

Drawn to the Lodestone

In such risings of fire and risings of sea, three years were consumed. Three more birthdays of little Lucie had been woven by the golden thread into the peaceful life of her home.

Many a night and many a day had its residents listened to the echoes in the street corner, with hearts that failed them when they heard the rushing feet. For the footsteps had become to their minds as the footsteps of a people, tumultuous under a red flag and with their country declared in danger, changed into wild beasts.

Those members of the French aristocracy— the princes, princesses, dukes, lords, and other people of noble blood—took to their noble heels and fled the country. Those who could escape the angry clutches of the enflamed masses got away as fast as they could. The royal court was now vacant.

Numerous members of the French nobility fled to England. By the summer of 1792, Tellson's

Bank had become a headquarters of sorts for former French aristocrats. Some had seen the storm coming and had brought their fortunes out of France. Tellson's was the natural place for them to store their wealth, while they awaited better days. Nearly every newcomer from France reported in to Tellson's, almost as a matter of course. So Tellson's became the primary source of news about events in France. Sometimes, a clerk would even post the latest bulletin in the Bank windows, for all who cared to read.

On a steaming, misty afternoon in August, Mr. Lorry sat at his desk. Charles Darnay stood leaning on it, talking with him in a low voice. It was within half an hour of closing time.

"Even though you have the energy of someone half your age," said Charles Darnay, rather hesitating, "I must still suggest to you—"

"I understand. That I am too old?" said Mr. Lorry.

"Unsettled weather, a long journey, uncertain means of traveling, a disorganized country, a city that may not be even safe for you."

"My dear Charles," said Mr. Lorry, with cheerful confidence, "you mention some of the reasons for my going, not for my staying away. It is safe enough for me. Nobody will interfere with an old fellow approaching his eightieth birthday. As to its being a disorganized city—if it were not a disorganized city, there would be no need to send somebody from our House here to our House there. As to the uncertain traveling and the long journey—if I were not prepared to submit myself to a few inconveniences for the sake of Tellson's, after all these years, who ought to be?"

"I wish I were going myself," said Charles Darnay, somewhat restlessly, and like one thinking aloud.

"You wish you were going yourself? And you a Frenchman born? You are a wise counselor. Hah!"

"My dear Mr. Lorry, it is because I am a Frenchman born, that the thought has passed through my mind often. I have some sympathy for the miserable people. I cannot help thinking that I might be listened to, and might have the power to bring about some restraint."

"The truth is, my dear Charles, you have no idea of the difficulty of our business there, and the danger to our books and papers. There would be terrible consequences to many people if some of our documents were seized or destroyed. And they might be, at any time, you know. Who can say that Paris will not be set afire today, or sacked tomorrow! Now, only I have the knowledge to select these particular documents and destroy them, or get them out of harm's way."

"And do you really go tonight?"

"I really go tonight. I cannot delay longer."

"And do you take no one with you?"

"I intend to take Jerry. Jerry has been my faithful servant and bodyguard, and I am used to him. Nobody will suspect Jerry of being anything but an English bulldog, or of having any idea in his head except to protect his master."

At that moment, a bank official approached Mr. Lorry. He placed a soiled and unopened letter before him, asking if he had yet located the person to whom it was addressed. The letter was placed so close to Darnay that he could read the name. It was his own.

The address, translated into English, was: "Extremely important. To Monsieur previously the Marquis St. Evrémonde, of France. In care of Messrs. Tellson and Co., Bankers, London, England."

On the marriage morning, Dr. Manette had urgently insisted that the secret of Charles's name should be kept between them. Nobody else knew it to be his name. Even his own wife did not know. Mr. Lorry did not know either.

"No," said Mr. Lorry, in reply to the banker. "I have referred it, I think, to everybody here, and no one can tell me where this gentleman is to be found."

Darnay, unable to restrain himself any longer, said: "I know the fellow."

"Will you take charge of the letter?" said Mr. Lorry. "You know where to deliver it?"

"I do. Do you start for Paris from here?"

"From here, at eight."

"I will come back, to see you off."

Very ill at ease, Darnay found a quiet place and

opened the letter. These were its contents:
Prison of the Abbaye, Paris.

June 21, 1792.
MONSIEUR PREVIOUSLY THE MARQUIS:

I have long been in danger of my life at the hands of the village. Now I have been seized, with great violence and indignity, and brought a long journey on foot to Paris. On the road I have suffered a great deal. Nor is that all. My house has been destroyed—burned to the ground.

The crime for which I am imprisoned, and for which I shall be tried, and shall lose my life (without your so generous help), is, they tell me, treason against the people. They say I have acted against them for an emigrant—one who no longer lives in France. I have told them that I have acted *for* them, and not against, as you have instructed me. I say that, before the seizure of your property, I had used it to pay their taxes, and that I had collected no rent from them. It is useless. Their only response is, that I have acted for an emigrant, and where is that emigrant?

Ah! most gracious Monsieur previously the Marquis, where is that emigrant? I demand of Heaven, will he not come to save me? No answer. Ah, Monsieur previously the Marquis, I send my desperate cry across the sea, hoping it may perhaps reach your ears through the great bank of Tellson known at Paris!

For the love of Heaven, of justice, of generosity, of the honor of your noble name, I beg you to release me. My fault is, that I have been true to you. Oh Monsieur previously the Marquis, I pray you be true to me!

From this prison here of horror, where every hour I come nearer and nearer to destruction, I send you, Monsieur previously the Marquis, the assurance of my sorrowful and unhappy service.

Your afflicted
GABELLE

This letter affected Darnay deeply. Gabelle was an old servant and a good one, whose only crime was faithfulness to himself and his family. This realization made Darnay decide what he had to do. Like the sailor in the old story, the winds and streams had driven him within the influence of the Lodestone Rock. A magnet was drawing him to itself, and he could not resist. He must go to Paris. He decided that neither Lucie nor her father must know of it until he was gone.

Soon it was time to return to Tellson's and say goodbye to Mr. Lorry. As soon as he arrived in Paris, he would present himself to this old friend. But he must say nothing of his intention now.

A carriage with post-horses was ready at the Bank door, and Jerry was booted and equipped.

"I have delivered that letter," said Charles Darnay to Mr. Lorry. "Will you take a verbal answer?"

"I will," said Mr. Lorry, "if it is not dangerous."

"Not at all. Though it is to a prisoner in the Abbaye."

"What is his name?" said Mr. Lorry, with his notebook in his hand.

"Gabelle."

"Gabelle. And what is the message to the unfortunate Gabelle in prison?"

"Simply, 'that he has received the letter, and will come.'"

"Any time mentioned?"

"He will start upon his journey tomorrow night."

"Any person mentioned?"

"No."

Darnay helped Mr. Lorry to wrap himself in a number of coats and cloaks. They went out together from the warm atmosphere of the old Bank, into the misty air of Fleet Street. "My love to Lucie, and to little Lucie," said Mr. Lorry, "and

take precious care of them till I come back."
Charles Darnay shook his head and doubtfully
smiled, as the carriage rolled away.

That night—it was the fourteenth of
August—he sat up late and wrote two letters. One
was to Lucie, explaining why he felt it necessary to
go to Paris. He also assured her that he would suffer no danger there. The other letter was to the
doctor, confiding Lucie and their dear child to his
care. To both, he wrote that he would send letters
to prove his safety immediately after he arrived.

The next day passed quickly. Early in the
evening he hugged Lucie, and her scarcely less
dear namesake, and explained that he had to go
out for a while. He had already, in secret, packed a
suitcase with his clothes. And so he went into the
heavy mist of the heavy streets, with a heavier
heart.

The unseen magnet was drawing him quickly
to itself, now, and all the tides and winds were
pushing him toward it. He left his two letters with
a trusty porter, to be delivered half an hour before
midnight, and no sooner. Then he took horse for
Dover and began his journey. "For the love of
Heaven, of justice, of generosity, of the honor of
your noble name!" This was the poor prisoner's
cry with which Darnay strengthened his sinking
heart, as he left all that was dear on earth behind
him, and floated away for the Lodestone Rock.

A TALE OF TWO CITIES

BOOK THE THIRD:

The Track of a Storm

CHAPTER
1

In Secret

In the autumn of 1792, travel from London to Paris was slow and tedious. In addition to the usual bad roads, rickety carriages, and unhealthy horses, the traveler had to contend with recently established obstacles in France. Every town and village had its band of citizen-patriots, armed and ready. They stopped all travelers, cross-questioned them, inspected their papers, looked for their names in lists of their own, turned them back, or sent them on, or simply stopped them and made them wait. Thus were the conditions at the dawning of the Republic One and Indivisible, of Liberty, Equality, Fraternity—or Death.

At least twenty times a day, Darnay was delayed by passing through such checkpoints. He had been days upon his journey in France alone, when he went to bed tired out, in a little town still a long way from Paris.

Only the production of Gabelle's letter, from his prison of the Abbaye, had gotten Darnay this far. His difficulty at the guard house in this small town had been so great that he wondered whether he would be allowed to proceed any further.

Darnay was awakened in the middle of the night. A timid local official and three armed patriots in rough red caps entered his room and sat down on the bed. "Emigrant," said the official, "I am going to send you on to Paris, with an escort."

"Citizen, I want to get to Paris, though I could do without the escort."

"Silence!" growled a red-cap, striking at the coverlet with his gun. "Peace, aristocrat!"

"It is as the good patriot says," the official added. "You are an aristocrat, and must have an escort—and must pay for it."

"I have no choice," said Charles Darnay.

"Choice! Listen to him!" cried the same scowling red-cap. "As if it was not a favor to be protected from being hanged from a lamp!"

"It is always as the good patriot says," said the official. "Rise and dress yourself, emigrant."

Darnay complied and was taken back to the guard house. There, other patriots in rough red caps were smoking, drinking, and sleeping, by a watch fire. He paid a heavy price for his escort, and he started with it on the wet roads at three o'clock in the morning.

The escort consisted of two mounted patriots in red caps decorated with tri-color cockades, symbols of the Revolution. They rode with him, one on each side, and were armed with guns and swords.

Darnay rode his own horse, but a loose line was attached to his bridle. One of the patriots kept its end tied round his wrist. In this state they set forth with the sharp rain driving in their faces. They traveled in the night, halting an hour or two after daybreak, and waiting again until the twilight fell.

The two escorts were wretchedly clothed. To protect themselves from the mud and rain, they twisted straw round their bare legs and ragged shoulders. One of the patriots was often drunk, and carried his gun very carelessly. Still, Charles Darnay felt relatively free of anxiety.

But when they came to the town of Beauvais, he suddenly felt quite alarmed. As the three riders entered the town at twilight, the streets were filled with people. An ominous crowd gathered when he dismounted. Many voices called out loudly, "Down with the emigrant!"

He lifted himself onto his horse again, feeling safer there, and said: "Emigrant? I am here, in France, by my own choice!"

"You are a cursed emigrant," cried a worker. He charged up to him in a furious manner, hammer in hand. "And you are a cursed aristocrat!"

The town postmaster placed himself between the worker and Darnay. He soothingly said, "Let him be; let him be! He will be judged at Paris."

"Judged!" repeated the worker, swinging his hammer. "Ay! And condemned as a traitor." At this, the crowd roared approval.

As soon as he could be heard, Darnay called out, "Friends, you deceive yourselves, or you are deceived. I am not a traitor."

"He lies!" cried another. "He is a traitor since the decree. His cursed life is not his own!"

Darnay saw that the crowd, already in a frenzy, was about to pull him off his horse. At that moment, the postmaster led his horse into the yard, the escort rode in afterward, and the postmaster shut and barred the double gates. The worker struck the gates with his hammer, and the crowd groaned. However, they did nothing else.

"What is this decree?" Darnay asked the postmaster, when he had thanked him, and stood beside him in the yard.

"A decree for selling the property of emigrants."

"When was it passed?"

"On the fourteenth."

"The day I left England!"

"It is but one of several new laws. There will be others—if there are not already—banishing all emigrants, and condemning all to death who return. That is what he meant when he said your life was not your own."

"But there are no such decrees yet?"

"What do I know!" said the postmaster, shrugging his shoulders. "There may be, or there will be. It is all the same."

They rested on some straw in a loft until the middle of the night. Then they rode forward again when all the town was asleep. On and on they rode through the untimely cold and wet. They passed barren fields that had yielded no fruits of the earth that year. Occasionally they spotted the blackened remains of burnt houses, or they passed patriot patrols on the watch on all the roads.

Daylight at last found them before one of the gates outside Paris. The barrier was closed and strongly guarded.

"Where are the papers of this prisoner?" demanded an authority.

Charles Darnay, disturbed by the disagreeable word, told the speaker that he was a free traveler and French citizen, in charge of an escort which had been imposed upon him, and which he had paid for.

"Where," repeated the same official, without paying any attention to him whatever, "are the papers of this prisoner?"

The drunken patriot had them in his cap and produced them. Casting his eyes over Gabelle's letter, the same authority seemed surprised, and looked closely at Darnay.

He left Darnay and his escorts without saying a word and went into the guard-room. The gate was guarded by both soldiers and civilian patriots, the latter far outnumbering the former. Peasants bringing in supplies found it easy to enter the city. However, exiting it, for anyone, was extremely difficult. Before allowing anyone to leave Paris, the guards conducted a thorough examination and carefully checked that person's identity. The red cap and tri-color cockade were everywhere, worn by both men and women.

When he had sat in his saddle a half-hour, taking note of these things, Darnay found himself faced by the same man in authority. He directed the guard to open the gate to the city. Then he delivered, to the escorts, a receipt for the escorted, and requested him to dismount. Darnay did so, and the two patriots, leading his tired horse, turned and rode away.

Darnay accompanied his conductor into a guard-room, smelling of common wine and tobacco. Soldiers and patriots, asleep and awake, drunk and sober, and in various states in between, were standing and lying about. Some registers were lying open on a desk, and a coarse-looking officer presided over these.

"Citizen Defarge," said the officer to Darnay's conductor, as he took a slip of paper to write on. "Is this the emigrant Evrémonde?"

"This is the man."

"Your age, Evrémonde?"

"Thirty-seven."

"Married, Evrémonde?"

"Yes."

"Where married?"

"In England."

"Without doubt. Where is your wife, Evrémonde?"

"In England."

"Without doubt. You are consigned, Evrémonde, to the prison of La Force."

"Just Heaven!" exclaimed Darnay. "Under what law, and for what offence?"

The officer looked up from his slip of paper for a moment.

"We have new laws, Evrémonde, and new offences, since you were here." He said it with a hard smile and went on writing.

"I beg you to observe that I have come here voluntarily, in response to that written appeal of a fellow countryman which lies before you. I demand only the opportunity to go to him without delay. Is not that my right?"

"Emigrants have no rights, Evrémonde," was the grim reply. The officer wrote until he had finished, read what he had written, blotted it, and handed it to Defarge, with the words "In secret."

Defarge motioned to the prisoner that he must accompany him. The prisoner obeyed, and a guard of two armed patriots accompanied them.

"Is it you," said Defarge, in a low voice, as they went down the guard house steps, "who married the daughter of Dr. Manette, once a prisoner in the Bastille that is no more?"

"Yes," replied Darnay, looking at him with surprise.

"My name is Defarge, and I keep a wine shop in the Quarter Saint Antoine. Possibly you have heard of me."

"My wife came to your house to reclaim her father? Yes!"

The word "wife" seemed to serve as a gloomy reminder to Defarge. He said, with sudden impatience, "In the name of that sharp female newly-born, and called La Guillotine, why did you come to France?"

"You heard me say why, a minute ago. Do you not believe it is the truth?"

"A bad truth for you," said Defarge, speaking with knitted brows, and looking straight ahead.

"All here is so changed, so suddenly and unfairly, that I am absolutely lost. Will you render me a little help?"

"None," Defarge answered, still looking straight ahead.

"Will you answer a single question?"

"Perhaps. What is it?"

"In this prison that I am going to so unjustly, may I communicate with the world outside?"

"You will see."

"I am not to be buried there, prejudged, without any means of presenting my case?"

"You will see. But, what then? Other people have been similarly buried in worse prisons, before now."

"But never by me, Citizen Defarge."

Defarge glanced darkly at him and walked on in silence. The deeper he sank into this silence, the fainter hope there was—or so Darnay thought—of his softening in any slight degree. He hurried to say, "It is of the greatest importance to me that I should be able to communicate to Mr. Lorry of Tellson's Bank, an English gentleman who is now in Paris, that I have been thrown into the prison of La Force. Will you do that for me?"

"I will do nothing for you. My duty is to my country and the People. I am the sworn servant of both, against you. I will do nothing for you."

It was hopeless to plead with him. As they walked on in silence, Darnay could see how used the people were to watching prisoners passing along the streets. He admitted to himself that he might not have made this journey, if he could have foreseen the events of the last few days. With these thoughts, he arrived at the prison of La Force.

A man with a bloated face opened the strong gate, as Defarge presented "The Emigrant Evrémonde."

"What the Devil! How many more of them?" exclaimed the jailer.

Defarge took his receipt, without noticing the exclamation, and withdrew with his two fellow patriots.

"In secret, too," grumbled the jailer, looking at the written paper. "As if I was not already full to bursting!"

He stuck the paper on a file, in an ill humor, and Charles Darnay awaited his further pleasure for half an hour.

"Come!" said the jailer, finally taking up his keys, "come with me, emigrant."

The prison of La Force was a gloomy place, dark and filthy, with a horrible smell of foul sleep. Through the dismal prison twilight, Darnay accompanied him by corridor and staircase, many doors clanging and locking behind them. At last they came into a large, low, vaulted chamber, crowded with prisoners of both sexes. The women were seated at a long table, reading and writing, knitting, sewing, and embroidering. The men were for the most part standing behind their chairs, or walking up and down the room.

Naturally associating prisoners with shameful crime and disgrace, Darnay shrank from this company. But these aristocrats graciously stood to receive him. Their manners were elegant.

"In the name of the assembled companions in misfortune," said a gentleman of courtly appearance and address, coming forward, "I have the honor of welcoming you to La Force.

I sympathize with you for the misfortune that has brought you among us. May it soon end happily! May I be so bold as to ask your name and condition?"

Charles Darnay gave the required information, in words as suitable as he could find.

"But I hope," said the gentleman, "that you are not in secret?"

"I do not understand the meaning of the term, but I have heard them say so."

"Ah, what a pity! We so much regret it! But take courage. Several members of our society have been in secret, at first, and it has lasted but a short time." Then he added, raising his voice, "I grieve to inform the society—in secret."

There was a murmur of sympathy as Charles Darnay crossed the room to a grated door, where the jailer awaited him. Many voices—among which the soft and compassionate voices of women were noticeable—gave him good wishes and encouragement. He turned at the grated door and thanked them. It closed, and he found himself on a stone staircase, leading upward. When they had climbed forty steps, the jailer opened a low black door, and they passed into a solitary cell. It was cold and damp, but it was not dark.

"Yours," said the jailer.

"Why am I confined alone?"

"How do I know?"

"I can buy pen, ink, and paper?"

"Such are not my orders. You will be visited, and can ask then. At present, you may buy your food, and nothing more."

A chair, a table, and a straw mattress were the only furniture in the cell. When the jailer was gone, Darnay murmured to himself, "Now am I left, as if I were dead."

"Five paces by four and a half, five paces by four and a half, five paces by four and a half." The prisoner walked back and forth in his cell, measuring it. The roar of the city was like muffled drums. "He made shoes, he made shoes, he made shoes. Five paces by four and a half." With such thoughts tossing in his mind, the prisoner walked faster and faster, counting and counting, hearing the roar of the city and the wail of voices.

CHAPTER
2

The Grindstone

Tellson's Bank in Paris was in a wing of a large house belonging to a nobleman. It was approached by a courtyard and shut off from the street by a high wall and a strong gate. Its owner had lived in it until he fled from the troubles, in his own cook's clothing, and escaped the country. This nobleman was the same Monseigneur who had required three men, besides the cook, to prepare his chocolate.

Jarvis Lorry was, on the third night of September, living in the building that housed Tellson's Bank. On the opposite side of the courtyard was a large area, surrounded by columns, that had once housed Monseigneur's carriages. Against two of its columns were fastened two great flaring torches. A large grindstone also occupied the space. Mr. Lorry looked out the window, shivered, and returned to his seat by the fire.

From the streets beyond the high wall and the strong gate, there came the usual night sounds of the city. But every now and then, a weird and unearthly ringing sound could be heard.

"Thank God," said Mr. Lorry, clasping his hands, "that no one near and dear to me is in this dreadful city tonight. May He have mercy on all who are in danger!"

All was quiet again, when his door suddenly opened, and two figures rushed in. Lucie and her father! Lucie with her arms stretched out to him, and with a most serious look on her face.

"What is this?" cried Mr. Lorry, breathless and confused. "What is the matter? Lucie! Manette! What has brought you here?"

Lucie was pale. She fell into Mr. Lorry's arms, crying, "O my dear friend! My husband!"

"Your husband, Lucie?"

"Charles."

"What of Charles?"

"Here."

"Here, in Paris?"

"Has been here some days—three or four. I don't know how many—I can't collect my thoughts. An errand of generosity, something we knew nothing about, brought him here. He was stopped at the barrier and sent to prison."

Almost at the same moment, the bell of the great gate rang again. A loud noise of feet and voices came pouring into the courtyard.

"What is that noise?" asked the doctor, turning toward the window.

"Don't look!" cried Mr. Lorry. "Manette, for your life, don't touch the blind!"

The doctor turned, with his hand upon the fastening of the window, and said, with a cool, bold smile, "My dear friend, I have a charmed life in this city. I have been a Bastille prisoner. There is no patriot in Paris—in France—who, knowing that I was a prisoner in the Bastille, would harm me. This power has brought us through the barrier, and gained us news of Charles there, and brought us here. I knew it would be so; I knew I could help Charles out of all danger. I told Lucie so.—What is that noise?" His hand was again upon the window.

"Don't look!" cried Mr. Lorry, absolutely desperate. "No, Lucie, my dear, nor you!" He put his arm round her and held her. "Don't be so terrified. I solemnly swear to you that I know of no harm having happened to Charles. I had no suspicion even of his being in this fatal place. What prison is he in?"

"La Force!"

"La Force! Lucie, my child, you will calm yourself now and do exactly as I say. More depends upon it than you can imagine. There is nothing you can do for your husband tonight. You must instantly be obedient and quiet. You must let me put you in a room at the back here. You must leave your father and me alone for two minutes, and you must not delay."

"I will obey you. I see in your face that you know I can do nothing else than this. I know you are true."

The old man kissed her and hurried her into his room. He then rushed back to the doctor and opened the window and the blind. He put his hand on the doctor's arm and looked out with him into the courtyard.

There they saw forty or fifty men and women clustered about the grindstone. But such awful workers, and such awful work!

The grindstone had a double handle, which two men were turning madly. Their faces were all bloody and sweaty. Their eyes glared with beastly excitement and lack of sleep. As these ruffians turned and turned the grindstone wheel, their matted hair flung forward over their eyes or backward over their necks, some women held wine to their mouths so that they might drink. What with dropping blood, and dropping wine, and the stream of sparks struck out of the stone, the wicked atmosphere reeked with gore and fire. Everyone was smeared with blood. Men, stripped to the waist, were shoving each other to get to the sharpening stone. Blood stained their limbs, their bodies, their ragged clothing, and their weapons. Hatchets, knives, bayonets, swords, all brought to be sharpened, were all red with it. And as the frantic users of these weapons snatched them from the stream of sparks and tore away into the streets, the same red was in their frenzied eyes.

"They are"—Mr. Lorry whispered the words, glancing fearfully at the room where Lucie was—"murdering the prisoners. If you really have the power you think you have, make yourself known to these devils, and get taken to La Force. It may be too late—I don't know—but do not delay one instant!"

Dr. Manette pressed his hand, hurried out of the room, and was in the courtyard in an instant. His streaming white hair, his remarkable face, and the confidence of his manner, as he pushed the weapons aside like water, carried him swiftly to the stone. For a few moments, he spoke to those at the grindstone. Then Mr. Lorry saw him in the midst of a line of twenty men, all linked shoulder to shoulder. They hurried out with cries of "Live the Bastille prisoner! Help for the Bastille prisoner's family in La Force! Make room for the Bastille prisoner in front there! Save the prisoner Evrémonde at La Force!"

Lorry closed the window and the curtain. He hastened to Lucie, finding little Lucie and Miss Pross with her. He told her that her father, assisted by the people, was gone in search of her husband.

Lucie had, by that time, fallen into a faint on the floor at his feet, clinging to his hand. Throughout the long, long night, she wept and moaned. Throughout the long, long night, her father did not reappear, nor was there news of him.

Twice more in the darkness, the bell at the great gate sounded, and the grindstone whirled and spluttered. "What is it?" cried Lucie, frightened. "Hush! The soldiers' swords are sharpened there," said Mr. Lorry. "The place is national property now."

The great grindstone, Earth, had turned when Mr. Lorry looked out again, and the sun was red on the courtyard. But the lesser grindstone stood alone in the calm morning air. Upon it was a red that the sun had never given, and would never take away.

CHAPTER
3

The Shadow

Mr. Lorry, ever the man of business, soon realized that he had no right to put Tellson's in danger by sheltering the wife of an emigrant prisoner under the Bank's roof. He would have risked his own possessions, his safety, even his life for Lucie and her child. However, the great trust he held was not his own.

At noon, when the doctor had not yet returned, Mr. Lorry went out to look for lodging for Lucie. Soon, he found a suitable place not far from the bank, on a quiet back street.

To this house he at once brought Lucie, her child, and Miss Pross. He left Jerry with them, as a bodyguard of sorts, and returned to his own banking occupations. Slowly and heavily, the day dragged on. When the bank closed, he returned to his room. He was considering what to do next, when he heard a foot upon the stair. In a few moments, a man stood in his presence and addressed him by his name.

"Do you know me?" asked Mr. Lorry.

He was a strongly built man with dark curling hair, around forty-five to fifty years of age. He answered by repeating the words. "Do you know me?"

"I have seen you somewhere."

"Perhaps at my wine shop?"

Much interested and agitated, Mr. Lorry said: "You come from Dr. Manette?"

"Yes. I come from Dr. Manette."

"And what does he say? What does he send me?"

Defarge put an open scrap of paper into his anxious hand. On it, in the doctor's writing, were these words: "Charles is safe, but I cannot safely leave this place yet. The bearer has a short note from Charles to his wife. Let the bearer see his wife." It was dated from La Force, within the hour.

"Will you accompany me," said Mr. Lorry, joyfully relieved, "to where his wife is living?"

"Yes," returned Defarge.

Defarge spoke in a curiously reserved and mechanical way. Mr. Lorry, not noticing, put on his hat, and they went down into the courtyard. There, they found two women, one knitting.

"Madame Defarge, surely!" said Mr. Lorry, who had left her in exactly the same position some seventeen years ago.

"It is she," observed her husband.

"Does Madame go with us?" inquired Mr. Lorry, seeing that she moved as they moved.

"Yes. She wishes to be able to recognize the faces and know the persons. It is for their safety."

Mr. Lorry, noticing Defarge's manner, looked doubtfully at him, but led the way. Both the women followed. The second woman was The Vengeance.

They arrived at Lucie's quarters and were admitted by Jerry. They found Lucie weeping, alone. She was overjoyed by the news of her husband Mr. Lorry gave her, and clasped the hand that delivered his note. It read, "DEAREST,—Take courage. I am well, and your father has influence around me. You cannot answer this. Kiss our child for me."

That was all the writing. It was so much, however, to Lucie, that she turned from Defarge to his wife, and kissed one of the hands that knitted. It was a passionate, loving, thankful, womanly action. But the hand made no response—it dropped, cold and heavy, and took to its knitting again.

There was something in its touch that startled Lucie. She stopped putting the note away and looked terrified at Madame Defarge. Madame Defarge met Lucie's lifted eyebrows and forehead with a cold, impassive stare.

"My dear," said Mr. Lorry, attempting to reassure her, "there are frequent uprisings in the streets. It is not likely that they will ever trouble you. Still, Madame Defarge wishes to see those whom she will have the power to protect, so that she may identify them. I believe," said Mr. Lorry, with some uncertainty, "I state the case, Citizen Defarge?"

Defarge looked gloomily at his wife and nodded.

"You had better, Lucie," said Mr. Lorry, "have the dear child here, and our good Pross. Our good Pross, Defarge, is an English lady and knows no French."

The lady in question, convinced that she was more than a match for any foreigner, appeared with folded arms and said in English to The Vengeance, "Well, I am sure, Boldface! I hope *you* are pretty well!" She also bestowed a British cough on Madame Defarge.

"Is that his child?" said Madame Defarge, and pointing her knitting needle at little Lucie.

"Yes, madame," answered Mr. Lorry. "This is our poor prisoner's darling daughter and only child."

The shadow that accompanied Madame Defarge and her party seemed to fall so threatening and dark on the child, that her mother instinctively kneeled beside her and held her close. The shadow that accompanied Madame Defarge and her party seemed then to fall, threatening and dark, on both the mother and the child.

"It is enough, my husband," said Madame

Defarge. "I have seen them. We may go."

Her grim manner had enough of menace in it to alarm Lucie. She laid her appealing hand on Madame Defarge's dress and said, "You will be good to my poor husband. You will do him no harm. You will help me to see him if you can?"

"Your husband is not my business here," replied Madame Defarge, looking down at her calmly. "It is the daughter of your father who is my business here."

"For my sake, then, be merciful to my husband. For my child's sake! We are more afraid of you than of these others."

Madame Defarge received this as a compliment. Defarge, who had been uneasily biting his thumbnail and looking at her, collected his face into a sterner expression.

"What is it that your husband says in that little letter?" asked Madame Defarge. "Influence; he says something touching influence?"

"That my father," said Lucie, hurriedly taking out the paper, but with her alarmed eyes on her questioner, "has much influence around him."

"Surely it will release him!" said Madame Defarge. "Let it do so."

"As a wife and mother," cried Lucie, most earnestly, "I beg you to have pity on me. I beg you not to exercise your power against my innocent husband, but to use it in his behalf. O sister-woman, think of me. As a wife and mother!"

Madame Defarge looked, coldly as ever, at

Lucie, and said, turning to her friend The Vengeance, "The wives and mothers we have seen around us, since we were as little as this child, have not been kindly treated. We have known *their* husbands and fathers confined in prison and kept from them, often enough. All our lives, we have seen our sister-women suffer from poverty, nakedness, hunger, thirst, sickness, misery, oppression, and neglect."

"We have seen nothing else," returned The Vengeance.

"We have borne this a long time," said Madame Defarge, turning her eyes again upon Lucie. "Judge you! Is it likely that the trouble of one wife and mother would matter to us now?"

She resumed her knitting and went out. The Vengeance followed. Defarge went last and closed the door.

"Courage, my dear Lucie," said Mr. Lorry, as he raised her. "Courage, courage! So far all goes well with us—much, much better than it has gone with many poor souls. Cheer up, and have a thankful heart."

"I am not thankless, I hope. But that dreadful woman seems to throw a shadow on me and on all my hopes."

"Nonsense!" said Mr. Lorry. "A shadow indeed! No substance in it, Lucie."

But he could not forget the Defarges' threatening behavior. In his secret mind, it troubled him greatly.

CHAPTER
4

Calm in Storm

Dr. Manette did not return until four days later. In that time, eleven hundred defenseless prisoners of both sexes and all ages had been killed by the raging mob.

To Mr. Lorry, the doctor confided that the crowd had taken him through this scene of butchery to the prison of La Force. A self-appointed court was sitting at a table, before which the prisoners were brought. This court then rapidly ordered that they were to be taken out to be massacred, or to be released, or (in a few cases) to be sent back to their cells. Presented to this court, Dr. Manette had announced himself as having been, for eighteen years, a secret and unaccused prisoner in the Bastille. One of the judges had risen and identified him. This man was Defarge.

Dr. Manette learned, by reading the lists on the table, that his son-in-law was still alive. He pleaded for Charles Darnay's life and liberty. Darnay was brought before the court, and at first, the court seemed ready to grant the doctor's request. But then the judges conferred secretly and decided that the prisoner must remain in custody—for the doctor's sake, in safe custody. The prisoner was removed to the interior of the prison again. The doctor then strongly pleaded for permission to remain and assure himself that his son-in-law was in a safe part of the prison. The court granted this request, and so Dr. Manette stayed at La Force until the danger was over.

The sights he saw there, with brief snatches of food and sleep, were too dreadful to describe. There was one prisoner, he said, who had been released into the street free, but at whom a mistaken savage had thrust a pike. The doctor was asked to go to him and dress the wound. He found him in the arms of several killers, who were sitting on the bodies of their victims. The killers helped the doctor, and tended the wounded man with the gentlest care. They even put him on a stretcher and escorted him carefully from the spot. But then they caught up their weapons and plunged anew into butchery. It was so dreadful that the doctor covered his eyes and lost consciousness.

As Mr. Lorry listened, and as he watched the face of his friend, now sixty-two years of age, he became fearful. Might not such dread experiences revive Dr. Manette's old illness and turn him back into a shoemaker?

The doctor disagreed. He felt that his previous suffering had given him strength and power. "My imprisonment all tended to a good end, my friend. It was not mere waste and ruin. As my beloved child was helpful in restoring me to myself, I will be helpful now in restoring the dearest part of herself to her. By the aid of Heaven, I will do it!" And when Jarvis Lorry saw the doctor's shining eyes and determined face, he believed.

Dr. Manette displayed such medical skill, and used his personal influence so wisely, that he was soon the inspecting physician of three prisons, including La Force. He could now assure Lucie that her husband was no longer confined alone, but was mixed with the general body of prisoners. The doctor saw her husband every week and brought sweet messages to her straight from his lips.

All this time, the doctor tried to get Charles Darnay set free, or at least to get him brought to trial. However, events were moving too swiftly. A new era had begun. The king of France was tried, convicted, and beheaded. His wife, the queen, was put to death eight months later. The nation, like a sickly patient, raged in a fever. There was a revolutionary tribunal in the capital, and forty or fifty thousand revolutionary committees all over the land. New laws took away all guarantees of liberty or life, and handed over good and innocent persons to bad and guilty ones. Prisons were filled with people who had committed no offense and could obtain no hearing. Above all, one hideous figure grew as familiar as if it had existed since the beginning of time: the figure of the sharp female called La Guillotine.

People joked about La Guillotine. They said it cured headaches, prevented gray hair, and gave the complexion an unusual delicacy. They called it the National Razor, which shaved close. Those who kissed La Guillotine, they said, looked through the little window and sneezed into the sack. For many it replaced the Cross. Models of it were worn on necks from which the Cross was discarded. It was bowed down to and believed in where the Cross was denied.

It sheared off so many heads that it, and the ground it polluted, were a rotten red. It hushed the eloquent, struck down the powerful, abolished the beautiful and good. One morning it lopped off the heads of twenty-two victims in as many minutes.

Time passed, and Charles had been in prison one year and three months. By then, the Revolution had grown more wicked. Rivers were clogged with the bodies of those violently drowned by night. Prisoners were shot in lines and squares under the southern wintry sun. But through all these terrors, the doctor walked with a steady head. No man was better known in Paris. He used his medical skills in both hospital and prison, treating both assassins and victims. His skills, his striking appearance, and his well-known story—a Bastille Captive—made him unique and protected him. He remained confident in his power, never doubting that he would save Lucie's husband at last.

CHAPTER
5

The Wood-Sawyer

One year and three months. During all that time Lucie was never sure if her husband would survive another day. Daily, through the stony streets, the wagons jolted heavily, carrying the condemned to the guillotine. Lovely girls, bright women, young men and old, gentle born and peasant born—all red wine for La Guillotine. Every day, they were brought from the dark cellars of the loathsome prisons, and carried to her through the streets to quench her devouring thirst. Liberty, equality, fraternity, or death—the last, much the easiest to bestow, O Guillotine!

It would have been understandable if Lucie had sunk into idleness and despair. But Lucie was of a different nature. She remained true to her duties, as all the quietly loyal and good always do. As soon as they were established in their new home, she arranged the little household exactly as if her husband had been there. Everything had its appointed place and its appointed time. She taught little Lucie as regularly as if they had all been united in their English home.

Lucie did not greatly change in appearance. The plain dark dresses, which she and her child wore, were as neat and as well cared for as the brighter clothes of happier days. She lost her color, and the old serious expression was always on her face. Otherwise, she remained very pretty. Sometimes, at night, kissing her father, she would burst into the grief she had repressed all day. She then would tell him of her great trust in him. The doctor always answered, "Nothing can happen to him without my knowledge, and I know that I can save him, Lucie."

One evening, Dr. Manette said to Lucie, "My dear, there is an upper window in the prison, to which Charles can sometimes gain access at three in the afternoon. When he can get to it, he might see you in the street, he thinks, if you stood in a certain place that I can show you. But you will not be able to see him, my poor child. And even if you could, it would be unsafe for you to make a sign of recognition."

"O show me the place, my father, and I will go there every day."

From that time, in all weather, she waited

there two hours. As the clock struck two, she was there, and at four she turned sadly away. When it was not too wet or stormy for her child to be with her, they went together. She never missed a single day.

It was the dark and dirty corner of a small winding street. The only house to be found at that end of the street belonged to a wood-sawyer. His occupation was to cut wood into lengths for burning. On the third day of her being there, he noticed her.

"Good day, citizeness."

"Good day, citizen." This form of address was now law.

"Walking here again, citizeness?"

"You see me, citizen!"

The wood-sawyer, who had once been a mender of roads, pointed at the prison. Putting his ten fingers before his face to represent bars, he peeped through them. "But it's not my business," he said, and went on sawing his wood.

Next day he was looking out for her, and spoke to her the moment she appeared.

"What? Walking here again, citizeness?"

"Yes, citizen."

"Ah! A child too! Your mother, is it not, my little citizeness?"

"Do I say yes, Mamma?" whispered little Lucie, drawing close to her.

"Yes, dearest."

"Yes, citizen."

"Ah! But it's not my business. My work is my business. See my saw! I call it my Little Guillotine. La, la, la; la, la, la! And off his head comes!"

The chunk of wood fell as he spoke, and he threw it into a basket.

"I call myself the Samson of the firewood guillotine. See here again! Loo, loo, loo; loo, loo, loo! And off *her* head comes! Now, a child. Tickle, tickle; pickle, pickle! And off *its* head comes. All the family!"

Lucie shuddered as he threw two more chunks into his basket. It was impossible to be there while the wood-sawyer was at work, and not be in his sight. From that day, to secure his good will, she always spoke to him first, and often gave him drink-money, which he readily received.

He was an inquisitive fellow. Sometimes, thinking only of her husband, she would forget about him completely. Then she would be surprised to find him looking at her, with his saw stopped in its work. "But it's not my business!" he would say, and would start sawing again.

In all weather—the snow and frost of winter, the bitter winds of spring, the hot sunshine of summer, the rains of autumn, and again in the snow and frost of winter, Lucie spent two hours every day at this place. Her husband saw her (so she learned from her father) once in five or six times, sometimes two or three days in a

ow, other times not for a week or two. It was
nough that he did see her when he could. For
his, she would have waited the entire day, seven
ays a week.

These occupations brought her round to
he month of December. On a lightly-snowing
fternoon, she arrived at the usual corner. It was
 day of some wild rejoicing, and a festival. She
ad seen the houses, as she came along, deco-
ated with little pikes, and with little red caps
tuck upon them. Many of the houses also dis-
layed tri-colored ribbons. Some had the stan-
ard inscription: Republic One and Indivisible.
iberty, Equality, Fraternity, or Death!

On this day her father came to join her. "I
ft him climbing to the window," he said, "and
 came to tell you. There is no one here to see.
ou may kiss your hand toward that highest roof
here."

"I do so, Father, and I send him my soul
ith it!"

"You cannot see him, my poor dear?"

"No, Father," said Lucie, weeping as she
issed her hand, "no."

A footstep in the snow. Madame Defarge. "I
alute you, citizeness," said the doctor. "I salute
ou, citizen," she replied, without feeling, and
narched on.

Dr. Manette turned to Lucie. "Give me
our arm, my love. Pass from here with an air of
heerfulness and courage, for his sake. That was

well done," he said after they had left the spot. "It shall not be in vain. Charles is summoned for tomorrow."

"For tomorrow!"

"There is no time to lose. I am well prepared, but there are precautions to be taken, which could not be taken until he was actually called before the Tribunal. He will soon receive the notice that he will be removed to the Conciergerie for his trial. You are not afraid?"

She could scarcely answer, "I trust in you."

"Do so. Your suspense is nearly ended, my darling. He shall be restored to you within a few hours. Now, I must see Lorry."

He stopped. There was a heavy lumbering of wheels. They both knew too well what it meant. One. Two. Three. Three carts passing with their dread loads over the hushing snow.

"I must see Lorry," the doctor repeated, turning her another way, so she would not see the condemned being taken to the guillotine.

It was almost dark when they arrived at the Bank. The stately residence of Monseigneur was altogether blighted and deserted. Above a heap of dust and ashes in the court, ran the letters: National Property. Republic One and Indivisible. Liberty, Equality, Fraternity, or Death!

Who could that be with Mr. Lorry—the owner of the riding-coat upon the chair—who must not be seen? From whom, newly arrived, did Mr. Lorry come out, agitated and surprised, to take his favorite in his arms? To whom did he repeat Lucie's words, "Removed to the Conciergerie, and summoned for tomorrow"?

CHAPTER
6

Triumph

The dread tribunal of five judges, public prosecutor, and determined jury, sat every day. Their
lists went forth every evening, and were read
out by the jailers of the various prisons to their
prisoners. The standard jailer joke was, "Come
out and listen to the evening paper, you inside
there!"

"Charles Evrémonde, called Darnay!"

So at last began the evening paper at La
Force.

When a name was called, its owner stepped
apart into a spot reserved for those so fatally
recorded. Charles Evrémonde, called Darnay,
had reason to know the custom. He had seen
hundreds pass away so.

His jailer glanced over to assure himself that
he had taken his place, and went through the list,
making a similar short pause at each name. There
were twenty-three names, but only twenty were

present. One of the prisoners had died in jail and been forgotten, and two had already been guillotined and forgotten. The list was read in the same vaulted chamber where Darnay had met his fellow prisoners on the night of his arrival. Every one of those had perished in the massacre. Every human creature he had since cared for and parted with, had died on the scaffold.

There were hurried words of farewell and kindness, but the parting was soon over.

The passage to the Conciergerie was short and dark. Next day, fifteen prisoners were put to the bar before Charles Darnay's name was called. All the fifteen were condemned in the space of an hour and a half.

"Charles Evrémonde, called Darnay," was at length called forth.

Looking at the jury and the turbulent audience, Darnay might have thought that the usual order of things was reversed, and that the felons were trying the honest men. The lowest, cruelest, and worst people in the city were in charge. Most of the men were armed. Some of the women wore knives, some wore daggers, some ate and drank as they looked on, many knitted. One of these women held a spare piece of knitting under her arm as she worked. She was in a front row, by the side of a man whom he had not seen since his arrival at the barrier: Defarge. He noticed that she once or twice whispered in his ear. But what he most noticed in the two figures was that although they stood very close to him, they never looked toward him. They seemed to be waiting for something, and they looked at the jury, but at nothing else. Under the President sat Dr. Manette, in his usual quiet dress. So far as the prisoner could see, he and Mr. Lorry were the only men there unconnected with the Tribunal.

Charles Evrémonde, called Darnay, was accused by the public prosecutor as an emigrant, whose life was forfeit to the Republic, under the decree which banished all emigrants on pain of Death. It did not matter that the decree was enacted after his return to France. There he was, and there was the decree. He had been taken in France, and his head was demanded.

"Take off his head!" cried the audience. "An enemy to the Republic!"

The President rang his bell to silence those cries. He asked the prisoner whether it was not true that he had lived many years in England.

Undoubtedly it was.

Was he not an emigrant then? What did he call himself?

Not an emigrant, he hoped, within the sense and spirit of the law.

Why not? the President desired to know.

Because he had given up a title and a station in life that were distasteful to him. And he had left his country before the decree was passed, to earn his living in England, rather than to live on the hard work of the overburdened people of France.

What proof had he of this?

He handed in the names of two witnesses: Theophile Gabelle and Alexandre Manette.

But he had married in England? the President reminded him.

True, but not an English woman.

A citizeness of France?

Yes. By birth.

Her name and family?

"Lucie Manette, only daughter of Dr. Manette, the good physician who sits there."

This answer had a happy effect upon the audience. Cheers for the well-known good physician rang throughout the hall. So deeply were the people moved, that tears immediately rolled down several ferocious faces. A moment before, they had been glaring at the prisoner, as if impatient to pluck him out into the streets and kill him.

Charles Darnay had answered these questions exactly as Dr. Manette had told him to. Darnay continued to respond according to the doctor's careful preparation.

The President asked, why had he returned to France when he did, and not sooner?

He had not returned sooner, Darnay replied, simply because he had no means of living in France. In England, he lived by teaching the French language and literature. He had returned when he did because of the desperate appeal of a French citizen. He had come back to save a citizen's life. Was that criminal in the eyes of the Republic?

The populace cried enthusiastically, "No!" and the President rang his bell to quiet them. It did not, and they continued to cry "No!" until they were ready to stop.

The President required the name of that citizen. The accused explained that the citizen was his first witness. He also referred to the citizen's letter, which had been taken from him at the barrier, but which he was certain would be found among the papers then before the President.

The doctor had taken care that it should be there, and it was produced and read. Citizen Gabelle was called to confirm it, and did so.

Dr. Manette was next questioned. His high personal popularity, and the clearness of his answers, made a great impression. He explained that the accused was his first friend on his release from his long imprisonment. He added that the accused had remained in England, always faithful and devoted to his daughter and himself. He pointed out that Darnay, rather than being in favor with the aristocrat government there, had actually been tried for his life by it. At last, the Jury declared that they had heard enough, and that they were ready with their verdict.

At every vote, the people applauded. All the voices were in the prisoner's favor, and the President declared him free.

As soon as the acquittal was pronounced, tears were shed, as freely as blood had been at another time. Men and women rushed to embrace him. Darnay himself was in danger of fainting from exhaustion. He knew that the very same people, carried by another current, would have rushed at him with the very same intensity, to tear him to pieces and scatter him over the streets.

All the people who had witnessed Darnay's trial had followed him out of the building to the entrance gate. All the people except two, for whom he looked in vain. On his coming out, the crowd rushed at him again, weeping, embracing, and shouting. The very tide of the river, on whose bank the mad scene was acted, seemed to run mad, like the people on the shore.

They put him into a great chair. Over the chair they had thrown a red flag, and to the back of it they had bound a pike with a red cap on its top. In this car of triumph, Darnay was carried to his home on men's shoulders, with a confused sea of red caps heaving about him.

In wild dreamlike procession, embracing whom they met and pointing him out, they carried him on. Lucie's father had gone on before, to prepare her. When her husband stood before her, she fainted in his arms.

He held her to his heart, and turned her beautiful head between his face and the brawling crowd. As his tears and her lips met, a few of the people fell to dancing. Instantly, all the rest fell to dancing, and the courtyard overflowed with the Carmagnole, the wild dance of the Revolution. They elevated into the vacant chair a young woman from the crowd to be carried as the Goddess of Liberty. Swelling and overflowing out into the streets, and along the river's bank, and over the bridge, the Carmagnole whirled them away.

Darnay grasped the doctor's hand, as he stood victorious and proud before him. Then he turned to Mr. Lorry and grasped his hand. He kissed little Lucie, who was lifted up to clasp her arms round his neck. Finally he hugged the ever zealous and faithful Pross who lifted her. Then he took his wife in his arms and carried her up to their rooms.

"Lucie! My own! I am safe."

"O dearest Charles, let me thank God for this on my knees."

They reverently bowed their heads. When she was again in his arms, he said to her, "And now speak to your father, dearest. No other man in all this France could have done what he has done for me."

She laid her head upon her father's chest, as she had laid his poor head on hers, long, long ago. "You must not be weak, my darling," he declared. "Don't tremble so. I have saved him."

CHAPTER
7

A Knock at
the Door

"I have saved him." And yet Lucie trembled, and a vague but heavy fear was upon her.

All the air round was so thick and dark. The people were passionately revengeful. The innocent were constantly put to death because of vague suspicion or the desire to kill. Lucie could not forget that many as blameless as her husband, and as dear to others as he was to her, shared the fate from which he had been saved. Consequently, her heart could not be as carefree as she felt it ought to be. The shadows of the wintry afternoon were beginning to fall, and even now the dreadful carts were rolling through the streets.

Her father, cheering her, showed surprising strength. No attic, no shoemaking, no One Hundred and Five, North Tower, now! He had accomplished the task he had set himself. He had saved Charles. Let them all lean upon him.

Their housekeeping was of a very frugal kind. That was the safest way of life, involving the least offense to the people. Also, they were not rich. Charles, throughout his imprisonment, had had to pay heavily for his bad food, for his guard, and toward the upkeep of the poorer prisoners. They kept no servant. Jerry (almost wholly transferred to them by Mr. Lorry) had become their daily helper and slept there every night.

In the universal fear and distrust, all the usual harmless ways of life were changed. Food, drink, and other necessities were purchased every evening, in small quantities and at various small shops. This was done to avoid attracting notice, and to give as little occasion as possible for talk and envy.

For some months past, Miss Pross and Mr. Cruncher had assumed responsibility for making household purchases. Every afternoon, when the public lamps were lighted, they went forth on this duty. On this particular day, they followed their custom and left Lucie, her husband, her father, and the child, by a bright fire. Mr. Lorry was soon expected back from the bank. Miss Pross had lighted the lamp, but had put it aside in a corner, that they might enjoy the firelight undisturbed. Little Lucie sat by her grandfather with her hands clasped through his arm. The doctor was softly telling her a story of someone great and powerful who had opened a prison wall and let out a captive who had once done him a favor. All was subdued and quiet, and Lucie was more at ease than she had been.

"What is that?" she cried, all at once.

"My dear!" said her father, stopping in his story, and laying his hand on hers, "control yourself. What a disordered state you are in! The least thing—nothing—startles you!"

"I thought, my father," said Lucie, with a pale face and in a trembling voice, "that I heard strange feet upon the stairs."

"My love, the staircase is as still as Death."

As he said the word, a sudden loud noise was heard at the door.

"Oh Father, Father! What can this be? Hide Charles. Save him!"

"My child," said the doctor, rising, and laying his hand upon her shoulder, "I *have* saved him. What weakness is this, my dear! Let me go to the door."

He took the lamp in his hand, crossed the two outer rooms, and opened the door. A rude clattering of feet over the floor, and four rough men in red caps, armed with sabres and pistols, entered the room.

"The Citizen Evrémonde, called Darnay," said the first.

"Who seeks him?" answered Darnay.

"I seek him. We seek him. I know you, Evrémonde. I saw you before the Tribunal

today. You are again the prisoner of the Republic."

The four surrounded Darnay, where he stood with his wife and child clinging to him.

"Tell me how, and why, am I again a prisoner?"

"It is enough that you return immediately to the Conciergerie. You will know tomorrow. You are summoned for tomorrow."

Dr. Manette was standing absolutely still, with the lamp in his hand, as if he were a statue made to hold it. He put the lamp down and confronted the speaker. Taking him roughly by the loose front of his red woolen shirt, he said, "You know him, you have said. Do you know me?"

"Yes, I know you, Citizen Doctor."

"We all know you, Citizen Doctor," said the other three.

He looked from one to another, and said, in a lower voice, after a pause:

"Will you answer me then? How does this happen?"

"Citizen Doctor," said the first, reluctantly, "he has been denounced to the Section of Saint Antoine. This citizen," pointing out the second who had entered, "is from Saint Antoine."

The second citizen nodded his head, and added, "He is accused by Saint Antoine."

"Of what?" asked the doctor.

"Citizen Doctor," said the first, "ask no more. If the Republic demands sacrifices from you, you—as a good patriot—will be happy to make them. The Republic goes before all. The People is supreme. Evrémonde, we must leave."

"One word," the doctor appealed. "Will you tell me who denounced him?"

"It is against the rule," answered the first; "but you can ask the citizen of Saint Antoine."

The doctor turned his eyes upon that man. He moved uneasily on his feet, rubbed his beard a little, and finally said, "Well! Truly it is against the rule. But he is denounced—and gravely—by the Citizen and Citizeness Defarge. And by one other."

"What other?"

"Do *you* ask, Citizen Doctor?"

"Yes."

"Then," said he of Saint Antoine, with a strange look, "you will be answered tomorrow. Now, I have no more to say!"

CHAPTER
8

A Hand at Cards

Happily unconscious of the new disaster at home, Miss Pross threaded her way along the narrow streets. Mr. Cruncher, with the basket, walked at her side. It was a raw evening, and mist rose over the river.

They began by purchasing a few groceries and a small amount of oil for the lamp. All that was left to buy was some wine. Soon they found themselves at the entrance of a wine shop known as the Good Republican Brutus of Antiquity. Here one could buy wine to take out or to consume on the premises. By the smoky lights, Miss Pross and Cruncher observed a few people playing with limp cards and yellow dominoes. A bare-armed, sooty workman read a journal aloud, while others listened to him. Several of the customers wore weapons or laid them on the tables.

Miss Pross and Mr. Cruncher approached the counter and indicated what they wanted.

As their wine was being measured out, a man rose to depart. In going, he had to face Miss Pross. As he did so, Miss Pross uttered a scream and clapped her hands. Miss Pross was lost in amazement and agitation; Mr. Cruncher was himself in a state of the greatest wonder.

"What is the matter?" said the man who had caused Miss Pross to scream. He spoke softly, and in English.

"Oh, Solomon, dear Solomon!" cried Miss Pross, clapping her hands again. "After not see-ing you or hearing of you for so long a time, I find you here!"

"Don't call me Solomon. Do you want to be the death of me?"

"Brother, brother!" cried Miss Pross, burst-ing into tears. "Have I ever been so hard with you? Such a cruel question!"

"Then hold your meddlesome tongue," said Solomon, "and come outside, if you want to speak to me. Who's this man?"

Miss Pross said, through her tears, "Mr. Cruncher."

"Let him come out too," said Solomon. "Does he think me a ghost?"

Apparently, Mr. Cruncher did, to judge from his looks. He said nothing, however, and Miss Pross paid for her wine. As she did so, Solomon turned to the customers in the Good

Republican Brutus of Antiquity, and offered a few words of explanation in the French language. They immediately returned to their former places and pursuits.

"Now," said Solomon, stopping at the dark street corner, "what do you want?"

"How dreadfully unkind in a brother to speak to me that way and show me no affection," she replied, beginning to weep.

"If you expect me to be surprised," said her brother Solomon, "I am not surprised. I knew you were here. I know of most people who are here. If you really don't want to endanger my existence—which I half believe you do—go your ways as soon as possible, and let me go mine. I am busy. I am an official."

"My English brother Solomon," mourned Miss Pross, casting up her tear-stained eyes. "He could have been one of the best and greatest of men in his native country. Now an official among foreigners, and such foreigners! I would almost sooner have seen the dear boy lying in his—"

"I said so!" cried her brother, interrupting. "I knew it. You want to be the death of me. I shall be considered Suspected, by my own sister. Just as I am beginning to prosper!"

"The gracious and merciful Heavens forbid!" cried Miss Pross. "I would rather never see you again, dear Solomon, though I have ever loved you truly, and ever shall. Say just one affectionate word to me. Tell me there is nothing angry between us, and I will detain you no longer."

Good Miss Pross! As if any differences between them had been her fault. As if it were she, not her brother, that had spent her money and deserted her!

He was saying the affectionate word, however, when Mr. Cruncher, touching him on the shoulder, hoarsely interrupted. "I say! Might I ask the favor? Is your name John Solomon, or Solomon John?"

The official turned toward him with sudden distrust.

"Come!" said Mr. Cruncher. "Speak out. John Solomon, or Solomon John? She calls you Solomon, and she must know, being your sister. And *I* know you're John, you know. Which of the two goes first? And regarding that name of Pross, likewise. That warn't your name over the water, in England."

"What do you mean?"

"Well, I don't know all I mean, for I can't call to mind what your name was, over the water."

"No?"

"No. But I'll swear it was a name of two syllables."

"Indeed?"

"Yes. T'other one's was one syllable. I know you. You was a spy—witness at the Bailey. What was you called at that time?"

"Barsad," said another voice, striking in.

"That's the name for a thousand pound!" cried Jerry.

The speaker who struck in was Sydney Carton. "Don't be alarmed, my dear Miss Pross. I arrived at Mr. Lorry's, to his surprise, yesterday evening. I present myself here to beg a little talk with your brother. I wish you had a better employed brother than Mr. Barsad. I wish, for your sake, Mr. Barsad was not a Sheep of the Prisons."

"Sheep" was a slang word of the time for a spy, working for the jailers. The spy, who was pale, turned paler, and asked him how he dared—

"I'll tell you," said Sydney. "I saw you, Mr. Barsad, coming out of the prison of the Conciergerie, an hour or more ago. You have a face to be remembered, and I remember faces well. I decided to follow you. I walked into the wine shop here, close after you, and sat near you. Overhearing your conversation, I had no trouble in figuring out your occupation. And now, I have devised a plan of action, Mr. Barsad."

"What plan?" the spy asked.

"It would be troublesome, and might be dangerous, to explain in the street. Could you favor me with some minutes of your company— at the office of Tellson's Bank, for instance?"

"Under a threat?"

"Oh! Did I say that?"

"Then, why should I go there?"

"Really, Mr. Barsad, I can't say, if you can't."

Carton's negligent and reckless manner caused fear to arise in Solomon's heart.

"Now, I told you so," said the spy, casting a reproachful look at his sister. "If any trouble comes of this, it's your doing."

"Come, come, Mr. Barsad!" exclaimed Sydney. "Don't be ungrateful. Were it not for my great respect for your sister, I might not have been so pleasant about this business. Do you go with me to the bank?"

"I'll hear what you have to say. Yes, I'll go with you."

"Let us first conduct your sister safely to the corner of her own street. Let me take your arm, Miss Pross. This is not a safe city for you to be out in. Are we ready? Come then!"

Miss Pross pressed her hands on Sydney's arm and looked up in his face, begging him not to harm her brother. Afterward, she remembered that as she did so, she sensed a purpose in his arm and a kind of inspiration in his eyes. These not only contradicted his joking manner, but changed and raised the man. But she was too much occupied then, with fears for her brother, to pay much attention to what she observed.

They left her at the corner of the street, and Carton led the way to Mr. Lorry's, which was within a few minutes' walk. John Barsad, or Solomon Pross, walked at his side.

Mr. Lorry had just finished his dinner, and was sitting before a cheery little fire. He turned his head as they entered, and showed some surprise when he saw a stranger.

"Miss Pross's brother, sir," said Sydney. "Mr. Barsad."

"Barsad?" repeated the old gentleman, "Barsad? I seem to recall the name—and the face."

"I said you had a remarkable face, Mr. Barsad," observed Carton, coolly. "Please sit down."

As he took a chair himself, he supplied the link that Mr. Lorry wanted, by saying to him with a frown, "Witness at Darnay's trial." Mr. Lorry immediately remembered, and looked at his new visitor with open hatred.

"Mr. Barsad has been recognized by Miss Pross as the affectionate brother you have heard of," said Sydney, "and has admitted the relationship. There is worse news. Darnay has been arrested again."

Astonished, the old gentleman exclaimed, "How can this be! I left him safe and free within these two hours, and am about to return to him!"

"Arrested for all that. When was it done, Mr. Barsad?"

"Just now, if at all."

"Mr. Barsad is the best authority possible,

sir," said Sydney, "and I heard, in Mr. Barsad's conversation with a friend and fellow sheep over a bottle of wine, that the arrest has taken place. He left the messengers at the gate, and saw them admitted by the porter. There is no earthly doubt that he is retaken. Now, I trust that the name and influence of Dr. Manette may be as helpful tomorrow—you said he would be before the Tribunal again tomorrow, Mr. Barsad?—"

"Yes; I believe so."

"—As helpful tomorrow as they were today. But it may not be so. I admit to you, I am shaken, Mr. Lorry, by Dr. Manette's not having had the power to prevent this arrest."

"He may not have known of it beforehand," said Mr. Lorry.

"But that very circumstance would be alarming, when we remember how identified he is with his son-in-law."

"That's true," Mr. Lorry acknowledged, with his troubled hand at his chin, and his troubled eyes on Carton.

"In short," said Sydney, "this is a desperate time, when desperate games are played for desperate stakes. Let the doctor play the winning game. I will play the losing one. No man's life here is worth anything. Any one carried home by the people today may be condemned tomorrow. Now, the stake I have resolved to play for, in case of the worst, is a friend in the Conciergerie. And the friend I intend to win is Mr. Barsad."

"You will need good cards, sir," said the spy.

"I'll look them over. I'll see what I hold. Mr. Lorry, you know what a brute I am. I wish you'd give me a little brandy."

It was put before him, and he drank off a glassful—drank off another glassful—pushed the bottle thoughtfully away.

"Mr. Barsad," he went on, in the tone of one who really was looking over a handful of cards. "Sheep of the prisons, messenger of Republican committees, sometimes guard, sometimes prisoner, always spy and secret informer. He presents himself to his French employers under a false name. That's a very good card. Mr. Barsad, now employed by the republican French government, was formerly employed by the aristocratic English government, the enemy of the French Revolution. That's an excellent card. It is even possible that Mr. Barsad, still paid by the aristocratic English government, is secretly and treacherously working to defeat the revolutionary French government! That's a card not to be beaten. Have you followed my hand, Mr. Barsad?"

"Not to understand your play," returned the spy, somewhat uneasily.

"I play my ace: denunciation of Mr. Barsad to the nearest Section Committee of the Revolution. Look over your hand, Mr. Barsad, and see what you have. Don't hurry."

He drew the bottle near, poured out another

glassful of brandy, and drank it off. He saw that the spy was afraid that he was drinking himself into a fit state for immediate denunciation. Seeing it, he poured out and drank another glassful.

"Look over your hand carefully, Mr. Barsad. Take your time."

It was a poorer hand than he suspected. Mr. Barsad saw losing cards in it that Sydney Carton knew nothing of. After he had lost his employment in England, through too much unsuccessful testifying there, he had crossed the Channel and become a spy in France. At first, he spied his own countrymen. Gradually, he became a spy among the French. Under the royal government that was overthrown, he had been a spy upon Saint Antoine and Defarge's wine shop. He remembered with fear and trembling how Madame Defarge had knitted when he talked with her, and had looked threateningly at him as her fingers moved. He had since seen her, in the Section of Saint Antoine. Over and over again, she had produced her knitted registers, and denounced people whose lives the guillotine then swallowed up. He knew, as every spy did, that he was never safe. Escape was impossible; he was tied fast under the shadow of the axe, and a word might bring it down upon him. Once denounced, and on such grave grounds as Carton had just now suggested, the dreadful woman would produce that fatal register, and would crush his last chance at life.

"You scarcely seem to like your hand," said Sydney, calmly. "Do you play? I play my ace, Mr. Barsad, in a very few minutes. Now I believe I have another good card here. That friend and fellow sheep, who spoke of himself as pasturing in the country prisons—who was he?"

"French. You don't know him," said the spy, quickly.

"French, eh?" repeated Carton. "Well, he may be."

"Is, I assure you," said the spy; "though it's not important."

"No, it's not important. Yet I know the face."

"I think not. I am sure not. It can't be," said the spy.

"It—can't—be," muttered Sydney Carton, filling his glass (which fortunately was a small one) again. "Spoke good French. Yet like a foreigner, I thought?"

"Country accent," said the spy.

"No. Foreign!" cried Carton, striking his open hand on the table. "Cly! Disguised, but the same man. We had that man before us at the Old Bailey."

"Now, there you are hasty, sir," said Barsad, with a smile. "There you really give me an advantage over you. Cly (who, I will unreservedly admit, was a partner of mine) has been dead several years. I was with him in his last illness. He was buried in London, at the church of

Saint Pancras-in-the-Fields. I helped to lay him in his coffin."

Here, Mr. Lorry became aware, from where he sat, of a most remarkable shadow on the wall. It was caused by a sudden extraordinary rising and stiffening of all the hair on Mr. Cruncher's head.

"Let us be reasonable," said the spy, "and let us be fair. To show you how mistaken you are, I will lay before you a certificate of Cly's burial, which I happen to have with me." He quickly produced and opened it. "There it is. You may take it in your hand; it's no forgery."

At these words, Mr. Cruncher rose and stepped forward. He touched the spy on the shoulder and proclaimed, "That there Roger Cly — so *you* put him in his coffin?"

"I did."

"Who took him out of it?"

Barsad leaned back in his chair and stammered, "What do you mean?"

"I mean," said Mr. Cruncher, "that he warn't never in it. No! Not he! I'll have my head took off, if he was ever in it."

The spy looked round at the two gentlemen. They both looked in unspeakable astonishment at Jerry.

"I tell you," said Jerry, "that you buried paving-stones and earth in that there coffin. Don't go and tell me that you buried Cly. It was a fake. Me and two more knows it."

"How do you know it?"

"What's that to you?" growled Mr. Cruncher. "It's you I have got a grudge against, with your shameful treatment of tradesmen! I'd catch hold of your throat and choke you for half a guinea."

Sydney Carton, just as amazed as Mr. Lorry, now requested Mr. Cruncher to explain himself.

"At another time, sir," he returned, evasively. "The present time is ill-conwenient for explainin'. What I tell you, is, that he knows well wot that there Cly was never in that there coffin. Let him say he was, and I'll either catch hold of his throat and choke him for half a guinea, or I'll out and denounce him."

"Humph! I see one thing," said Carton. "I hold another card, Mr. Barsad. Impossible, here in raging Paris, with Suspicion filling the air, for you to survive denunciation, when you are in communication with another aristocratic spy. Especially one who pretended to die and came to life again! A plot in the prisons, of the foreigner against the Republic. A strong card—a certain Guillotine card! Do you play?"

"No!" returned the spy. "I give up. You are correct. There was no other way for Cly to escape the mob. Though how this man knows it was false is a wonder to me."

The spy then turned to Sydney Carton and said, "I go on duty soon. You told me you had a proposal. What is it? I will not put myself in danger. Now, what do you want with me?"

"Not very much. You have the keys to the Conciergerie?"

"I tell you once for all, escape is not possible," said the spy, firmly.

"Why do you tell me what I have not asked? You are a guard at the Conciergerie?"

"I am sometimes."

"You can be when you choose?"

"I can pass in and out when I choose."

Sydney Carton filled another glass with brandy and drank it with deliberation. Once it was gone, he stood and said to the spy, "So far, we have spoken before these two, so that others could judge the cards we held. Come into the next room, and let us have one final word alone."

CHAPTER
9

The Game Made

As Sydney Carton and the sheep of the prisons were speaking quietly in the adjoining room, Mr. Lorry looked at Jerry with mistrust. The honest tradesman's reaction did not inspire confidence. He changed the leg on which he rested as often as if he had fifty legs and were trying them all. He examined his fingernails with an unusual closeness of attention. Whenever Mr. Lorry's eye caught his, he coughed in a manner seldom seen in individuals of noble character.

"Jerry," said Mr. Lorry. "Come here."

Mr. Cruncher came forward sideways, with one of his shoulders before the other.

"What have you been, besides a messenger?"

After some hesitation, Mr. Cruncher replied, "Agricultooral character."

"I am greatly troubled," said Mr. Lorry, angrily shaking a forefinger at him. "It seems that you have used the respectable and great house of Tellson's as a cover for an unlawful and disrespectable occupation. If you have, don't expect me to be your friend in England. Don't expect me to keep your secret. Tellson's shall not be so used."

"I hope, sir," pleaded the embarrassed Mr. Cruncher, "that a gentleman like yourself wot I've had the honor of odd jobbing for, these many years, would think twice about harming me. I don't say it is so, but even if it wos so, there'd be two sides to it. There might be medical doctors banking at Tellson's, cocking their medical eyes at that tradesman on the sly. Well, that 'ud be imposing, too, on Tellson's. For you cannot sauce the goose and not the gander. Then, wot with undertakers, and wot with parish clerks, and wot with sextons, and wot with private watchmen (all awaricious and all in it), a man wouldn't get much by it, even if it wos so. And wot little a man did get, would never prosper with him, Mr. Lorry. He'd never have no good of it. He'd want all along to be out of the line, if he could see his way out—even if it wos so."

"Ugh!" cried Mr. Lorry, "I am shocked at the sight of you."

"Now, what I would humbly offer to you, sir," pursued Mr. Cruncher—"even if it wos so, which I don't say it is—would be this. Upon that there stool, at that there Bar, sets that there boy of mine. He will errand you, message you, general-light-job you, if such should be your wishes. If it wos so, which I still don't say it is, let that there boy keep his father's place, and take care of his mother."

"Say no more now," said Mr. Lorry. "I may still be your friend, if you deserve it, and repent in action—not in words. I want no more words."

Mr. Cruncher knuckled his forehead, as Sydney Carton and the spy returned from the dark room. "Goodbye, Mr. Barsad," said Carton. "Our arrangement is made; you have nothing to fear from me."

He sat down in a chair on the hearth next to Mr. Lorry. When they were alone, Mr. Lorry asked him what he had done.

"Not much. If it should go ill with Darnay, I have ensured access to him, once."

Mr. Lorry's face fell.

"It is all I could do," said Carton. "To ask too much would be to put this man's head under the axe. As he himself said, nothing worse could happen to him if he were denounced."

"But access to him," said Mr. Lorry, "if it should go ill before the Tribunal, will not save him."

"I never said it would."

Mr. Lorry's eyes gradually turned toward the fire. His sympathy for Lucie, and the heavy disappointment of Darnay's second arrest, saddened him greatly, and his tears fell.

"You are a good man and a true friend," said Carton. "Forgive me if I notice that you are moved. I could not see my father weep, and sit by, without caring. And I could not respect your sorrow more, if you were my father. You are free from that misfortune, however."

Though he said the last words with a slip into his usual manner, there were true feeling and respect in his tone. Mr. Lorry, who had never seen the better side of him, gave him his hand, and Carton gently pressed it.

"To return to poor Darnay," said Carton. "Don't tell *her* of this interview, or this arrangement. It would not enable her to go to see him. Don't speak of me to her. As I said to you when I first came, I had better not see her. I can do helpful work for her without that. You are going to her, I hope? She must be very sad tonight."

"I am going now, directly."

"I am glad of that. She has such a strong attachment to you and reliance on you. How does she look?"

"Anxious and unhappy, but very beautiful."

"Ah!"

It was a long, grieving sound, like a sigh—almost like a sob. The sound made Mr. Lorry look at Carton, who just then lifted his foot to put back a little flaming log, which was tumbling forward. He wore the white riding-coat and top-boots, then in style. The light of the fire made him look very pale, with his long brown hair, all untrimmed, hanging loose about him. His indifference to the fire brought a word of caution from Mr. Lorry. Carton's boot was still upon the hot embers of the flaming log, when it had broken under the weight of his foot.

"I forgot it," he said.

Mr. Lorry's eyes were again attracted to Carton's face. He noticed the wasted air which clouded the naturally handsome features. It reminded him of the expression he had seen on the faces of prisoners.

"And your duties here have drawn to an end, sir?" said Carton, turning to him.

"Yes. As I was telling you last night when Lucie came in so unexpectedly, I have done all that I can do here. I was hoping to leave them in perfect safety, and then to depart from Paris. I have my Leave to Pass. I was ready to go."

They were both silent.

"Yours is a long life to look back upon, sir?" said Carton, wistfully.

"I am in my seventy-eighth year."

"You have been useful all your life? Trusted, respected, and looked up to?"

"I have been a man of business, ever since I have been a man. Indeed, I may say that I was a man of business when I was a boy."

"See what a place you fill at seventy-eight. How many people will miss you when you leave it empty!"

"A solitary old bachelor," answered Mr.

Lorry, shaking his head. "There is nobody to weep for me."

"How can you say that? Wouldn't *she* weep for you? Wouldn't her child?"

"Yes, yes, thank God. I didn't quite mean what I said."

"It *is* a thing to thank God for; is it not?"

"Surely, surely."

Carton ended the conversation here, by rising to help him on with his outer coat.

"Are you going out?" Mr. Lorry inquired.

"I'll walk with you to her gate. You know my vagabond and restless habits. If I should prowl about the streets a long time, don't be uneasy. I shall reappear in the morning. You go to the court tomorrow?"

"Yes, unhappily."

"I shall be there, but only as one of the crowd. My spy will find a place for me. Take my arm, sir."

Mr. Lorry did so, and they went downstairs and out in the streets. A few minutes brought them to Mr. Lorry's destination. Carton left him there, but stayed longer. He had heard of her going to the prison every day. "She came out here," he said, looking about him, "turned this way, must have walked on these stones often. Let me follow in her steps."

It was ten o'clock at night when he stood before the prison of La Force, where she had stood hundreds of times. A little wood-sawyer, having closed his shop, was smoking his pipe at his shop door.

"Good night, citizen," said Sydney Carton, pausing in going by. The man eyed him with curiosity.

"Good night, citizen."

"How goes the Republic?"

"You mean the Guillotine. Not bad. Sixty-three today. We shall have a hundred soon. The executioner and his men complain sometimes of being exhausted. Ha, ha, ha! Such a barber!"

"Do you often go to see him—"

"Shave? Every day. You have seen him at work?"

"Never."

"Go and see him when he has a good batch. Figure this to yourself, citizen; he shaved sixty-three today, in less than two pipes! Word of honor!"

The grinning little man held out the pipe he was smoking, to explain how he timed the executioner. Carton was so aware of a rising desire to strike the life out of him that he turned away.

"But you are not English," said the wood-sawyer, "though you wear English dress?"

"Yes," said Carton, pausing again, and answering over his shoulder.

"You speak like a Frenchman."

"I am an old student here."

"Aha, a perfect Frenchman! Good night, Englishman."

"Good night, citizen."

Sydney Carton had not gone far, when he stopped in the middle of the street under a glimmering lamp, and wrote with his pencil on a scrap of paper. Then, walking along several dark and dirty streets, he entered a drugstore, which the owner was closing with his own hands. A small, dim, crooked shop, kept in a twisting, uphill street, by a small, dim, crooked man.

Carton laid the scrap of paper before him. "Whew!" the druggist whistled softly, as he read it. "For you, citizen?"

"For me."

"You will be careful to keep them separate, citizen? You know the consequences of mixing them?"

"Perfectly."

Certain small packets were made and given to him. He put them, one by one, in the pocket of his coat, counted out the money for them, and deliberately left the shop. "There is nothing more to do," said he, glancing upward at the moon, "until tomorrow. I can't sleep." He uttered these words in the settled manner of a tired man, who had wandered and struggled and gotten lost, but who had finally found his road and saw its end.

Long ago, when Sydney Carton was thought to be a young man with a brilliant future, he had followed his father to the grave. His mother had died, years before. These solemn words, which had been read at his father's grave, arose in his mind as he went down the dark streets, among the heavy shadows, with the moon and the clouds sailing on high above him. "I am the resurrection and the life, saith the Lord: he that believeth in me, though he were dead, yet shall he live: and whosoever liveth and believeth in me, shall never die."

With these thoughts, Carton walked on through the streets of Paris. Riders in coaches were liable to be suspected, and gentility hid its head in red nightcaps, and trudged in heavy shoes. But the theaters were all well filled, and the people poured cheerfully out as he passed, and went chatting home. At one of the theater doors, there was a little girl with a mother, looking for a way across the street through the mud. He carried the child over, and before the timid arm was loosed from his neck, asked her for a kiss.

"I am the resurrection and the life, saith the Lord: he that believeth in me, though he were dead, yet shall he live: and whosoever liveth and believeth in me, shall never die."

The night wore out. Carton stood upon the bridge listening to the water as it splashed the river walls of Paris. The day came coldly, looking like a dead face out of the sky. He walked by the river, far from the houses. In the light and warmth of the sun, he fell asleep on the bank.

When he awoke, he lingered there yet a little longer, watching a little current that turned and turned without purpose, until the stream absorbed it, and carried it on to the sea.—"Like me."

Mr. Lorry was already out when he got back, and it was easy to guess where the good old man was gone. Sydney Carton drank nothing but a little coffee and ate some bread. After he washed and changed his clothing, he went to the place of trial.

The court was all astir and a-buzz. Mr. Lorry was there, and Dr. Manette was there. *She* was there, sitting beside her father.

When her husband was brought in, Lucie turned to look at him. Her expression was so encouraging, so full of love and tenderness and courage, for his sake, that it brightened his glance, and animated his heart. If there had been any eyes to notice the influence of her look on Sydney Carton, those eyes would have seen the same thing.

Before that unjust Tribunal, there was little or no order of procedure. No accused person received a reasonable hearing. There could have been no Revolution, if all laws, forms, and ceremonies, had not first been so monstrously abused. The suicidal vengeance of the Revolution had scattered them all to the winds.

Every eye was turned to the jury. It was made up of the same determined patriots and good republicans as yesterday and the day before. One eager man was prominent among them. He had a craving face, and his fingers perpetually hovered about his lips. A bloodthirsty, cannibal-looking juryman: this was Jacques Three of Saint Antoine.

Every eye then turned to the five judges and the public prosecutor. They all looked stern and murderous.

Charles Evrémonde, called Darnay. Released yesterday. Reaccused and retaken yesterday. Indictment delivered to him last night. Suspected and denounced enemy of the Republic, aristocrat, one of a family of tyrants, who had used their abolished privileges to oppress the people. Charles Evrémonde, called Darnay, one of a race proscribed, absolutely dead in law. So spoke the public prosecutor.

The President asked, was the accused openly denounced or secretly?

"Openly, President."

"By whom?"

"Three voices. Ernest Defarge, wine vendor of Saint Antoine."

"Good."

"Thérèse Defarge, his wife."

"Good."

"Alexandre Manette, physician."

A great uproar took place in the court. In the midst of it, Dr. Manette was seen, pale and trembling, standing where he had been seated.

"President, I indignantly protest. This is a forgery and a fraud. You know the accused to be the husband of my daughter. My daughter, and those dear to her, are far dearer to me than my life. Who is the false conspirator who says that I denounce the husband of my child!"

"Citizen Manette, be quiet. Submit to the authority of the Tribunal. Dearer to you than life? Nothing can be so dear to a good citizen as the Republic."

Loud cheers hailed this rebuke. The President rang his bell, and with warmth resumed.

"If the Republic should demand the sacrifice of your child herself, you would have the duty to sacrifice her. Listen to what is to follow. Meanwhile, be silent!"

Frantic acclamations were again raised. Dr. Manette sat down, with his eyes looking around, and his lips trembling. His daughter drew closer to him. The craving man on the jury rubbed his hands together, and returned his hand to his mouth.

Defarge was produced. When the court was quiet enough to hear him, he rapidly told the story of the imprisonment, when he was a young servant in the doctor's house. He told of the doctor's release, and of the state of the prisoner when released and delivered to him.

"You did good service at the taking of the Bastille, citizen?"

"I believe so."

Here, an excited woman screeched from the crowd: "You were one of the best patriots there. Why not say so? You were a cannoneer that day there, and you were among the first to enter the accursed fortress when it fell. Patriots, I speak the truth!"

It was The Vengeance who thus spoke out. The President rang his bell. However, The Vengeance, encouraged by the crowd, shrieked, "I defy that bell!"

"Inform the Tribunal of what you did that day within the Bastille, citizen."

"I knew," said Defarge, looking down at his wife, "I knew that this prisoner had been confined in a cell known as One Hundred and Five, North Tower. He knew himself by no other name than One Hundred and Five, North Tower, when he made shoes under my care. I resolved, when the place should fall, to examine that cell. It falls. I climb up to the cell, with a fellow citizen who is one of the jury. I examine it, very closely. In a hole in the chimney, where a stone has been worked out and replaced, I find a written paper. This is that written paper. I have examined some specimens of the writing of Dr. Manette. This is the writing of Dr. Manette. I confide this paper, in the writing of Dr. Manette, to the hands of the President."

"Let it be read."

There was dead silence and stillness. The

prisoner looked lovingly at his wife. His wife looked back, except for some quick glances at her father. Dr. Manette kept his eyes fixed on the reader. Madame Defarge never took hers from the prisoner. Defarge stared steadily at his wife. All the other eyes in the courtroom were intent upon the doctor, who saw none of them. The paper was read, as follows.

CHAPTER
10

The Substance of the Shadow

"I, Alexandre Manette, unfortunate physician, native of Beauvais, and afterward resident in Paris, write this melancholy paper in my cell in the Bastille, during the last month of the year 1767. I write it at stolen intervals, under every difficulty. I am hiding it in the wall of the chimney, where I have slowly and laboriously made a hiding place for it. Some pitying hand may find it there, when I and my sorrows are dust.

"I write these words with a rusty iron point. I write with great difficulty, in scrapings of soot and charcoal from the chimney, mixed with blood, in the last month of the tenth year of my captivity. I no longer have hope. I already see signs that my mind will not long remain clear. However, I solemnly declare that I am at this time in the possession of my right mind—that my memory is exact.

271

"One cloudy moonlight night, in the third week of December, 1757, I was walking along a bank of the Seine to enjoy the frosty air. A carriage came along behind me, driven very fast. As I stood aside to let it pass, fearful that it might otherwise run me down, the carriage stopped.

"A voice called to me by my name. I answered. Two gentlemen opened the door and stepped down.

"I observed that they were both wrapped in cloaks, and appeared to conceal themselves. As they stood side by side near the carriage door, I also observed that they looked about my own age, or rather younger. They were greatly alike, in stature, manner, voice, and (as far as I could see) face too.

"'You are Dr. Manette?' said one.

"I am."

"'Dr. Manette, formerly of Beauvais,' said the other; 'the young physician, originally an expert surgeon? Who has become well-known in Paris within the last year or two?'

"'Gentlemen,' I returned, 'I am that Dr. Manette of whom you speak so graciously.'

"'We have been to your residence,' said the first. 'Not being so fortunate as to find you there, and being informed that you were walking in this direction, we followed, hoping to overtake you. Will you please enter the carriage?'

"Their request was more like a command. As they spoke, they both moved, so that I was between them and the carriage door. They were armed. I was not.

"'Gentlemen,' said I, 'pardon me. I must inquire who does me the honor to seek my assistance, and what is the nature of the case to which I am summoned.'

"The reply to this was made by the second man. 'Doctor, your clients are people of wealth. As to the nature of the case, our confidence in your skill assures us that you will ascertain it for yourself. Enough. Will you please enter the carriage?'

"I could do nothing but comply, and I entered it in silence. They both entered after me—the last springing in, after putting up the steps. The carriage turned around and drove on at its former speed.

"I repeat this conversation exactly as it occurred. I describe everything exactly as it took place. Where I make the broken marks that follow here, I leave off for the time, and put my paper in its hiding place. . . .

"The carriage left the streets behind, passed the North Barrier, and emerged upon the country road. At two-thirds of a league from the Barrier, it turned from the main road and stopped at a solitary house. We all three stepped down, and walked, by a damp footpath in a garden where a neglected fountain had overflowed, to the door of the house. It was not opened immediately, in answer to the ringing of the bell.

One of my two guides struck the servant who opened it across the face with his heavy riding glove.

"There was nothing in this action to attract my particular attention. I had seen common people struck more commonly than dogs. But the other of the two, being angry likewise, struck the man in like manner with his arm. The look and bearing of the brothers were then so exactly alike, that I then realized they were twin brothers.

"From the time of our arrival, I had heard cries coming from an upper chamber. I was conducted to this chamber immediately. The cries grew louder as we ascended the stairs. In the chamber, I found a patient in a high fever of the brain, lying on a bed.

"The patient was a woman of great beauty, not much past twenty. Her hair was torn and ragged, and her arms were bound to her sides with sashes and handkerchiefs. I noticed that these bonds were all portions of a gentleman's dress. On one of them, a fringed scarf, I saw the crest of a noble family, and the letter E.

"In her restless movements, the patient had turned over onto her face on the edge of the bed and had pulled the end of the scarf into her mouth. She was in danger of suffocation. I turned her gently over, placed my hands upon her to calm her and keep her down, and looked into her face. Her eyes were wild. She constantly uttered piercing shrieks, and repeated the words,

'My husband, my father, and my brother!' and then counted up to twelve, and said, 'Hush!' For an instant, and no more, she would pause to listen, and then the piercing shrieks would begin again, and she would repeat the cry, 'My husband, my father, and my brother!' and would count up to twelve, and say, 'Hush!' There was no variation in the order, or the manner.

"'How long,' I asked, 'has this lasted?'

"To distinguish the brothers, I will call them the elder and the younger. By the elder, I mean the one who seemed in charge. It was the elder who replied, 'Since about this hour last night.'

"'She has a husband, a father, and a brother?'

"'A brother.'

"'I do not address her brother?'

"He answered with great contempt, 'No.'

"'She has some recent association with the number twelve?'

"The younger brother impatiently replied, 'With twelve o'clock.'

"'See, gentlemen,' said I, still keeping my hands upon her, 'how useless I am! If I had known what I was coming to see, I could have brought proper medicines. As it is, time must be lost. There are no medicines to be obtained in this lonely place.'

"The elder brother looked to the younger, who said haughtily, 'There is a case of medicines here.' He brought it from a closet and put it on the table. . . .

"I opened some of the bottles, smelt them, and put the stoppers to my lips. They were all narcotics, no better than poisons.

"'Do you doubt them?' asked the younger brother.

"'You see, monsieur, I am going to use them,' I replied, and said no more.

"I made the patient swallow, with great difficulty, and after many efforts, the dose that I desired to give. I intended to repeat it after a while. Since it was necessary to watch its influence, I then sat down by the side of the bed. There was a timid woman in attendance (the wife of the man downstairs), who had retreated into a corner. The house was damp and decayed, carelessly furnished—evidently recently occupied and temporarily used. Some thick old hangings had been nailed up at the windows to deaden the sound of the shrieks. She continued to repeat them in the same order, crying, 'My husband, my father, and my brother!' counting up to twelve, and then saying 'Hush!' Her frenzy was so violent that I had not removed the bandages that restrained her arms. The only spark of encouragement in the case was that touching the sufferer calmed her for a few minutes at a time. It had no effect upon the cries, though. No pendulum could be more regular.

"I had sat by the side of the bed for half an hour, with the two brothers looking on, before the elder said, 'There is another patient.'

"I was startled and asked, 'Is it an urgent case?'

"'You had better see,' he carelessly answered as he took up a light. . . .

"We proceeded to a back room in a sort of loft over a stable. The details are as vivid in my cell in the Bastille, near the close of the tenth year of my captivity, as I saw them that night.

"On some hay on the ground, with a cushion thrown under his head, lay a handsome peasant boy. He was not more than seventeen. He lay on his back, with his teeth set, his right hand clenched on his chest, and his glaring eyes looking straight upward. I could not see where his wound was, as I kneeled on one knee over him. However, I could see that he was dying of a wound from a sharp point.

"'I am a doctor, my poor fellow,' said I. 'Let me examine it.'

"'I do not want it examined,' he answered. 'Let it be.'

"It was under his hand, and I convinced him to let me move his hand away. The wound was a sword-thrust, received from twenty to twenty-four hours before, but no skill could have saved him. He was dying fast. The elder brother was looking down at this handsome boy, whose life was ebbing out, as if he were a wounded bird or hare or rabbit, not a fellow human being.

"'How has this been done, monsieur?' I asked.

"'A crazed young common dog! A serf! Forced my brother to duel, and has fallen by my brother's sword—like a gentleman.'

"There was no touch of pity or shared humanity in this answer. The speaker seemed to suggest that the boy's death, there in his castle, was an inconvenience. He should have died in some out-of-the-way place, like the rest of his kind.

"The boy's eyes had slowly moved to him as he had spoken. They now slowly moved to me.

"'Doctor, they are very proud, these nobles. They plunder us, outrage us, beat us, kill us. But we common dogs have a little pride left, sometimes. She—have you seen her, Doctor?'

"The shrieks and the cries could still be heard there, though subdued by the distance. I said, 'I have seen her.'

"'She is my sister, Doctor. They have had their shameful rights, these nobles, in violating the modesty and virtue of our sisters, many years. But we have had good girls among us. I know it, and have heard my father say so. She was a good girl. She was engaged to a good young man, too, a tenant of his. We were all tenants of his—that man's who stands there. The other is his brother, the worst of a bad race.'

"It was extremely difficult for the boy to speak, but his spirit spoke with a dreadful emphasis.

"'We were robbed by that man who stands

there, as all we common dogs are by those superior beings. We were taxed by him without mercy. We were forced to work for him without pay, grind our corn at his mill, feed his tame birds on our wretched crops, although we could not keep a single tame bird of our own. When we chanced to have a bit of meat, we ate it in fear, with the door barred and the shutters closed, so that his people should not see it and take it from us. We were so robbed, and hunted, and were made so poor, that our father told us it was a dreadful thing to bring a child into the world. What we should most pray for, he said, was that our women might be barren and our miserable race die out!'

"I had never before seen such strong resentment. I had supposed that it must be present in the people somewhere. But I had never seen it burst forth, until I saw it in the dying boy.

"'Nevertheless, Doctor, my sister married. Her lover was ailing at that time, poor fellow, and she married him so that she might care for him in our cottage—our dog-hut, as that man would call it. She had not been married many weeks, when that man's brother saw her and admired her, and asked that man to lend her to him! My sister was good and virtuous, and hated his brother with a hatred as strong as mine. What did the two do then, to persuade her husband to use his influence with her, to make her willing?'

"The boy's eyes, which had been fixed on mine, slowly turned to the nobleman. I saw in the two faces that all he said was true. I can see their opposing kinds of pride, even in this Bastille. The gentleman's pride—all negligent indifference. The peasant's—all trodden-down sentiment and passionate revenge.

"'You know, Doctor, that it is among the rights of these nobles to harness us common dogs to carts and drive us. They so harnessed him and drove him. You know that it is among their rights to keep us in their grounds all night, quieting the frogs, so that their noble sleep may not be disturbed. They kept him out in the unwholesome mists at night, and ordered him back into his harness in the day. But he was not persuaded. No! Taken out of harness one day at noon, to feed—if he could find food—he sobbed twelve times, once for every stroke of the bell, and died in her arms.'

"Nothing human could have held life in the boy but his determination to tell his story. He forced back the gathering shadows of death, as he forced his clenched right hand to remain clenched, and to cover his wound.

"'Then, with that man's permission and even with his aid, his brother took her away for his pleasure. I saw her pass me on the road. When I brought the news home, our father's heart burst, and he died on the spot. I took my younger sister (for I have another) to a place beyond the reach of this man, and where, at least, she will never be *his* vassal. Then, I followed the brother here, and last night climbed in—a common dog, but sword in hand.—Where is the loft window? It was somewhere here?'

"The room was darkening to his sight; the world was narrowing around him. I glanced around, and saw that the hay and straw on the floor were trampled, as if there had been a struggle.

"'She heard me, and ran in. I told her not to come near us till he was dead. He came in and first tossed me some pieces of money. Then he struck at me with a whip. But I, though a common dog, so struck at him as to make him draw his sword. He had to defend himself with all his skill to save his life.'

"My glance had fallen, a few moments before, on the fragments of a broken sword, lying among the hay. That weapon was a gentleman's. Nearby lay an old sword that seemed to have been a soldier's.

"'Now, lift me up, doctor; lift me up. Where is he?'

"'He is not here,' I said, supporting the boy, and thinking that he referred to the brother.

"'He! Proud as these nobles are, he is afraid to see me. Where is the man who was here? Turn my face to him.'

"I did so, raising the boy's head against my knee. But, feeling a brief surge of strength, he raised himself completely. I rose too, or I could not have still supported him.

"'Marquis,' said the boy, facing him with his eyes open wide, and his right hand raised. 'In the days when all these things are to be answered for, I summon you and yours, to the last of your bad race, to answer for them. I mark this cross of blood upon you, as a sign that I do it. I summon your brother, the worst of the bad race, to answer for them separately. I mark this cross of blood upon him, as a sign that I do it.'

"Twice, he put his hand to the wound in his chest, and with his forefinger drew a cross in the air. He stood for an instant with the finger yet raised. As it dropped, he dropped with it, and I laid him down dead. . . .

"When I returned to the bedside of the young woman, I found her raving as before. I knew that this might last for many hours, and that it would probably end in the silence of the grave.

"I repeated the medicines I had given her, and I sat at the side of the bed until the night was far advanced. She never softened the piercing quality of her shrieks, never changed the order of her words. They were always, 'My husband, my father, and my brother! One, two, three, four, five, six, seven, eight, nine, ten, eleven, twelve. Hush!'

"This lasted twenty-six hours from the time when I first saw her. I had come and gone twice, and was again sitting by her, when she began to weaken. I did what little I could. Soon she sank into unconsciousness, and lay like the dead.

"It was as if the wind and rain had lulled at last, after a long and fearful storm. I released her arms and called the woman to assist me in making her more comfortable. It was then that I realized she was in the beginning stage of pregnancy, and it was then that I lost the little hope I had had for her.

"'Is she dead?' asked the Marquis, the elder brother, coming into the room.

"'Not dead,' I answered; 'but likely to die.'

"'What strength there is in these common bodies!' he said, looking down at her with some curiosity.

"'There is enormous strength,' I answered, 'in sorrow and despair.'

"He first laughed at my words, and then frowned at them. He moved a chair with his foot near to mine, ordered the woman away, and said in a subdued voice, 'Doctor, finding my brother in this difficulty with these beasts, I recommended that your aid should be invited. Your reputation is high, and you must think of your future. The things that you see here are not to be spoken of.'

"I listened to the patient's breathing and avoided answering.

"'Do you honor me with your attention, Doctor?'

"'Monsieur,' said I, 'in my profession, the communications of patients are always received in confidence.' I was guarded in my answer, for I was troubled by what I had heard and seen. Looking around as I resumed my seat, I saw both the brothers looking intently at me. . . .

"I write with so much difficulty. The cold is so severe. I am fearful of being detected and transferred to an underground cell and total darkness. I must shorten this narrative. There is no confusion or failure in my memory. I can recall every word that was ever spoken between me and those brothers.

"She lingered for a week. Toward the last, I could understand a few syllables that she said to me, by placing my ear close to her lips. She asked me where she was, and I told her; who I was, and I told her. She would not tell me her family name. She faintly shook her head upon the pillow, and kept her secret, as the boy had done.

"I had no opportunity of asking her any question, until I had told the brothers she was sinking fast and could not live another day. Until then, one or other of the brothers had always sat behind the curtain at the head of the bed when I was there.

"I always observed that their pride bitterly resented the younger brother's (as I call him) having crossed swords with a peasant, and that peasant a boy. This seemed highly disgraceful to the family. The younger brother's expression, when he looked at me, told me that he disliked me deeply, because of what the boy had said to me.

"My patient died two hours before midnight. I was alone with her, when her forlorn young head drooped gently on one side, and all her earthly wrongs and sorrows ended.

"The brothers were waiting in a room downstairs, impatient to ride away. I had heard them striking their boots with their riding-whips, and walking up and down.

"'At last she is dead?' said the older brother, when I went in.

"'She is dead,' said I.

"'I congratulate you, my brother,' were his words.

"He had before offered me money, which I had postponed taking. He now gave me a piece of gold. I took it from his hand, but laid it on the table. I had resolved to accept nothing.

"'Please excuse me,' said I. 'Under the circumstances, no.'

"They exchanged looks, but bent their heads to me as I bent mine to them, and we parted without another word on either side. . . .

"Early in the morning, the piece of gold was left at my door in a little box, with my name on the outside. From the first, I had anxiously considered what I ought to do. I decided, that day, to write privately to the Minister, describing everything about these two cases, including the monstrous injustices that were part of them.

"I was very busy that day, and could not complete my letter that night. I rose long before my usual time next morning to finish it. It was the last day of the year. The letter was lying before me just completed, when I was told that a lady waited, who wished to see me. . . .

"I am growing more and more unequal to the task I have set myself. It is so cold, so dark, my senses are so numb, and the gloom upon me is so dreadful.

"The lady was young and attractive, but not marked for long life. She was very nervous. She presented herself to me as the wife of the Marquis St. Evrémonde. I connected the title, by which the boy had addressed the elder brother, with the letter embroidered on the scarf.

"My memory is still accurate, but I cannot write the words of our conversation. I suspect that I am watched more closely than I was. I do not know at what times I may be watched.

"She had in part suspected, and in part discovered, the main facts of the cruel story. She knew of her husband's share in it, and my being summoned. She did not know that the girl was dead. Her hope had been, she said in great distress, to show her, in secret, a woman's sympathy. Her hope had been to turn aside the wrath of Heaven from a house that had long been hateful to the suffering peasants.

"She had reasons for believing that there was a younger sister living. Her greatest desire was to help that sister. I could tell her only that there was such a sister. In coming to me, she had hoped that I could tell her the sister's name and address. Unfortunately, even in this wretched hour, I am ignorant of both. . . .

"These scraps of paper fail me. One was taken from me, with a warning, yesterday. I must finish my record today.

"She was a good, compassionate lady, and not happy in her marriage. How could she be! The brother distrusted and disliked her. She stood in dread of him, and in dread of her husband too. When I escorted her to the door, there was a child, a pretty boy about two or three years old, in her carriage.

"'For his sake, Doctor,' she said, pointing to him in tears, 'I would do all I can to make amends for this wrong. He will never prosper in his inheritance otherwise. I am afraid that if no other atonement is made for this, it will one day be required of him. What I have left to call my own—it is little beyond the worth of a few jewels—I will urge him to offer to this injured family, if the sister can be discovered.'

"She kissed the boy and said, 'It is for your own dear sake. You will be faithful, little Charles?' The child answered her bravely, 'Yes!' I kissed her hand, and she went away. I never saw her again.

"I sealed my letter and, not trusting it out of my own hands, delivered it myself that day.

"That night, the last night of the year, toward nine o'clock, a man in a black dress appeared at my gate, demanded to see me, and softly followed my young servant, Ernest Defarge, upstairs. When my servant came into the room where I sat with my wife—O my wife, beloved of my heart! My fair young English wife!—we saw the man, who was supposed to be at the gate, standing silent behind him.

"An urgent case in the Rue St. Honoré, he said. It would not take long to go there. He had a coach in waiting.

"As soon as I was away from the house, a black muffler was drawn tightly over my mouth from behind, and my arms were pinned down. The two brothers crossed the road from a dark corner and identified me with a single gesture. The Marquis took from his pocket the letter I had written, showed it to me, burned it in the light of a lantern, and extinguished the ashes with his foot. Not a word was spoken. I was brought here. I was brought to my living grave.

"If it had pleased God to inspire the hard heart of either of the brothers, in all these frightful years, to grant me any news of my dearest wife—just to let me know by a word whether she was alive or dead—I might have thought that He had not quite abandoned them. But now I believe that the mark of the red cross is fatal to them, and that they have no part in His mercies. And them and their descendants, to the last of their race, I, Alexandre Manette, unhappy prisoner, do this last night of the year 1767, in my unbearable agony, denounce to the times when all these things shall be answered for. I denounce them to Heaven and to earth."

A terrible sound arose when the reading was complete. It was a sound of craving and eagerness for blood. The document called up the most revengeful passions of the time. Any head in the nation would have dropped because of it.

There was little need to show how the Defarges had not made the paper public, with the other captured Bastille memorials. They had kept it, biding their time. There was little need to show that this family name of Evrémonde had long been despised by Saint Antoine, and was knitted into the fatal register. No man, however virtuous, could have overcome such denunciation.

What made it even worse for the doomed man was that the denouncer was a well-known citizen, his friend, the father of his wife. The President of the Tribunal even declared that the good physician would deserve the Republic's praise for rooting out an obnoxious family of aristocrats, and would surely feel a sacred glow and joy in making his daughter a widow and her child an orphan. At these words, there was wild excitement, patriotic fervor, and not a hint of human sympathy.

"Much influence around him, has that doctor?" murmured Madame Defarge, smiling to

The Vengeance. "Save him now, my doctor, save him!"

At every juryman's vote, there was a roar. Another and another.

Unanimously voted. At heart and by descent an aristocrat, an enemy of the Republic, a notorious oppressor of the People. Back to the Conciergerie, and Death within twenty-four hours!

CHAPTER
11

Dusk

The judges had to take part in a public demonstration out of doors, so the Tribunal adjourned. As everyone left the courtroom, Lucie stood stretching out her arms toward her husband. There was nothing in her face but love and consolation.

"If I might touch him! If I might embrace him once! O, good citizens, if you would have so much compassion for us!"

Only a single jailer was left, along with two guards and Barsad. The people had all poured out to the show in the streets. Barsad suggested, "Let her embrace him; it is but a moment." It was agreed, and they let her go to him.

"Farewell, dear darling of my soul. My parting blessing on my love. We shall meet again, where the weary are at rest!" These were her husband's words, as he held her close.

"I can bear it, dear Charles. I am supported

from above. Don't suffer for me. A parting blessing for our child."

"I send it to her by you. I kiss her by you. I say farewell to her by you."

"My husband. No! A moment!" He was tearing himself from her. "We shall not be separated long. I feel that this will break my heart before long. But I will do my duty while I can. When I leave her, God will provide friends for her, as He did for me."

Her father had followed her. He would have fallen on his knees to both of them, but Darnay cried, "No, no! What have you done that you should kneel to us? We know now what a struggle you made. We know now what you felt when you suspected my descent, and when you knew it. We know now the natural hatred you fought against, and conquered, for her dear sake. We thank you with all our hearts. Heaven be with you!"

Dr. Manette's only answer was to draw his hands through his white hair, and wring them with a shriek of anguish.

"It could not be otherwise," said Darnay. "It was my attempt to carry out my poor mother's wishes that first brought my fatal presence near you. A happy ending could not come from so unhappy a beginning. Be comforted, and forgive me. Heaven bless you!"

As the guards pulled him away, his wife stood looking after him. She placed her hands together as if in prayer. As Darnay went out at the prisoners' door, she turned, tried to speak to her father, and collapsed at his feet.

Then, issuing from the dark corner from which he had never moved, Sydney Carton came and took her up. Only her father and Mr. Lorry were with her. Carton's arm trembled as it raised her and supported her head. Yet there was an air about him that had a flush of pride in it.

He carried her to the door and laid her tenderly down in a coach. Her father and their old friend got into it, and he took his seat beside the driver.

When they arrived at the gateway where he had paused in the dark not many hours before, he lifted her again, and carried her up the staircase to their rooms. There, he placed her on a couch, where her child and Miss Pross wept over her.

"Don't wake her up," he said, softly, to the latter. "She is better so."

"Oh, Carton, Carton, dear Carton!" cried little Lucie, springing up and throwing her arms around him, in a burst of grief. "Now that you have come, I think you will do something to help mamma, something to save papa! O, look at her, dear Carton! Can you, of all the people who love her, bear to see her so?"

He bent over the child, and laid her cheek against his face. He put her gently from him, and looked at her unconscious mother.

"Before I go," he said, and paused—"may I kiss her?"

It was remembered afterward that when he bent down and touched her face with his lips, he murmured some words. The child, who was nearest to him, heard them. She told her grandchildren, when she was a handsome old lady, that she heard him say, "A life you love."

When he had gone into the next room, Carton turned suddenly to Mr. Lorry and her father, who were following, and said to the latter, "You had great influence yesterday, Dr. Manette. Let it at least be tried. These judges, and all the men in power, are very friendly to you and appreciate your services. Is this not so?"

"I had the strongest assurances that I could save him," Dr. Manette answered, with great trouble, and very slowly.

"Try them again. The hours between now and tomorrow afternoon are few and short, but try."

"I intend to try. I will not rest a moment."

"Good. I have known such energy as yours do great things before now—though never," he added, with a smile and a sigh together, "such great things as this. But try."

"I will go," said Dr. Manette, "to the Prosecutor and the President immediately, and I will go to others whom it is better not to name. I will write too, and—But wait! There is a celebration in the streets, and no one will be available until dark."

"True. Well! It is a slim hope at the best,

and will not suffer much for being delayed. I should like to know how you do, though. Mind, I expect nothing! When are you likely to see these dread powers, Dr. Manette?"

"Immediately after dark, I should hope. Within an hour or two from now."

"It will be dark soon after four. If I go to Mr. Lorry's at nine, shall I hear what you have done, either from our friend or from yourself?"

"Yes."

"May you succeed!"

Mr. Lorry followed Sydney Carton to the outer door and touched him on the shoulder. "I have no hope," said Mr. Lorry, in a low and sorrowful whisper.

"Nor have I."

"I doubt if any of these men would spare him after the demonstration in the court."

"And so do I. I heard the fall of the axe in that sound."

"Yes, yes, yes," returned Mr. Lorry, drying his eyes, "you are right. He will perish; there is no real hope."

"Yes. He will perish; there is no real hope," echoed Carton. And he walked with a settled step downstairs.

CHAPTER
12

Darkness

Sydney Carton paused in the street, unsure of where to go. "At Tellson's banking house at nine," he said to himself. "Shall I, in the meantime, show myself? I think so. It is best that these people should know there is such a man as I here." And he turned his face toward Saint Antoine.

Defarge had described himself, that day, as the keeper of a wine shop in the Saint Antoine district. It was not difficult, for one who knew the city well, to find his shop. Having discovered its location, Carton took his dinner and fell sound asleep. For the first time in many years, he had no strong drink. Since last night he had taken nothing but a little light thin wine. Last night, he had placed the brandy slowly down on Mr. Lorry's hearth, like a man who had done with it.

It was as late as seven o'clock when Carton awoke refreshed and went out into the streets again. As he walked toward Saint Antoine, he stopped at a shop window, where there was a mirror. He straightened his loose necktie and coat collar, and he combed his wild hair. This done, he went on to Defarge's, and went in.

The only customer in the shop was Jacques Three, of the restless fingers and the croaking voice. This man, whom he had seen upon the jury, stood drinking at the little counter, in conversation with the Defarges. The Vengeance was there, as well.

Carton walked in and took a seat. He asked (in very poor French) for a small measure of wine. Madame Defarge cast a careless glance at him, and then looked closely, and then looked even more closely. She walked up to him herself, and asked him what it was he had ordered.

He repeated what he had already said.

"English?" asked Madame Defarge, raising her dark eyebrows.

After looking at her, as if he were having trouble with the French language, he answered, in his former strong foreign accent. "Yes, madame, yes. I am English!"

Madame Defarge returned to her counter to get the wine. Carton took up a Jacobin journal and pretended to read it. He heard her say, "I swear to you, like Evrémonde!"

Defarge brought him the wine, and wished him a good evening.

"Oh! Good evening, citizen," filling his

glass. "Ah! and good wine. I drink to the Republic."

Defarge went back to the counter and said, "Certainly, a little like." Madame sternly retorted, "I tell you a good deal like." Jacques Three remarked, "He is so much in your mind, see you, madame." The amiable Vengeance added, with a laugh, "And you are looking forward with so much pleasure to seeing him once more tomorrow!"

Carton followed the lines and words of his paper with a slow forefinger, and with a studious and absorbed face. They were all leaning their arms on the counter close together, speaking low. After a silence of a few moments, during which they all looked toward him without distracting him from the journal, they resumed their conversation.

"It is true what madame says," observed Jacques Three. "Why stop? There is great force in that."

"Well, well," reasoned Defarge, "but one must stop somewhere. But where?"

"At extermination," said madame.

"Magnificent!" croaked Jacques Three. The Vengeance, also, highly approved.

"Extermination is good doctrine, my wife," said Defarge, rather troubled. "In general, I say nothing against it. But this doctor has suffered much. You saw him today. You observed his face when the paper was read."

"I have observed his face!" repeated madame, scornfully and angrily. "Yes. I have observed his face to be not the face of a true friend of the Republic. Let him take care of his face!"

"And you have observed, my wife," said Defarge, "the suffering of his daughter, which must be a dreadful distress to him!"

"I have observed his daughter," repeated madame. "Yes, I have observed his daughter, more times than one. I have observed her in the court, and I have observed her in the street by the prison. Let me but lift my finger—!" She seemed to raise it (the listener's eyes were always on his paper), and to let it fall with a rattle on the ledge before her, as if the axe had dropped.

"The citizeness is superb!" croaked the Juryman.

"She is an angel!" said The Vengeance, and embraced her.

"As to you," pursued madame, sternly, addressing her husband, "if it depended on you—which, happily, it does not— you would rescue this man even now."

"No!" protested Defarge. "Not if to lift this glass would I do it! But I would leave the matter there. I say, stop there."

"See you then, Jacques," said Madame Defarge, wrathfully; "and see you, too, my little Vengeance. Listen! For previous crimes as tyrants and oppressors, I have this family a long time on my register, doomed to destruction and extermination. Ask my husband, is that so."

"It is so," agreed Defarge, without being asked.

"In the beginning of the great days, when the Bastille falls, he finds this paper that was read today, and he brings it home. And in the middle of the night, when this shop is shut, we read it, here on this spot, by the light of this lamp. Ask him, is that so."

"It is so," replied Defarge.

"That night, I tell him, when the paper is read through, that I have now a secret to communicate. Ask him, is that so."

"It is so," replied Defarge again.

"I communicate to him that secret. I tell him, 'Defarge, I was brought up among the fishermen of the seashore. That peasant family so injured by the two Evrémonde brothers is *my* family. Defarge, that sister of the mortally wounded boy upon the ground was my sister. That husband was my sister's husband. That unborn child was their child. That brother was my brother. That father was my father. Those dead are my dead. And that summons to answer for those things descends to me!' Ask him, is that so."

"It is so," replied Defarge once more.

"Then tell wind and fire where to stop," replied Madame Defarge; "but don't tell me."

Both her listeners derived a horrible enjoyment from her deadly anger, and both highly praised it. Defarge, a weak minority, added a few words, reminding them of the compassionate wife of the Marquis. But Madame Defarge merely repeated her last reply: "Tell the wind and the fire where to stop, not me!"

The English customer paid for his wine and made a point of being confused about his change. He then asked, as a tourist normally would, to be directed toward the National Palace. Madame Defarge took him to the door, and put her arm on his, pointing out the road. The English customer thought fleetingly that it might be a good deed to seize that arm, lift it, and stab under it sharp and deep.

But he went his way, and was soon swallowed up in the shadow of the prison wall. At the appointed hour, he arrived at Mr. Lorry's room, where he found the old gentleman walking back and forth in restless anxiety. He said he had been with Lucie until just now, and had only left her for a few minutes, to come and keep his appointment. Her father had not been seen since he had left the banking house around four o'clock, trying to do something to save Charles. The doctor had been gone more than five hours. Where could he be?

Mr. Lorry waited until ten. Dr. Manette had not returned. Since he was unwilling to leave Lucie any longer, it was arranged that Mr. Lorry should go back to her, and come to the banking house again at midnight. In the meanwhile,

Carton would wait alone by the fire for the doctor.

He waited and waited. The clock struck twelve, but Dr. Manette did not come back. Mr. Lorry returned with no news of him. Where could he be?

They were discussing this question, and were beginning to feel some slight hope, due to his prolonged absence, when they heard him on the stairs. The instant he entered the room, it was plain that all was lost.

"I cannot find it," said he, "and I must have it. Where is it?"

His head and throat were bare. As he spoke, with a helpless look, he took his coat off, and let it drop on the floor.

"Where is my bench? I have been looking everywhere for my bench, and I cannot find it. What have they done with my work? Time presses. I must finish those shoes."

They looked at one another, and their hearts died within them.

"Come, come!" said he, in a whimpering miserable way. "Let me get to work. Give me my work."

Receiving no answer, he tore his hair, and beat his feet upon the ground, like a distracted child. "Don't torture a poor forlorn wretch," he begged them, with a dreadful cry, "but give me my work! What is to become of us, if those shoes are not done tonight?"

Lost, utterly lost!

It was so clearly beyond hope to reason with him, or try to restore him. As if by agreement, they each put a hand upon his shoulder, and persuaded him to sit down in front of the fire, promising that he should have his work soon. He sank into the chair, and stared at the embers, and shed tears.

Carton was the first to speak. "The last chance is gone. Dr. Manette should be taken to be with his daughter. But, before you take him, will you, for a moment, listen closely to me? Don't ask me why I make the requests I am going to make, and exact the promise I am going to exact. I have a reason—a good one."

"I do not doubt it," answered Mr. Lorry. "Say on."

The doctor was all the time rocking back and forth and moaning. They spoke in the same tone they would have used if they had been watching by a sickbed in the night.

Carton stooped to pick up the coat, which lay at his feet. As he did so, a small case, in which the doctor kept the lists of his day's duties, fell lightly on the floor. Carton picked it up and found a folded paper in it. "We should look at this!" he said. Mr. Lorry nodded. Carton opened it, and exclaimed, "Thank God!"

"What is it?" asked Mr. Lorry, eagerly.

"A moment! Let me speak of it in its place." He put his hand in his coat and took another paper from it. "This is the certificate which enables me to pass out of this city. Look at it. You see—Sydney Carton, an Englishman?"

Mr. Lorry held it open in his hand, gazing into his earnest face.

"Keep it for me until tomorrow. I shall see Darnay tomorrow, you remember, and I had better not take it into the prison."

"Why not?"

"I don't know. I prefer not to do so. Now, take this paper that Dr. Manette has carried about him. It is a similar certificate, enabling him and his daughter and her child, at any time, to pass the barrier and to leave France! You see?"

"Yes!"

"Perhaps he obtained it as his last and utmost precaution against evil, yesterday. Keep it carefully with mine and your own. It is good until recalled. But it may be soon recalled. I have reason to think it will be."

"They are not in danger?"

"They are in great danger. They are in danger of denunciation by Madame Defarge. I heard it from her own lips. Since then, I have seen the spy. He confirms what I am saying. He knows that a wood-sawyer, living by the prison wall, is under the control of the Defarges. This man has been prepared by Madame Defarge to swear he has seen *her*"—he never mentioned Lucie's name—"making signs and signals to prisoners. She could be accused of helping carry out a prison plot. This could place her life at risk—and perhaps her child's—and perhaps her father's—for both have been seen with her at that place. Don't look so horrified. You will save them all."

"Heaven grant I may, Carton! But how?"

"I am going to tell you how. It will depend on you, and it could depend on no better man. This new denunciation will certainly not take place until after tomorrow; probably not until two or three days afterward. You know it is a capital crime, to mourn for, or sympathize with, a victim of the Guillotine. She and her father would unquestionably be guilty of this crime. Are you following me?"

"Absolutely."

"You have money, and can buy the means of traveling to the seacoast as quickly as the journey can be made. Your preparations have been completed for some days, to return to England. Early tomorrow have your horses ready, so that you may leave at two o'clock in the afternoon."

"It shall be done!"

His manner was so eager and fervent, that Mr. Lorry too was inspired.

"You are a noble heart. Tell her, tonight, that you know her child and her father are in danger as well as she. Dwell upon that, for she would lay her own fair head beside her husband's cheerfully." He faltered for an instant, then went on as before. "For the sake of her child and her father, convince her to leave Paris, with them and you, at that hour. Tell her that it was her husband's last wish. Tell her that more depends upon it than she dare believe, or hope. Have all these arrangements made in the courtyard here. Then take your own seat in the carriage. The moment I come to you, take me in, and drive away for England. We are now pledged to one another. Promise me solemnly that nothing will influence you to change this course."

"Nothing, Carton."

"Remember these words tomorrow. Change the course, or delay in it—for any reason—and no life can possibly be saved, and many lives will be sacrificed."

"I will remember them. I hope to do my part faithfully."

"And I hope to do mine. Now, goodbye!"

Carton said it with a grave smile of earnestness. Though he even put the old man's hand to his lips, he did not leave him then. He helped him rouse and escort the doctor to the house where Lucie waited through the awful night. He entered the courtyard and remained there for a few moments alone, looking up at the light in the window of her room. Before he went away, he breathed a blessing toward it, and a farewell.

CHAPTER
13

Fifty-Two

In the prison of the Conciergerie, the doomed of that day awaited their fate. There were as many as the weeks of the year. Fifty-two were to roll that afternoon on the life-tide of the city to the boundless, everlasting sea. Before they left their cells, new occupants were appointed. Before their blood ran into the blood spilled yesterday, the blood that was to mingle with theirs tomorrow was already set apart.

Charles Darnay sat alone in a cell. In every line of the document that had been read, he had heard his condemnation. He knew that no personal influence could possibly save him.

Nevertheless, it was not easy, with the face of his beloved wife fresh before him, to compose his mind to what it must bear. His hold on life was strong, and it was very, very hard, at first, to loosen.

Before long, Darnay realized that there was no disgrace in the fate he must meet. Many others who did not deserve to die had traveled the same road. This gave him some comfort. Being allowed to purchase the means of writing, and a light, he sat down to write until such time as the prison lamps would be put out.

He wrote a long letter to Lucie. In it he explained that he had known nothing of her father's imprisonment, until he had heard of it from herself. He also wrote that he had not known of his father's and uncle's responsibility for that misery, until the paper had been read in court. He had already explained to her that his concealment of the name he had given up was the one condition—fully understandable now—that her father had attached to their marriage. He begged her, for her father's sake, never to ask him whether he remembered the paper, or had had it recalled to him, by the story of the Tower, on that old Sunday under the dear old plane tree in the garden. If he had recalled it, he must have thought it destroyed with the Bastille. There had been no mention of it among the relics of prisoners which the people had discovered there. He begged Lucie to assure her father that he did not deserve blame. He urged her to remember his own grateful love and blessing, to try to overcome her sorrow, and to devote herself to their dear child until they should meet in Heaven.

To Dr. Manette, he wrote a similar message. He also told the doctor that he entrusted his wife and child to his care.

To Mr. Lorry, he entrusted them all, and explained his worldly affairs. That done, with many added sentences of grateful friendship and warm attachment, he was finished. He never thought of Carton. His mind was so full of the others that he never once thought of him.

He had time to complete these letters before the lights were put out. When he lay down on his straw bed, he thought he had finished with this world.

But it beckoned him back in his sleep. He dreamed that he was free and happy, back in the old house in Soho. He was with Lucie again, and she told him it was all a dream, and he had never gone away. When he awoke in the gloomy morning, he did not know where he was or what had happened. Then it flashed upon his mind, "This is the day of my death!"

Thus had he come to the day when the fifty-two heads were to fall. He was calm, and hoped that he could meet the end with quiet heroism.

The hours went on as he walked up and down, and the clocks struck the numbers he would never hear again. Nine gone forever, ten gone forever, eleven gone forever, twelve coming on to pass away. The worst of the strife was over. He could walk up and down, free from distracting fancies, praying for himself and for those he loved.

Twelve gone forever.

He had been told that the final hour was three. He knew he would be summoned some time earlier, since the wagons jolted heavily and slowly through the streets. Therefore, he resolved to keep two before his mind, as the hour. He would strengthen himself until then. He might be able, after that time, to strengthen others.

Walking regularly up and down with his arms folded on his chest, he heard one o'clock struck away from him, without surprise. The hour had measured like most other hours. He thought, "There is just one more now," and turned to walk again.

Footsteps sounded in the stone passage outside the door. He stopped.

The key was put in the lock, and turned. Before the door was opened, a man said in a low voice, in English: "He has never seen me here. I have kept out of his way. Go in alone; I wait nearby. Lose no time!"

The door was quickly opened and closed. Before him, face to face, quiet, with a smile on his features, and a cautionary finger on his lip, stood Sydney Carton.

There was something so bright and remarkable in his look that at first, the prisoner thought he was a ghost. But Carton spoke, and it was his voice. He took the prisoner's hand, and it was his real grasp.

"Of all the people upon earth, you least expected to see me?" Carton said.

"I could not believe it was you. I can scarcely believe it now. You are not"—the apprehension came suddenly into his mind—"a prisoner?"

"No. I am accidentally possessed of a power over one of the keepers here. Because of this, I stand before you. I come from her—your wife, dear Darnay."

The prisoner wrung his hand.

"I bring you a request from her."

"What is it?"

"A most earnest, pressing, and emphatic entreaty, addressed to you in the most pathetic tones of the voice so dear to you."

The prisoner turned his face partly aside.

"You have no time to ask me why I bring it, or what it means. I have no time to tell you. You must comply with it. Take off those boots you wear, and put on mine."

There was a chair against the wall of the cell, behind the prisoner. Carton had already, with the speed of lightning, sat him down on it, and stood over him, barefoot.

"Put on these boots of mine. Quickly!"

"Carton, there is no escaping from this place. It never can be done. You will only die with me. It is madness."

"It would be madness if I asked you to escape, but do I? When I ask you to walk out that door, tell me it is madness, and remain here. Exchange that necktie for mine, that coat for mine. While you do it, let me take this ribbon from your hair, and shake out your hair like mine!"

With wonderful quickness, and with a strength both of will and action, Carton forced all these changes upon him. The prisoner was like a young child in his hands.

"Carton! Dear Carton! It is madness. It cannot be accomplished, it never can be done. It has been attempted, and has always failed. I beg you not to add your death to the bitterness of mine."

"Do I ask you, my dear Darnay, to go through the door? When I ask that, refuse. There are pen and ink and paper on this table. Is your hand steady enough to write?"

"It was when you came in."

"Steady it again, and write what I shall dictate. Quickly, friend, quickly!"

Pressing his hand to his bewildered head, Darnay sat down at the table. Carton, with his right hand in his pocket, stood close beside him.

"Write exactly as I speak."

"To whom do I address it?"

"To no one."

"Do I date it?"

"No."

The prisoner looked up, at each question. Carton, standing over him with his hand in his pocket, looked down.

"'If you remember,'" said Carton, dictating, "'the words that passed between us, long ago, you will understand this when you see it. You do remember them, I know. It is not in your nature to forget them.'"

He was taking his hand from his pocket. The prisoner looked up in hurried wonder as he wrote. The hand stopped, closing upon something.

"Have you written 'forget them'?" Carton asked.

"I have. Is that a weapon in your hand?"

"No; I am not armed."

"What is it in your hand?"

"You shall know soon enough. Write on; there are just a few words more." He dictated again. "'I am thankful that the time has come when I can prove them. That I do so is no subject for regret or grief.'" As he said these words, with his eyes fixed on the writer, his hand slowly and softly moved down close to the writer's face.

The pen dropped from Darnay's fingers on the table, and he looked about him vacantly.

"What vapor is that?" he asked.

"Vapor?"

"Something that I smell."

"I am conscious of nothing. There can be nothing here. Take up the pen and finish. Hurry, hurry!"

The prisoner made an effort to focus his attention. As he looked at Carton with clouded eyes and with an altered manner of breathing, Carton—his hand again in his pocket—looked steadily at him.

"Hurry, hurry!"

The prisoner bent over the paper, once more.

"'If it had been otherwise'"—Carton's hand was again slowly and softly moving down—"'I never should have had this opportunity. If it had been otherwise'"—the hand was at the prisoner's face—"'I should have had so much more to answer for. If it had been otherwise—'" Carton looked at the pen and saw it was trailing off into meaningless signs.

Carton's hand did not move. The prisoner sprang up with a reproachful look. But Carton's hand was close and firm at his nostrils, and Carton's left arm caught him round the waist. For a few seconds Darnay faintly struggled with the man who had come to lay down his life for him. Within a minute, he was stretched unconscious on the ground.

Quickly, but with hands as true to the purpose as his heart was, Carton dressed himself in the clothes the prisoner had laid aside. He combed back his hair and tied it with the ribbon the prisoner had worn. Then he softly called, "Come in!" and the spy presented himself.

"You see?" said Carton, looking up, as he kneeled on one knee beside the unconscious prisoner, putting the paper in Darnay's pocket.

"Is your danger very great?"

"Mr. Carton," the spy answered, "there is no danger, if you are true to the whole of your bargain."

"Don't fear me. I will be true to the death."

"You must be, Mr. Carton, if the count of fifty-two is to be right. Being made right by you, dressed as you are, I shall have no fear."

"Have no fear! I shall soon be out of the way of harming you. The others will soon be far from here, please God! Now, get help and take me to the coach."

"You?" said the spy nervously.

"Him, man, with whom I have exchanged. You go out at the gate by which you brought me in?"

"Of course."

"Tell the guards I was weak and faint when you brought me in, and I am fainter now. The parting interview overpowered me. Such a thing has happened here, often. Your life is in your own hands. Quick! Call for help!"

"You swear not to betray me?" said the trembling spy, as he paused for a last moment.

"Man, man!" returned Carton, stamping his foot. "I have sworn a solemn vow already. Why do you waste the precious moments now? Take him yourself to the courtyard you know of, and place him yourself in the carriage. Tell Mr. Lorry yourself to give him no restorative but air. Tell him to remember what I said last night, and what he promised last night, and drive away!"

Carton seated himself at the table, resting his forehead on his hands. The spy withdrew, and returned immediately, with two men. They raised the unconscious figure, placed it on a stretcher they had brought to the door, and bent to carry it away.

"The time is short, Evrémonde," said the spy, in a warning voice.

"I know it well," answered Carton. "Be careful of my friend, I beg you, and leave me."

"Come, then, my friends," said Barsad. "Lift him, and come away!"

The door closed, and Carton was left alone. He listened for any sound that might mean suspicion or alarm. There was none. Keys turned, doors clashed, footsteps passed along distant passages. No unusual cry was raised, or hurry made. Breathing more freely in a little while, he sat down at the table, and listened again until the clock struck two.

Sounds that he was not afraid of, for he knew their meaning, then began to be audible. Several doors were opened in succession, and finally his own. A jailer, with a list in his hand, looked in, merely saying, "Follow me, Evrémonde!" He followed the jailer into a large dark room. It was a dark winter day, with shadows inside, and shadows outside. He could hardly see the others who had been brought there to have their arms bound. Some were standing;

some seated. Some were lamenting, and moving restlessly, but these were few. Most were silent and still, looking fixedly at the ground.

As Carton stood by the wall in a dim corner, one man stopped in passing, to embrace him, as if he knew him. Carton was terrified that he would be discovered, but the man went on. A few moments later, a young woman, with a slender girlish form, a sweet, thin, pale face, and large, widely opened, patient eyes, rose from the seat where he had observed her, and came to speak to him.

"Citizen Evrémonde," she said, touching him with her cold hand. "I am a poor little seamstress, who was with you in La Force."

He murmured an answer: "True. I forget what you were accused of."

"Plots. Though the just Heaven knows that I am innocent of any. Who would think of plotting with a poor little weak creature like me?"

The sad smile with which she said this touched him. Tears started from his eyes.

"I am not afraid to die, Citizen Evrémonde, but I have done nothing. I am willing to die, if the Republic, which is to do so much good to us poor, will profit by my death. But I do not know how that can be, Citizen Evrémonde. Such a poor weak little creature!"

Carton's heart warmed and softened to this pitiable girl. It was the last thing on earth that his heart would warm and soften to.

"I heard you were released, Citizen Evrémonde. I hoped it was true."

"It was. But I was again taken and condemned."

"If I may ride with you, Citizen Evrémonde, will you let me hold your hand? I am not afraid, but I am little and weak, and it will give me more courage."

As the patient eyes were lifted to his face, he saw a sudden doubt in them, and then astonishment. He pressed the work-worn, hunger-worn young fingers, and touched his lips.

"Are you dying for him?" she whispered.

"And his wife and child. Hush! Yes."

"O, will you let me hold your brave hand, stranger?"

"Hush! Yes, my poor sister; to the last."

• • •

The same shadows that are falling on the prison, are falling, in that same hour of the early afternoon, on the Barrier with the crowd about it. A coach going out of Paris drives up to be examined.

"Who goes here? Who is within? Papers!"

The papers are handed out, and read.

"Alexandre Manette. Physician. French. Which is he?"

The inarticulately murmuring, wandering old man is pointed out.

"Apparently the Citizen-Doctor is not in his right mind? The Revolution-fever was too much for him?"

Greatly too much for him.

"Hah! Many suffer with it. Lucie. His daughter. French. Which is she?"

She is identified.

"Lucie, the wife of Evrémonde, is it not?"

It is.

"Hah! Evrémonde has an appointment elsewhere. Lucie, her child. English. This is she?"

She is shown.

"Kiss me, child of Evrémonde. Now, you have kissed a good Republican, something new in your family. Remember it! Sydney Carton. Advocate. English. Which is he?"

Lying in a corner of the carriage, he too is pointed out.

"Apparently the English advocate is in a swoon?"

It is hoped he will recover in the fresher air. He is not in strong health, and has separated sadly from a friend who is under the displeasure of the Republic.

"Is that all? It is not a great deal, that! Many are under the displeasure of the Republic, and must look out at the little window. Jarvis Lorry. Banker. English. Which is he?"

"I am he. Necessarily, being the last."

It is Jarvis Lorry who has replied to all the previous questions. It is Jarvis Lorry who has stepped down and stands with his hand on the coach door, replying to a group of officials.

They leisurely walk round the carriage. They leisurely mount the box, to look at what little luggage it carries on the roof. The country people hanging about press nearer to the coach doors and greedily stare in. A little child, carried by its mother, has its short arm held out for it, that it may touch the wife of an aristocrat who has gone to the Guillotine.

"Here are your papers, Jarvis Lorry, countersigned."

"We may depart, citizen?"

"You may depart. A good journey!"

"I salute you, citizens," Mr. Lorry declared. And, to the coach passengers, in a hushed voice, "The first danger passed!"

There is terror in the carriage, there is weeping, there is the heavy breathing of the unconscious traveler.

"Are we not going too slowly? Can they not be made to go faster?" asks Lucie, clinging to the old man.

"It would seem like flight, my darling. I must not urge them too much. It would rouse suspicion."

"Look back, look back, and see if we are pursued!"

"The road is clear, my dearest. So far, we are not pursued."

Houses in twos and threes pass by us, solitary farms, collapsed buildings; then, open country and avenues of leafless trees. The hard uneven

A TALE OF TWO CITIES

pavement is under us. Soft deep mud is on either side. Sometimes, we swerve into the mud, to avoid the stones that clatter and shake us. Sometimes, we stick in ruts. Our impatience is then so great, that in our wild alarm and agony we are for getting out and running—hiding— doing anything but stopping.

Out of the open country, in again among run-down buildings, solitary farms, cottages in twos and threes, avenues of leafless trees. Have these men deceived us, and taken us back by another road? Is not this the same place again? Thank Heaven, no. A village. Look back, look back, and see if we are pursued! Hush! The posting house.

Leisurely, our four horses are detached from the carriage. The horseless carriage waits, seemingly forever, in the street. Finally, the new horses come into view, one by one. Leisurely, the new coach drivers follow, snapping and braiding the lashes of their whips. Leisurely, the old coach drivers count their money, make mistakes, and count again. All the time, our frantic hearts are beating at a rate faster than the fastest gallop of the fastest horses ever born.

At last the new coach drivers are in their saddles, and the old are left behind. We are through the village, up the hill, and down the hill, and on the low watery grounds. Suddenly, the drivers exchange speech with animated gestures. The horses are pulled up, almost on their haunches. We are pursued?

"Ho! Within the carriage there. Speak then!"

"What is it?" asks Mr. Lorry, looking out the window.

"How many did they say?"

"I do not understand you."

"At the last post. How many to the Guillotine today?"

"Fifty-two."

"I said so! A brave number! My fellow driver here would have it forty-two; ten more heads are worth having. The Guillotine goes handsomely. I love it. Whoop!"

The night comes on, dark. The drugged passenger moves. He is beginning to revive and to speak. He thinks he and Carton are still together in the cell. He speaks to Carton, calling him by name and asking what he has in his hand. O pity us, kind Heaven, and help us! Look out, look out, and see if we are pursued.

The wind is rushing after us, and the clouds are flying after us, and the moon is plunging after us, and the whole wild night is in pursuit of us. But, so far, we are pursued by nothing else.

CHAPTER
14

The Knitting Done

As the fifty-two awaited their fate, Madame Defarge was meeting with The Vengeance and Jacques Three of the Revolutionary Jury. They conferred in the shed of the wood-sawyer, formerly a mender of roads. The wood-sawyer was not part of the conference, but waited a short distance away.

"But our Defarge," said Jacques Three, "is undoubtedly a good Republican? Eh?"

"There is no better," The Vengeance protested shrilly, "in France."

"Peace, little Vengeance," said Madame Defarge, laying her hand with a slight frown on her lieutenant's lips. "Hear me speak. My husband, fellow citizen, is a good Republican and a bold man. He has deserved well of the Republic, and possesses its confidence. But my husband has his weaknesses. He might support whatever the doctor wishes."

"It is a great pity," croaked Jacques Three, shaking his head, with his cruel fingers at his hungry mouth. "It is not what is expected of a good citizen. It is a thing to regret."

"See you," said madame, "I care nothing for this doctor. He may wear his head or lose it, for all I care. But, the Evrémonde people are to be exterminated, and the wife and child must follow the husband and father."

"She has a fine head for it," croaked Jacques Three. "I have seen blue eyes and golden hair there, and they looked charming when Samson held them up." Although he was an ogre, he spoke like a gourmet.

Madame Defarge cast down her eyes and thought a little.

"The child also," observed Jacques Three, "has golden hair and blue eyes. And we seldom have a child at the guillotine. It is a pretty sight!"

"In a word," said Madame Defarge, ending her silence, "I cannot trust my husband in this matter. Since last night, I sense that I dare not confide to him the details of my projects. I also fear that if I delay, there is danger of his giving warning. Then they might escape."

"That must never be," croaked Jacques Three. "No one must escape. We have not half enough as it is. We ought to have hundreds of heads each day."

"In a word," Madame Defarge went on, "my husband does not have my reason for pursuing this family to annihilation. I must act for myself, therefore. Come hither, little citizen."

The wood-sawyer advanced fearfully, with his hand to his red cap.

"Concerning those signals, little citizen," said Madame Defarge, sternly, "that she made to the prisoners. Are you ready to bear witness to them this very day?"

"Yes, yes, why not!" cried the sawyer. "Every day, in all weathers, from two to four, always signaling, sometimes with the little one, sometimes without. I know what I know. I have seen with my eyes."

He made all manner of gestures while he spoke, imitating signals he had never seen.

"Clearly plots," said Jacques Three.

"There is no doubt of the jury?" inquired Madame Defarge, letting her eyes turn to him with a gloomy smile.

"Rely upon the patriotic jury, dear citizeness. I answer for my fellow jurymen."

"Now, let me see," said Madame Defarge, thinking again. "Can I spare this doctor for my husband's sake? I have no feeling either way. Can I spare him?"

"He would count as one head," observed Jacques Three, in a low voice. "We really have not heads enough. It would be a pity, I think."

"He was signaling to the prisoner with her

when I saw her," argued Madame Defarge. "I cannot speak of one without the other. I do not feel I can trust the case wholly to this little citizen here. For I am not a bad witness."

The Vengeance and Jacques Three exclaimed that she was the most admirable and marvelous of witnesses. The little wood-sawyer, not to be outdone, declared her to be a heavenly witness.

"The doctor must take his chance," said Madame Defarge. "No, I cannot spare him! You are engaged at three o'clock; you are going to see the batch of today executed.—You?"

The question was addressed to the wood-sawyer, who hurriedly said yes. He quickly added that he was the most ardent of Republicans. He would be the most miserable of Republicans if anything prevented him from smoking his afternoon pipe in the company of the national barber.

"I," said madame, "am equally engaged at the same place. After it is over—say at eight tonight—come see me, in Saint Antoine, and we will give information against these people at my Section."

The wood-sawyer said he would be proud and flattered to accompany the citizeness.

Madame Defarge beckoned the juryman and The Vengeance a little nearer to the door. She then explained to them, "She will now be at home, awaiting the moment of Evrémonde's death. She will be mourning and grieving. She will be in a state of mind to challenge the justice of the Republic. She will be full of sympathy with its enemies. I will go to her and gather evidence against her."

"What an admirable woman; what an adorable woman!" exclaimed Jacques Three, rapturously. "Ah, my cherished!" cried The Vengeance, and embraced her.

"Take my knitting," said Madame Defarge, placing it in her lieutenant's hands. "Have it ready for me in my usual seat by the guillotine. Keep my usual chair for me. Go there, at once, for there will probably be a greater crowd than usual, today."

"I willingly obey the orders of my chief," said The Vengeance, kissing her cheek. "You will not be late?"

"I shall be there before the first head falls."

"Be sure you are there, my soul," said The Vengeance, "before the wagons arrive!"

Madame Defarge waved her hand, to imply that she heard, and would arrive in good time. She walked through the mud and around the corner of the prison wall. The Vengeance and the Juryman, looking after her as she walked away, spoke with appreciation of her fine figure and her superb moral character.

There were many women, at that time, whom the Revolution had made cruel. But not one among them was more to be dreaded than this ruthless woman, now stalking her way along the streets. Madame Defarge was strong and fearless, shrewd, and greatly determined. From childhood, she had had a brooding sense of wrong, and a deep-rooted hatred of the aristocracy. Now she was like a tigress, absolutely without pity.

It meant nothing to her that an innocent man was to die for the sins of his forefathers. She saw not him, but them. It meant nothing to her that his wife was to be made a widow and his daughter an orphan. That was insufficient punishment. They were her natural enemies and her prey, and as such had no right to live. Appealing to her was hopeless. She had no sense of pity, even for herself. If she had been laid low in the streets, in any of the many encounters in which she had been engaged, she would not have pitied herself. Even if she had been ordered to the guillotine tomorrow, she would have felt no sorrow—only a fierce desire to change places with whoever had sent her there.

Such a heart Madame Defarge carried under her rough dress. She walked with the confident tread of a woman who had often walked in her girlhood, barefoot and barelegged, on the brown sea-sand. Lying hidden in her dress was a loaded pistol. Lying hidden at her waist was a sharpened dagger. Thus prepared, Madame Defarge took her way along the streets.

Now, when Mr. Lorry had planned the

journey from Paris, the difficulty of including Miss Pross had greatly concerned him. He did not want to overload the coach. Also, the time occupied in examining it and its passengers had to be the barest minimum. Their escape might depend on the saving of only a few seconds. So he had proposed that Miss Pross and Jerry, who were at liberty to leave the city, should leave at three o'clock in the lightest-wheeled vehicle available. Without the burden of luggage, they would soon overtake the coach. They could then order its new horses in advance. This would speed their progress during the precious hours of the night, when delay was the most to be dreaded.

Miss Pross joyfully consented to this arrangement. She and Jerry had seen the coach start, had known who it was that Solomon brought, and had spent some ten minutes in suspense. As Madame Defarge, taking her way through the streets, now drew nearer and nearer, they were concluding their arrangements to follow the coach.

"Now, Mr. Cruncher," said Miss Pross, so distressed that she could hardly speak, or stand, or move, "what do you think of our not starting from this courtyard? Another carriage has already gone from here today. It might awaken suspicion."

"My opinion, miss," returned Mr. Cruncher, "is as you're right. Likewise I'll stand by you, right or wrong."

"I am so distracted with fear and hope for our precious creatures," said Miss Pross, wildly crying, "that I am incapable of forming any plan. Are *you* capable of forming any plan, my dear Mr. Cruncher?"

"Respectin' any present use o' this here blessed old head o' mine, miss," returned Mr. Cruncher, "I think not."

"Oh, for gracious sake!" cried Miss Pross, still wildly crying. "My poor darlings!"

And still Madame Defarge, pursuing her way along the streets, came nearer and nearer.

"If you were to go on ahead," said Miss Pross, "and were to wait somewhere for me, wouldn't that be best?"

Mr. Cruncher thought it might be best.

"Where could you wait for me?" asked Miss Pross.

Mr. Cruncher was so bewildered that he could think of no locality but Temple Bar. Alas! Temple Bar was hundreds of miles away in London, and Madame Defarge was drawing very near indeed.

"By the cathedral door," said Miss Pross. "Would it be much out of the way, to take me in, near the great cathedral door between the two towers?"

"No, miss," answered Mr. Cruncher.

"Then go to the posting-house right away and make that change."

"I am doubtful," said Mr. Cruncher, hesitating and shaking his head, "about leaving you, you see. We don't know what may happen."

"Heaven knows we don't," returned Miss Pross, "but have no fear for me. Take me in at the cathedral, at three o'clock, or as near to it as you can. I am sure it will be better than our going from here. I feel certain of it. There! Bless you, Mr. Cruncher! Think not of me, but of the lives that may depend on both of us!"

This plea, and Miss Pross's two hands clasping his, convinced Mr. Cruncher. With an encouraging nod or two, he immediately went out to change the arrangements. She would follow later, as she had suggested.

Miss Pross was greatly relieved by this change of plans. She then realized that she needed to change her appearance so that it should attract no special notice in the streets. It was twenty minutes past two. She had no time to lose, but must get ready at once.

Miss Pross got a basin of cold water and began washing her eyes, which were swollen and red. In her extreme anxiety, she was afraid of the deserted rooms. She half imagined faces peeping from behind every open door. Haunted by her fears, she constantly paused and looked round to make sure that there was no one watching her. In one of those pauses she shrank back and cried out. There was a figure standing in the room.

The basin fell to the ground broken, and the water flowed to the feet of Madame Defarge.

Madame Defarge looked coldly at her, and said, "The wife of Evrémonde; where is she?"

Miss Pross realized that the doors were all standing open, suggesting escape. Her first act was to shut them. There were four in the room, and she shut them all. She then stood in front of the door of the room which Lucie had occupied.

Madame Defarge's dark eyes followed her through this rapid movement, and rested on her when it was finished. Miss Pross had nothing beautiful about her. Years had not tamed the wildness, or softened the grimness, of her appearance. But she too was a determined woman, and she measured Madame Defarge with her eyes, every inch.

"You might, from your appearance, be the wife of the devil," said Miss Pross, in English. "Nevertheless, you shall not get the better of me. I am an Englishwoman."

Madame Defarge looked at her scornfully. She knew full well that Miss Pross was the family's devoted friend. Miss Pross knew full well that Madame Defarge was the family's evil enemy.

"I am on my way to the guillotine," said Madame Defarge, in French, with a slight movement of her hand toward the fatal spot, "where they reserve my chair and my knitting for me. I am come to make my compliments to the wife of Evrémonde. I wish to see her."

"I know that your intentions are evil," said Miss Pross. "And you may depend upon it, I'll hold my own against them."

Each spoke in her own language. Neither understood the other's words. Both were very watchful, trying to deduce, from look and manner, what the strange words meant.

"It will do her no good to keep herself concealed from me at this moment," said Madame Defarge. "Good patriots will know what that means. Let me see her. Go tell her that I wish to see her. Do you hear?"

"No, you wicked foreign woman. I am as strong as you."

"Imbecile and pig-like woman!" said Madame Defarge, frowning. "I take no answer from you. I demand to see her. Either tell her that I demand to see her, or stand aside and let me go to her!" This, with an angry wave of her right arm.

"I little thought," said Miss Pross, "that I should ever want to understand your nonsensical language. But I would give all I have, except the clothes I wear, to know whether you suspect the truth, or any part of it."

Neither of them for a single moment released the other's eyes. Madame Defarge had not moved from the spot where she stood when Miss Pross first became aware of her. She now advanced one step.

"I am a Briton," said Miss Pross. "I am desperate. I don't care an English twopence for myself. I know that the longer I keep you here, the greater hope there is for my Ladybird. I'll not leave a handful of that dark hair upon your head, if you lay a finger on me!"

Thus Miss Pross, with a shake of her head and a flash of her eyes between every rapid sentence, and every rapid sentence a whole breath. Thus Miss Pross, who had never struck a blow in her life.

Miss Pross's courage was of an emotional

nature; it brought tears into her eyes. This was a courage that Madame Defarge did not understand. She mistook it for weakness. "Ha, ha!" she laughed, "you poor wretch! What are you worth? I address myself to that doctor." Then she raised her voice and called out, "Citizen Doctor! Wife of Evrémonde! Child of Evrémonde! Any person but this miserable fool, answer the Citizeness Defarge!"

Either the following silence, or something in the expression of Miss Pross's face, whispered to Madame Defarge that they were gone. She opened three of the doors swiftly, and looked in.

"Those rooms are all in disorder. There has been hurried packing; there are odds and ends upon the ground. There is no one in that room behind you! Let me look."

"Never!" said Miss Pross, who understood the request as perfectly as Madame Defarge understood the answer.

"If they are not in that room, they are gone, and can be pursued and brought back," said Madame Defarge to herself.

"As long as you don't know whether they are in that room or not, you are uncertain what to do," said Miss Pross to herself. "And you shall not know that, if I can prevent your knowing it. Anyhow, you shall not leave here so long as I can hold you."

"I have been in the streets from the first.

Nothing has stopped me. I will tear you to pieces, but I will move you from that door," said Madame Defarge.

"We are alone at the top of a high house in a solitary courtyard. We are not likely to be heard. I pray for bodily strength to keep you here. Every minute you are here is worth a hundred thousand guineas to my darling," said Miss Pross.

Madame Defarge lunged at the door. Miss Pross seized her around the waist in both her arms. It was in vain for Madame Defarge to struggle and to strike. Miss Pross, with the powerful strength of love—always so much stronger than hate—clasped her tightly, and even lifted her from the floor as they struggled. The two hands of Madame Defarge battered and tore her face. But Miss Pross, with her head down, held her around the waist, and clung to her like a drowning woman.

Soon, Madame Defarge's hands stopped striking, and felt at her encircled waist. "It is under my arm," said Miss Pross, in smothered tones. "You shall not draw it. I am stronger than you. I bless Heaven for it. I will hold you till one or the other of us faints or dies!"

Madame Defarge's hands were inside her dress. Miss Pross looked up, saw what she held, struck at it. There was a flash and a crash, and Miss Pross stood alone—blinded with smoke.

All this was in a second. The smoke cleared,

leaving an awful stillness. It passed out on the air, like the soul of the furious woman whose body lay lifeless on the ground.

In the first fright and horror of her situation, Miss Pross walked around the body as far from it as she could, and ran down the stairs to call for help. Happily, she thought of the consequences of what she did in time to stop herself and go back. It was dreadful to go in at the door again. But she did go in, and even went near it, to get the bonnet and other things that she must wear. These she put on and ran down the staircase, first shutting and locking the door and taking away the key. She sat on the stairs a few moments to breathe and to cry, and then got up and hurried away.

By good fortune, she had a veil on her bonnet. Otherwise, she could not have gone through the streets without being stopped. By good fortune, too, she was already peculiar in appearance. She needed both advantages, for the marks of gripping fingers were deep in her face, her hair was torn, and her dress (hastily arranged with unsteady hands) was dragged a hundred ways.

In crossing the bridge, Miss Pross dropped the door key in the river. She arrived at the cathedral a few minutes before Jerry Cruncher. Waiting there, she thought: What if the key were already taken in a net? What if it were identified? What if the door were opened and the remains discovered? What if she were stopped at the gate, sent to prison, and charged with murder! In the midst of these fluttering thoughts, Mr. Cruncher appeared, took her in, and took her away.

"Is there any noise in the streets?" she asked him.

"The usual noises," Mr. Cruncher replied, looking surprised by the question and by her appearance.

"I don't hear you," said Miss Pross. "What do you say?"

It was useless for Mr. Cruncher to repeat what he said. Miss Pross could not hear him. "So I'll nod my head," thought Mr. Cruncher. "She'll see that." And she did.

"Is there any noise in the streets now?" asked Miss Pross again.

Again Mr. Cruncher nodded his head.

"I don't hear it."

"Gone deaf in an hour?" said Mr. Cruncher, disturbed. "Wot's come to her?"

"I feel," said Miss Pross, "as if there had been a flash and a crash, and that crash was the last thing I should ever hear in this life."

"Blest if she ain't in a queer condition!" said Mr. Cruncher, more and more disturbed. "Wot can she have been a takin', to keep her courage up? Listen! There's the roll of them dreadful carts! You can hear that, miss?"

"I can hear," said Miss Pross, seeing that he

spoke to her, "nothing. O, my good man, there was first a great crash, and then a great stillness. And that stillness seems to be fixed and unchangeable, never to be broken as long as I live."

"If she don't hear the roll of those dreadful carts, now very near their journey's end," said Mr. Cruncher, glancing over his shoulder, "it's my opinion that indeed she never will hear anything else in this world."

And indeed she never did.

CHAPTER
15

The Footsteps Die Out For Ever

Along the Paris streets, the death-carts rumble, hollow and harsh. Six wagons carry the day's wine to La Guillotine. Crush humanity out of shape once more, under similar hammers, and it will twist itself into the same tortured forms. Sow the same seed of unrestrained privilege and oppression over again, and it will surely yield the same fruit.

As the dismal wheels of the six carts go around, they seem to plow a long crooked furrow among the populace in the streets. Ridges of faces are thrown to this side and to that, and the plows go steadily onward. The regular inhabitants of these houses are so used to the spectacle that many do not even bother to look out their windows.

Some of the riders in the carts observe these things with an impassive stare. Others, seated with drooping heads, are sunk in silent despair.

Several close their eyes, and think, or try to collect their straying thoughts. Only one, a miserable crazed creature, is so shattered and made drunk by horror that he sings and tries to dance. Not one of the whole number appeals, by look or gesture, to the pity of the people.

There is a guard of horsemen riding beside the carts. Faces are often turned up to some of them, and they are asked a question. It would seem to be always the same question, for it is always followed by a press of people toward the third cart. The horsemen beside that cart frequently point out one man in it with their swords. That man stands at the back with his head bent down, speaking to a young woman who sits on the side of the cart and holds his hand. He has no curiosity or care for the scene about him; he speaks only to the young woman. Here and there in the long street of St. Honoré, cries are raised against him. If they move him at all, it is only to a quiet smile, as he shakes his hair a little more loosely about his face. He cannot easily touch his face, his arms being bound.

On the steps of a church, awaiting the carts, stands the spy and prison-sheep. He looks into the first of them: not there. He looks into the second: not there. He already asks himself, "Has he sacrificed me?" when his face clears, as he looks into the third.

"Which is Evrémonde?" says a man behind him.

"That. At the back there."

"With his hand in the girl's?"

"Yes."

The man cries, "Down, Evrémonde! To the Guillotine all aristocrats! Down, Evrémonde!"

"Hush, hush!" the spy pleads, timidly.

"And why not, citizen?"

"He is going to pay his penalty. It will be paid in five minutes more. Let him be at peace."

But the man continues to exclaim, "Down, Evrémonde!" The face of Evrémonde is turned toward him for a moment. Evrémonde then sees the spy, and looks attentively at him, and goes on.

The clocks are striking three o'clock, and the furrow plowed among the populace is turning round into the place of execution. The ridges thrown on either side now close behind the last plow as it passes on. All are following to the Guillotine. In front of it, seated in chairs, as if in a public garden, are a number of women, busily knitting. On one of the front chairs stands The Vengeance, looking around for her friend.

"Thérèse!" she cries, in her shrill tones. "Who has seen her? Thérèse Defarge!"

"She never missed before," says a knitting-woman of the sisterhood.

"No, nor will she miss now," cries The Vengeance, annoyed. "Thérèse!"

"Louder," the woman recommends.

Ay! Louder, Vengeance, much louder, and still she will not hear you. Louder yet,

Vengeance, with a little oath or so added; it will not bring her. Send other women to seek her. Although they have done awful deeds, they will probably not want to go far enough to find her!

The Vengeance, stamped her foot on the chair. "Here are the wagons! Evrémonde will be executed in a wink, and she is not here! See her knitting in my hand, and her empty chair ready for her. I cry with vexation and disappointment!"

As The Vengeance descends from her chair, the carts begin to discharge their loads. The ministers of Sainte Guillotine are robed and ready. Crash!—A head is held up, and the knitting women, who scarcely lifted their eyes to look at it a moment ago, when it could think and speak, count One.

The second cart empties and moves on. The third comes up. Crash! —And the knitting women, never pausing in their work, count Two.

The supposed Evrémonde descends, and the seamstress is lifted out next after him. He has not let go of her patient hand in getting out, but still holds it as he promised. He gently places her with her back to the crashing engine that constantly whirrs and falls, and she looks into his face and thanks him.

"But for you, dear stranger, I should not be so calm. I am naturally a poor little thing, faint of heart. Nor should I have been able to raise my thoughts to Him who died for our sins, that we might have hope and comfort here today. I think you were sent to me by Heaven."

"Or you to me," says Sydney Carton. "Keep your eyes upon me, dear child, and mind no other object."

"I mind nothing while I hold your hand. I shall mind nothing when I let it go, if they are rapid."

"They will be rapid. Fear not!"

The two stand in the fast-thinning crowd of victims. They speak as if they were alone. Eye to eye, voice to voice, hand to hand, heart to heart—these two, otherwise so different, have come together on the dark highway, to go home together.

"Brave and generous friend, will you let me ask you one last question? I am very ignorant, and it troubles me—just a little."

"Tell me what it is."

"I have a cousin, an only relative and an orphan, like myself. I love her very dearly. She is five years younger than I, and she lives in a farmer's house in the south country. Poverty parted us, and she knows nothing of my fate, for I cannot write. And if I could, how should I tell her! It is better as it is."

"Yes, yes: better as it is."

"What I have been thinking as we came along, and what I am still thinking now, as I look into your kind strong face which gives me so much support, is this. If the Republic really does good to the poor, and they become less hungry, and suffer less, she may live a long time. She may even live to be old."

"What then, my gentle sister?"

Her eyes shone with tears, and her lips trembled. "Do you think," she said, "that it will seem long to me, while I wait for her in the better place where both you and I will be mercifully sheltered?"

"It cannot be, my child. There is no time there, and no trouble there."

"You comfort me so much! I am so ignorant. Am I to kiss you now? Is the moment come?"

"Yes."

She kisses his lips; he kisses hers; they solemnly bless each other. Her hand does not tremble as he releases it. Nothing worse than a sweet, bright faithfulness is in her patient face. She goes next before him—is gone. The knitting women count Twenty-Two.

"I am the Resurrection and the Life, saith the Lord: he that believeth in me, though he were dead, yet shall he live: and whosoever liveth and believeth in me shall never die."

The murmuring of many voices, the upturning of many faces, the pressing on of many footsteps in the back of the crowd, so that it swells forward in a mass. Like one great heave of water, all flashes away. Twenty-Three.

• • •

They said of him, about the city that night, that it was the most peaceful face ever seen there. Many added that he looked noble and prophetic.

One of the most remarkable sufferers by the same axe—a woman—had asked at the foot of the same scaffold, not long before, to be allowed to write down her final thoughts. If he had done the same, and if his thoughts were prophetic, this is what Sydney Carton would have written:

"I see Barsad, and Cly, Defarge, The Vengeance, the Juryman, the Judge—all the new oppressors who have risen by destroying the old—perishing by this sharp instrument. I see a beautiful city and a brilliant people rising from this abyss. I see, in the years to come, their struggles to be truly free, their triumphs, their defeats. I see the evil of this time, and of the previous time of which this is the natural birth, gradually fading away.

"I see the lives for which I lay down my life, peaceful, useful, prosperous and happy, in that England which I shall see no more. I see *her* with a child, who bears my name. I see her father, aged and bent, but otherwise restored, healing the sick, and at peace. I see Jarvis Lorry, so long their friend, in ten years' time enriching them with all he has, and passing quietly to his reward.

"I see that I hold a sanctuary in their hearts, and in the hearts of their descendants, generations from now. I see her, an old woman, weeping for me on the anniversary of this day. I see her and her husband, at the end of their lives, lying side by side in their last earthly bed. And I know that each was not more honored and held sacred in the other's soul, than I was in the souls of both.

"I see that child, who was given my name, become a man, succeeding in that path of life which once was mine. I see him succeeding so well that my name is distinguished because of his. I see the blots I threw upon it, faded away. I see him, a famous judge and an honored man, bringing a boy named for me, with a forehead like mine and golden hair, to this place. On that future day, this place will be fair to look upon, without a trace of this day's disfigurement. And

I hear him tell the child my story, in a tender and trembling voice.

"It is a far, far better thing that I do, than I have ever done. It is a far, far better rest that I go to, than I have ever known."

AFTERWORD

About the Author

One of the major themes of *A Tale of Two Cities* is injustice. Instances of unfair treatment occur as early as page 1. We see people brought to trial and condemned—sometimes to death—for crimes they did not commit, or that were not crimes at all. We see other innocent people imprisoned without even having a trial. We see the French nobility's mistreatment of the common people and, later, the French revolutionaries' similar mistreatment of the nobility. This focus on injustice is hardly surprising, for Charles Dickens himself experienced ill-treatment, both as a child and as a young man—and he never forgot it.

Charles Dickens was born in 1812, just about twenty years after the events he relates in *A Tale of Two Cities*. He was the second of eight children; several other brothers and sisters died in infancy. His father, John Dickens, worked as a clerk in the Navy Pay Office. This was a good position, and his salary should have enabled the Dickens family to lead a comfortable middle-class life. However, John Dickens was poor at managing money. In addition, every time John was transferred to a new position—often along with a cut in pay—the family had to move. Life in the Dickens family was full of uncertainties, especially financial ones.

Despite the moves and the financial problems, Charles's first ten years were relatively happy. He spent five of them in the seacoast town of Chatham, where he became involved with books at an early age. He loved reading adventure stories, such as *Robinson Crusoe* and *The Arabian Nights,* and pretending he was the hero. His father and uncle took him to see plays at the local theater. They also took him to taverns, where he would stand on the counter and sing funny songs. Even as a child, Charles was creative, enjoyed jokes, and loved to perform. He did well at school, which he also enjoyed; and he seemed destined for success.

But then disaster struck. In 1822, John Dickens was transferred to London, where the cost of living was much higher than in Chatham, and bill collectors were always at the door. His parents could no longer afford to keep Charles at school. So young Charles, just a few days after his twelfth birthday, was forced to take a job at a shoe polish factory on the Thames River. Here the sensitive, intelligent twelve-year-old spent from 8 a.m. to 8 p.m., six days a week, attaching labels to bottles of shoe polish—and breathing in the unhealthy fumes of the shuttered, rat-infested factory—for six shillings a week (about 60 cents today). At the end of each long workday, Charles walked three miles to a lonely rented room in a lodging house in North London. Charles felt as if he were in prison. Later Dickens wrote that he wondered "how I could have been so easily cast away at such an age."

Matters soon became worse. On February 20, John Dickens was arrested for debt and sent to the Marshalsea debtors' prison. In Dickens's time, debtors' prisons provided living quarters for the families of the inmates. The rest of the Dickens family (except for Charles and his older sister Fanny, who had a scholarship to study music at the Royal Academy) soon joined him there. Charles, already devastated by his own imprisonment at the factory, now had to endure the further humiliation of seeing his father (and his mother and brothers and sisters) in jail.

Three months later, John Dickens was declared a bankrupt and released from prison. Not long afterward, he rescued Charles from the shoe polish factory and placed him again in school. However, his mother, Elizabeth Dickens, had wanted Charles to remain at the factory. After all, he *was* earning money, and his earnings helped the family. Dickens, understandably, resented his mother's attitude. Many years later, Dickens wrote, "I never afterwards forgot, I never can forget, that my mother was [eager to send] me back."

Charles Dickens eventually graduated from school at age fifteen and found a job as a clerk in a law firm. He soon became bored with the law and its endless details and delays (which he would later make fun of in his own writing). His creativity and sense of fun were very much out of place in a law firm. So he studied shorthand and became a court reporter, astonishing his colleagues with how fast and accurately he could reproduce what was said during a trial. Following this, he was a newspaper reporter—and then, finally, a very famous and successful author. But he never forgot the childhood injustices—the months of mindless work in the dreary factory, the betrayal by both parents, the stigma of his father's imprisonment. Abandoned children, lonely orphans, evil authority figures, and dismal prison scenes recur in all the novels he wrote.

While he was still a clerk, however, Dickens resumed a habit from his childhood. He took long, leisurely walks through London's streets, seeking out the more dangerous areas where poverty and crime were common. On these walks, Dickens, who was extremely observant, saw hundreds of interesting people whose facial expressions, speech, and habits would later appear in the characters he invented.

Also, while he was still a clerk, and before he became famous, Charles Dickens fell in love. The woman he adored, Maria Beadnell, was a flirtatious blonde beauty two years older than Dickens.

She was very popular, and admirers were always visiting her home. Perhaps because she was so popular, or perhaps because her family assumed Dickens would be poor all his life and could never support her, she treated Dickens quite badly. During the four years that he courted Maria, she occasionally refused his gifts, did not answer his love letters, insulted him in public, and finally stopped writing to him altogether. Dickens was completely devastated by this new example of injustice. When he finally did marry, he chose a quiet, submissive woman, someone as unlike Maria as possible.

Dickens's full-time writing career began when he was in his early 20s. In 1833, he began to contribute short stories and essays to magazines. A collection of these short pieces, *Sketches by Boz* (Boz was the family's nickname for his youngest brother) appeared in 1836 and was a great success. That same year, Dickens published the first installments of *The Pickwick Papers*, another collection of stories about London life and the fictional adventures of the members of the Pickwick Club. This was the book that made Dickens world-famous. Readers loved his vivid word-pictures, not realizing that the characters Dickens described were based on real people he had met on his wanderings.

You may have noticed the word *installments* in the previous paragraph. In Dickens's time, books were not published all at once, as they are today. Instead, like our soap operas, they appeared a little at a time, in short sections called installments. These sections were printed and sold either separately or as part of a monthly magazine. After the final installment appeared, the publisher collected all the parts and reprinted them as a complete book. This type of publication makes a great deal of sense. Authors had more time to finish their stories (although they had strict deadlines for each part). Publishers could see how well the installments sold before going to the extra expense of printing a hardcover book. The only people who might have objected were the readers. Once they were "hooked" on a story, they had to suffer in suspense for weeks while waiting for the next few chapters to appear.

By 1836, then, Dickens was internationally popular. In that year he married Catherine Hogarth, the eldest daughter of his editor. Although they had ten children, their marriage was not a happy one, and they finally separated in 1858. Perhaps contributing to their unhappiness was Dickens's obvious infatuation with Catherine's younger sister Mary, who had come to live with the couple shortly after their marriage. Dickens referred to her as "the grace and life of our home," and when she died suddenly a year later, he was devastated. Until his own death, he wore on his finger a ring that had belonged to her. Mary's place was taken by another of Catherine's sisters, Georgiana, and Dickens is thought to have loved her, as well. He also had a long relationship with a much younger actress, Ellen Ternan, which resulted in the final breakup of his marriage. Throughout Dickens's novels we can find examples of lovely, angelic women, whose gentle efforts make life delightful for those who love them, and who inspire men to do great things. Were these characters based on Mary, or Georgiana, or Ellen, or all three? Only Dickens could have answered this question.

Dickens's fame and popularity continued to grow throughout his lifetime. He went on to write fifteen major novels, of which *A Tale of Two Cities*—one of the last, and one of the least humorous—is also one of the most acclaimed. He also traveled; he first visited the United States in 1841, and more trips followed. On these tours, and others he made within Great Britain, Dickens gave paid readings of his works, an activity Dickens loved as much as his audience. His dramatic performances of scenes from his writings, some humorous and some hair-raising, thrilled everyone who came to see them. Although these readings always tired him, more so as he grew older, Dickens continued to perform onstage for the last fifteen years of his life. He had always wanted to be an actor since the days he stood on the counter as a child and sang funny songs. He loved the cheers of his audiences as much as he appreciated the income that they provided. In addition to writing novels and giving performances, Dickens founded various journals and wrote hundreds of essays, often on the social evils of the day.

The furious pace of Dickens's life eventually took a serious toll on his health. The work, particularly the dramatic readings, simply exhausted him, yet he would not even think of giving them up. In 1869 he collapsed after one of his public performances, and his doctors ordered him to stop performing. However, he ignored their advice. The following year, while only part way through writing his final novel, *The Mystery of Edwin Drood*, he suffered a massive stroke and died the next day.

Dickens is buried at Westminster Abbey in London—the greatest honor possible for a British author. The inscription on his tombstone reads: "He was a sympathiser to the poor, the suffering, and the oppressed; and by his death, one of England's greatest writers is lost to the world."

About the Book

"It was the best of times; it was the worst of times." You might have wondered, as you read the first sentence of *A Tale of Two Cities*, "How can it be the best of times *and* the worst of times at the *same* time?" The answer is that Charles Dickens is showing us the same events from two different points of view. For the powerful and privileged ruling classes, it was "the best of times." For the suffering common people, it was "the worst of times." And just as there can be different opinions about the same period of time, there can be different opinions about the book that describes them. *A Tale of Two Cities* can be viewed as five books in one. It is a historical novel. It is a mystery story. It is a love story. It is a stern warning that the lessons of history cannot be ignored. Finally, it is a thrilling story of rebirth.

A Tale of Two Cities is one of the most famous historical novels ever written. As its name suggests, a historical novel is a story whose major characters are fictional, but whose setting is real—a previous century or event. As the backdrop for *A Tale of Two Cities,* Charles Dickens chose one of the most significant events in European history, the French Revolution. This upheaval began in 1789 and played itself out over the next few years. The effects of the Revolution in France eventually spread throughout Western Europe. Before 1789, a tiny class of privileged aristocrats enjoyed immense wealth, status, and power. This class is represented in the novel by the arrogant castle-owner Monseigneur. By the time the Revolution had done its work, this extravagant ruling minority had been replaced by the common men and women. Kings and queens were gone. The forces of democracy had taken over.

In telling us about the French Revolution, Dickens does not offer a comprehensive historical account. Rather, he illuminates certain features, just as a flash of lightning reveals only the tallest buildings of a cityscape. The plight of the ordinary citizens of France is represented by the inhabitants of the Saint Antoine district of Paris. Hunger, poverty and hopelessness mark the boundaries of their lives. Given their lot in life, it is not difficult to understand the murderousness of their actions once the Revolution begins. Madame Defarge represents these people at their most extreme. Similarly, the French nobility is represented by the Marquis St. Evrémonde. The nobility's dismissive and contemptuous attitude toward the common people is vividly expressed when the Marquis's coach runs over Gaspard's son. The nobleman's main concern is not the death of an innocent child, but the possible injury to his horses. Another example of the monstrous injustice of the pre-Revolutionary regime is the imprisonment of Dr. Manette. The doctor had committed no crime. His mistake was in reporting the crimes of a noble family. To silence him, Dr. Manette was kept in solitary confinement for almost eighteen years in prison cell 105 in the North Tower of the Bastille. These few details would not meet the historian's test of providing a full and balanced account of the French Revolution. However, they do convey in extremely vivid brushstrokes the nature of the times and the motivations of the central characters.

A Tale of Two Cities is also a mystery story—or, more accurately, a series of mysteries. Throughout *A Tale of Two Cities*, Dickens presents us with unanswered questions. What is the meaning of the strange message, "Recalled to Life"? Why has Dr. Manette been in prison for eighteen years? Why is Charles Darnay on trial for treason? Exactly what does Jerry Cruncher do—besides odd jobs for Tellson's Bank—to earn his living, and why are his fingers rusty? Why does Sydney Carton drink so much and stay up so late at night? Who is Monseigneur, and why are he and the Marquis so cruel? Why is Madame Defarge constantly knitting, and why is she so eager for the Revolution to begin? Finally, what do all these separate stories in *A Tale of Two Cities* have to do with each other? It is a tribute to Dickens's talent as a writer that he gradually weaves these separate tales together, like strands of hair that form a braid.

Dickens's skillful use of minor characters adds to the mystery. When we first meet Miss Pross, Jerry Cruncher, Roger Cly, Gaspard, and John Barsad, we are inclined to pay little attention to them. Some disappear from the story for over a hundred pages. Yet each will have his or her part to play in the outcome. For example, Miss Pross's long-lost brother seems little more than a humorous afterthought when we first encounter him. Toward the end of the novel, however, he is an important part of Sydney Carton's plan for Charles Darnay. Each of these minor characters has a crucial role to play in the unfolding of the story. There are no loose ends—or unnecessary people—in *A Tale of Two Cities.*

A Tale of Two Cities is also a book about the

power of love. The most obvious love story, of course, is that of Lucie Manette and Charles Darnay—who fall in love at first sight. In keeping with the style of the nineteenth century, Dickens does not describe in detail the passionate embraces of his characters. Compared to contemporary novels and films, the love between Lucie and Charles seems tame indeed. However, Dickens's own readers would not have felt that way, and they would have enjoyed the descriptions of this devoted couple in their happy English home. But this is only one of the love stories in *A Tale of Two Cities*. Lucie's devotion to her father is deep and unselfish. Dr. Manette returns this love, even approving of his daughter's marriage. Surely, Dr. Manette knows that, despite Lucie's pledge of undivided love for her father, her marriage will create some distance between father and daughter. But his daughter's happiness is more important. Sydney Carton reveals yet another type of love. In his self-denying love for Lucie, Carton scales the heights of heroic love. He even offers his own life to ensure her happiness. Finally, Miss Pross exemplifies yet another type of love. Her unfailing care for Lucie since birth culminates in a fight to the death with Madame Defarge, a fight whose outcome Dickens hints at when he writes that Miss Pross has "the powerful strength of love—always so much stronger than hate."

There's a famous quotation by the philosopher George Santayana that states, "Those who do not remember the past are condemned to repeat it." Dickens certainly would agree. In *A Tale of Two Cities*, he warns us that unless we learn from our mistakes, or those of others, we will make similar mistakes and suffer the consequences. One of the greatest mistakes we can make is to oppress other human beings. As another philosopher, Lord Acton, once wrote, "Power corrupts, and absolute power corrupts absolutely." The once-powerful French aristocrats write their own death sentence. Their crimes bring about their downfall at the hands of the common people they have mistreated for so long. Eventually, as Sydney Carton predicts, the revolutionaries, themselves corrupted by power, will also perish at the guillotine. Dr. Manette and Madame Defarge, both victims of oppression, want to mercilessly avenge themselves on those who have injured them. Both will live to regret it. Dickens even extends his warning to his readers—then and now. Near the end of *A Tale of Two Cities*, he writes, "Crush humanity out of shape once more, under similar hammers, and it will twist itself into the same tortured forms. Sow the same seed of unrestrained privilege and oppression over again, and it will surely yield the same fruit." Sadly, recent violent events in our 21st century have proved Dickens was right. Those who think they are victimized will strike back against those whom they hold responsible—and thousands of people will perish.

"I am the resurrection and the life, saith the

Lord: he that believeth in me, though he were dead, yet shall he live: and whosoever liveth and believeth in me, shall never die." These words, which Sydney Carton heard at his father's funeral, suggest the greatest message of the book. *A Tale of Two Cities* is, most of all, a story of rebirth. Dr. Manette is "recalled to life" after nearly eighteen years as a prisoner in the Bastille. Charles Darnay is faced with three sentences of death; each time, he is given a new lease on life. Jerry Cruncher is jokingly referred to as a "resurrection man"—and in a sense, he does bring the dead to life. Sydney Carton, a self-doomed failure, redeems himself with his glorious sacrifice; and a son of Lucie and Charles, named Sydney Carton Darnay, will redeem his name—giving Sydney a symbolic rebirth. Even France, a country of death in 1793, will be reborn. In his final vision, Sydney imagines the Paris of the future, "a beautiful city and a brilliant people rising from this abyss. . . . I see the evil of this time, and of the previous time of which this is the natural birth, gradually fading away."

A Tale of Two Cities is many stories—historical, mysterious, romantic, threatening. But its final message is one of hope. If we can learn from the past, if we realize the futility of violence and oppression, if we can place love above hatred— then we can turn "the worst of times" into "the best of times."